'What happens when Paradis
was fortunate enough to reac ̣ and I knew
from the first few lines that this was destined to be a very special
book. The betrayal of the First Nation Americans and the legacy
of that betrayal is examined here with a gimlet eye for vivid
detail and a hugely empathetic heart. It's a book about manhood
and community, about fitting in and fighting back and how the
trauma of war can infect a family bloodline for generations. It
is also very beautifully written. Robin de Rosario has penned
a gloriously epic and sweeping novel that asks hard and timely
questions about the foundations of America. It will be read and
re-read for generations to come.'
Russ Litten

'Reminiscent of Leslie Marmon Silko's *Ceremony*, *Coyote* delves
into the storytelling tradition of First Nation people to explore
and reinvent the Western genre, shining a light on the dark
inception of the modern United States, from the perspective
of the communities who fell victim to greed and prejudice. De
Rosario's novel is the moving story of a family stretched across
cultures and the staggering landscape of the Southwest. A
stunning debut that will grip your attention from start to finish.'
Sophie Buchaillard

'Robin de Rosario's novel *Coyote* is beautifully composed and
fiercely written. The prose acts as a vessel of grace, and draws
readers into a gritty, transcendent world. A western work of art
and radiance. Buy the book. Read it for its uncommon latent
strength. *Coyote* is elegant, profound, and powerful. This novel
fulfills the night dream.'
Shann Ray

COYOTE

ROBIN DE ROSARIO

LUCENT DREAMING

First Edition

Coyote
Published by Lucent Dreaming Ltd.
103 Bute Street, Cardiff, CF10 5AD

Cover illustrations © Cerys Knighton 2025

ISBN 978-1-916632-06-6

Lucent Dreaming acknowledges the financial support
of Books Council of Wales and Creative Wales.

CYNGOR LLYFRAU CYMRU
BOOKS COUNCIL of WALES

To those who came before

Prologue

Coyote lay in shadow, his head on his forelegs, his empty belly resting on the slab beneath him. He watched the doe antelope and, as he contemplated the imminent slaughter, his stomach growled. Her pale tail rose and trembled. Slick and black, the head of a fawn appeared, inching out. She lay down and raised a hind leg. Coyote lifted his head and waited. She jumped up as it slipped from her onto the ground, the sack glistening. He rose to his feet. She stooped, cleaning it with her mouth. A second muzzle squeezed into view; she rotated so that the newborn would fall next to its sibling. He sprinted from the rocks. Without breaking stride, he snatched the firstborn, cracking its neck with his jaws. The antelope turned, seeing Coyote, she leapt at him, head lowered in attack. Abandoned, her second fawn cried out a thin squeak. The doe halted, paralysed. With her eyes, she followed the slack body in Coyote's mouth as he loped west, her head rising and falling again and again as her high, keening calls echoed back to her unanswered.

Coyote stopped on a hummock. Overlooking an

Anaii village on flatland framed by rock outcrops, he chose the spot for its field of vision. The settlement was near-deserted, its inhabitants out hunting or tending to flocks. He dropped his prey and started in on the tender corpse, burying his nose deep in its ribcage. Flies crowded the air in a dark halo.

When the Akote raiders came into view, the sun was near the top of its climb making the legs of their galloping ponies shimmer in the haze from the sand. Coyote looked towards the village. A young woman emerged from her hogan carrying a basket. She tilted her head to listen, then shaded her eyes and looked north. She dropped the basket. Peaches rolled across the dirt. She ran towards the next hogan shouting the alarm. Coyote nuzzled in the fawn, found the liver, and ripped it out. He chewed as he observed.

The woman turned and raced back inside, emerging moments later with two young boys and a knife. She stopped and looked south. More raiders.

A few women, children and the elderly fled from the mouths of their hogans. A handful of Anaii warriors stood in the open, arrows notched, shouting for them to run towards the outcrop at their backs. Coyote swallowed the last morsel of liver. The villagers reached the base of the rock and, one at a time, started up a narrow path which vanished within a few paces into the folds of sandstone. Dust clouded the air and the ground shook as the raiders swept in.

The young woman turned her knife so that the handle was concealed by her fingers, the long blade along the inside of her forearm. She pushed her sons behind her, the three of them waiting to ascend. One by one the mounted raiders picked off the defending Anaii with their arrows. When the last of them fell, the Akote kicked their horses on towards the woman. She glanced over her shoulder. The path was clear. She shouted at the younger boy to go, the older one to follow him. The younger disappeared into the rock; his brother remained by his mother. She screamed at him in Spanish, 'Go, go! Now!'

An Akote warrior, slight and not much older than her children, leapt from his pony and ran at her, raising his knife above his head as he closed the few paces between them. She jumped forward towards him, swinging her arm in an arc across his neck, slitting its full width. He fell, trying to stem the gash with his hands. Behind him, an older, broader warrior strode towards them. The boy left his mother's side and charged. The man backhanded him across the head, the blow lifting him off his feet to land face down, unconscious. The woman screamed and surged forward, her knife arm weaving back and forth like a spider making its web. The warrior ducked left, left again then right, stabbing his blade up under her ribs. She backed towards the rock, slashing with one arm, the fingers of her free hand plugging the wound.

Coyote concentrated on the fawn once more, taking his time, carefully excising the sweet kidneys and soft lungs. Only when he had swallowed the last of the heart did he raise his head, licking blood from his muzzle, his tongue savouring fat and salt.

The village was empty. Coyote watched the boy come

to in the full midday sun, its heat a place of suffocation between sky and sand. The child saw his mother's body at the base of the rock, one leg beneath her, the opposite arm outstretched. He tried to shake her back to life. When he failed, he knelt and rested his head on her chest. Hearing the beat of hooves, the boy turned to see a lone Akote horseman leaning down, arm extended, galloping towards him. He ran so fast his growing legs could not keep pace with his will to survive and he stumbled as the man's arm struck, sweeping him bodily onto the horse and knocking the boy's breath from his chest. They galloped east to rejoin the raiding party. Coyote left the fawn and trotted down from his hummock. He sniffed at the woman's hands, remembering her ferocity as she slashed and sliced her enemies. A ferocity no man can know – the frenzy of a mother protecting her young.

Coyote lay down next to her and started to lick her fingers. He tasted her bloodline, its future, mixed with the blood of the Akote. He jumped to his feet, recoiling. His guts spasmed, his jaws opened wide to regurgitate the sour taint of betrayal.

Part One

Hawk

In the void, the God calls me. I awaken to his howl. I open my eyes and look out through the doorway of the hogan. The milky predawn touches the silt floor of the canyon and its red walls. My eyes are drawn to a ledge halfway up. There he sits: Coyote. Above him, the sky stretches from rim to rim like a pale drumskin. I nod my acknowledgement. He stands, stretches, and starts the climb up the rock face.

I turn to Willow Tree, my wife. I look at her slender throat and jet hair as she kneels at her prayers, watching the trickle of smoke from the floor curl despite the stillness of the air outside. An omen. She is reckoning the omens. The sadness in her voice twists my stomach, but in my chest, the fast beating of Coyote's heart. A gift. He brings a gift. Have our prayers been heard? An eagle shrieks far above. She wipes her tears with the back of her hand. Despite the strength in my arms and legs, I am impotent. But the dream. Coyote brought the rain: a single drop of Life making its way through the mud roof to drip onto Willow Tree's belly.

A gentle hiss from along the canyon grows into the sound of a hundred women whispering as the aspen shake their leaves awake in the breeze. It strokes the skin of my face then catches the smoke at the chimney hole and bustles it westwards. The sun breaks from behind Bear Rock through the open doorway, washing over the yellow cobs stacked beside Willow Tree, making them glow. In this instant, each particle of smoke is like a new-born Sun God, gleaming, rising into its journey. The sweetness of the corn cooking in the dirt of the floor fills the space. I watch her breathe it deep for comfort. I did the same as a child in my mother's home. The corners of her mouth creep into a smile.

I am in the gloom at the back of the hogan. I cough to let her know I am awake, so as not to startle her. She turns to watch me emerge from the darkness. I see her face flush with the first warmth of the summer's day and something else. Desire. I harden.

'The air is good, Hawk.'

'The air is good, my wife, but why must my wife be the most hard-working of the tribe, waking me before the other men?'

'To show my respect to the Dawn, to make my husband comfortable, and perhaps to stop him getting fat.' She grins, waiting.

My reach is enough to scoop a cob with my fingertips. I throw it to miss her by a finger's breadth. Deep laughter forces itself up from her belly. 'That laugh! Sometimes Wife, I wonder if I have married a man.'

Her face becomes earnest again, 'Hawk – the omens this morning, so many! Today will be a blessing.'

Should I tell her my dream? 'Willow Tree –'

'No, Husband, today will be a blessing.'

I look through the doorway at the day beginning in the canyon, then back at her. I feel my frown ease. The smoke rises from the floor. 'It smells good in here – like breakfast and Wife.'

She laughs again, reaches for the cob, and hurls it back at me. I catch it, surprising her with the speed of my arm. I rise and cross the space between us. Her fingers press into my shoulder blades as I push her gently onto her back.

*

The sun is climbing the bluebird sky. Clouds, white as rabbits' tails, cast shadows the shape of their flat undersides on the canyon floor. We walk towards the eastern edge of the village, as we have so many times. The canyon floor stretches before us, orchards and shallow cornfields lining the base of the rockface in the silt. The wash trickles, almost dry. Willow Tree leads the fattest sheep from her flock by a halter. Trotting to keep up, it bleats in protest.

We have not eaten, and the tang of ripening melons makes Willow Tree's stomach grind aloud. The womenfolk are weaving on looms as high as their hogans, the hum of their words broken now and then by laughter. As Willow Tree passes, they glance up to smile at her. Despite her apprehension, she makes herself nod and smile back, then turns to me, slightly ahead. I acknowledge the older men by looking to the side of them. The younger men, and some my age, meet me in this way. Although I am not a father, she is proud that I am held in respect.

Sudden barking close by makes her jump. She turns. Across the path behind her, children chase a dog. It is trying to shake itself free of twig antlers tied to its head with twine: a stag but not a stag, goaded. Older boys sitting with their menfolk – notching, and binding arrow weed – call out for their siblings to play elsewhere. A woman shares a peach between her grandchildren; as she parts the flesh, the juice drips dark spots into the dust. She licks her fingers. Willow Tree is staring at the children. She forgets herself sometimes, then realises and the shame burns her. It has been five summers since the breaking of the corncake to mark her womanhood, but still no child. The emptiness inside her aches, I know. I feel it. Perhaps it is mine. She blames only herself. She sighs and looks away, hurrying to make up ground. We continue. I feel her eyes on the back of my legs. She told me that I never chide her for being childless, that never once has she felt anything but loved. But it could be me, not her, my seed lifeless. We draw close to Mountain Song's hogan. I sense the resonance of his voice through my feet as we approach. My mind clears. I feel the power of his medicine before I see him.

There he is, small and bare-chested, necklaces of seed pods and animal bones hanging over his ribs. For as long as I have been here, he has looked this way, his face lined like a dry riverbed. Willow Tree's breath is quickening – she cannot wait to list the signs she witnessed this morning. I should tell him about the drop of rain in my dream if only to be put out of the misery of hope. A ram stands foursquare and confident before him. He rocks, and at a rising point in the chant, showers the animal with cornmeal from a skin pouch. The chant ends. Silence. He looks at the ground and nods, calling us into the space. We step forward and I greet him.

'The air is good, Mountain Song.'

'The air is good, Hawk.'

Willow Tree cannot wait. Once again, she breaks with tradition and speaks first, 'This morning smoke from the fire turned sunwise though the air was still, then –'

I flinch. She sees and Mountain Song cuts her off, 'Willow Tree, has your husband lost his voice?'

She turns to me. I cannot chide her. I smile and look at my feet.

'No, but –'

'Have you chanted as I told you?'

She shakes her hands in impatience, 'Yes, of course –'

'Have you used the cornmeal as I said?'

'I have, and –'

'Have you listened carefully for the Spirit Winds?' My wife is a girl now, tugging at the end of her shawl, moving from foot to foot, desperate to be heard. Mountain Song continues, 'Have you prayed to Spider Woman as you weave so that –'

'She weaves balance and harmony in me, yes! And this morning there was a web between the blankets and the door frame, the wind blew from the East and the Eagle came before dawn.'

'Well then, come forward.' Closing his eyes, he floats the trembling palm of his right hand over her abdomen. How many times will she have to endure this before the disappointment breaks her spirit? I remember the dream. What hope can there be if it is not fulfilled? I breathe in the sharpness of his sweat and the smokiness of burnt herbs.

Mountain Song opens his eyes, 'As I suspected.' He glances at me, mischievous. 'She who holds all life in her web has chosen me for a blessing.'

Willow Tree shakes her head, she is desperate now, 'You?'

He blinks. 'She has decided to make the life of an old medicine man easier by granting your request. Remember the ceremonies your mother taught you, keep your thoughts pure, your prayers daily at dawn. No butchering of animals until after the birth.' I feel my head shake, I hear the words but cannot hold them, my breath rises into my throat. Willow Tree looks back and forth between me and Mountain Song. He continues. 'Be peaceful, Hawk. No arguments.' She bursts into thanks and tears. I cannot show mine; I swallow them back.

Mountain Song shakes his head, 'Not me – in prayer. Both of you. I, too, saw the Eagle here at daybreak.' He looks at me once more, 'I saw Coyote come, also.' He kneels on a blanket in front of his hogan, chanting under his breath as he drizzles brilliant white grains into a zigzag round the circumference of the sand painting before him. He finishes and stands.

Willow Tree is struggling to remain still. She focuses on the raven perched on a high branch behind him. It drops and glides just above us. We feel the cooling downdraft of its wings on our heads. Mountain Song gestures us towards a second blanket. We sit.

'The child will be a girl,' he says, looking through me.

I know other men would want a son, but it has been so long, and a girl for Willow Tree to teach and love. A child like my wife, her beauty continued. My spirit is filled with the sunlight of it. Willow Tree has covered her mouth with her hand in gladness and anxiety. She looks at me. We lean closer to Mountain Song and wait.

'Willow Tree, this life that you carry is particular.' My stomach tenses with fear that the happiness so recently given is already to be taken. 'Your family will come to be of vital importance to the future of the Akote. This spirit will be the twine that binds the family together. She must be allowed her own choices in a way our women are usually not, and so must her offspring. This will be difficult for her, but more so for you. She, not you, will choose her husband, and he will be a man who risks his life for her before he knows her. Know also that her blood will return to the rock.'

Before Willow Tree can speak, Mountain Song stills her with a raised hand and gestures towards the centre of the painting. She calms herself, takes a breath, and steps in from the East onto an image of a woman surrounded by a turquoise sky, an infant with jet black hair in her belly. On the ground, around her, are symmetrical representations of the ancestors and Mountain Song himself, their backs straight and their arms lined by their sides.

Willow Tree is breathing shallow as tears roll down her cheeks. I cannot go to her without breaking the medicine. Mountain Song's voice rises to a chant. He dips his hand into a bowl of water and herbs. Willow Tree closes her eyes as he rubs the sacred liquid into her hair and skin. She holds out her hand, into which he pours cornmeal. She showers herself with it and offers the remainder up to the wind, checking between her fingers to ensure every grain is taken so that her gratitude is clear. I know how strong it is; how strong mine is. I sing it under my breath.

Mountain Song brings her out of the circle with a movement of his arm then he crouches down to scoop the sands onto a skin to scatter in the desert. We are still thanking him as he gestures us away, laughing and muttering to himself.

*

I feel like I am soaring above the village. I lift Willow Tree up into the air by her waist and spiral around and around. I stop and put her gently down. I must take great care of her now. I cradle her in my arm as we walk back through the settlement. Already the heat shimmers off the silt. The others are seeking shade under the rough-trunked cottonwood trees.

A bead of sweat on Willow Tree's forehead. I wipe it with my finger. She stops and turns, the words bursting out of her, 'I told you, Hawk, I told you I saw the signs, so many signs.' She slips free of my arm and skips around me as she speaks, bumping into my flank.

'Be careful Willow Tree, I fear for the unborn child. You cannot be as rough with yourself as you were with the sheep you brought for Mountain Song.'

She laughs at my seriousness and slows to a walk, then halts once more to look me up and down. 'The father of my child.' I brush the hair out of her eyes. She grins at me, outshining the sun, then looks around to check no one can see before she shoves me forward with her free hand. 'That was my best sheep,' she calls after me. 'You're the offering next time, Husband.'

*

I honour the great blessing we were granted yesterday by respecting Mountain Song's advice. He told me to be gentle with Willow Tree and the others in the village – especially in training the young of the tribe in the ways of hunting. The new caution in my demeanour already causes amusement to the other men.

The student I am teaching with the bow this morning has forgotten his leather wrist protector once again. I start to chide the boy, but check myself, remembering the medicine man's words. I force my voice to be softer and my face to smile, 'You must remember the protector, so you do not suffer from the string striking your skin. Hurry now and fetch it. Remember it next time.' He runs off.

Pale Horse, taller and broader than any man in the canyon, looks across from the next stand and grins at me. I know what is coming. 'Hawk! We have powerful medicine. A warrior who can wrestle a bear and ride a horse as well as any man now speaks as softly as my grandmother. Our enemies will run!'

Crowsfoot, on my other side, joins him. 'They will scatter like cottontails, but not in fear, in confusion!'

They laugh until they are bent double. I feel my own laughter rising, but hide it, shake my head and glower at them. Pale Horse staggers towards me and slaps me on the back. The weight of his arm jars my spine. 'Brother, we are happy for you and Willow Tree. We know there are customs to observe while your child is carried.'

Crowsfoot is howling now like a wolf bitch, spitting words between gasps, 'Yes – and you will only – have to endure it – seven more months!'

Clucking breaks from the cottonwoods ahead of us. I snatch up my bow with my left hand, notch an arrow with my right, aim and loose. Twenty paces ahead the noise becomes a blur of beating feathers as a wild turkey leaves the ground, heading for the far side of the canyon. It reaches the apex of its flight and the pale underside of its wings flashes as it locks them to glide. At that instant, the arrow takes it in the breast, punching it backwards, shocking the others into silence as I knew it would.

I keep my face like the rock. 'When you can shoot like this grandmother then you can cry with laughter. Now, who wants to practise the bow?'

We are cut short by the noise of a galloping horse. It is Straight Tree, our war chief. He reins in hard and speaks without greeting. 'Mescalero Apache. Their attacks have reached the eastern edge of the settlement. My granddaughter Butterfly has been taken. Summon your men. We counter raid without delay.'

*

In the hogan, I feel Willow Tree's eyes on my back, watching me gather my weapons. She says nothing, but we both know the life awaiting her and our child should I fall. No word is spoken between us, but as I go to leave, she puts the palm of her hand on my cheek and smiles at me. I ache with her sadness and my own.

Our war party rides east. It was a matter of time before they came here. Mexicans and the hostile tribes have been raiding increasingly across our lands. Ute, Mescalero Apache and Anaii Akote rustle stock to swell their herds and take our women and children for slaves. I am side by side with Pale Horse at Straight Tree's right hand. This unbroken pursuit risks pushing our animals to lameness. I spare my horse as best I can.

It is dusk, we have reached a point near the end of the canyon, its walls stretching away towards the mountains. Beyond the next outcrop I see a rising spark. The tell-tale smoke reveals the raiders' camp. I whisper to Straight Tree who nods at me to scout. I dismount and creep forward. I still my thoughts, allowing my vision to absorb the scene. The Apache have made a cook fire in the dust and are roasting deer, counting the day's prizes. Beyond them, the flames reveal our women and children imprisoned in an alcove in the rock face. Two sentries sit guard. Something is unaccounted for. A westerly breeze carries the smell of venison towards us.

Straight Tree points his head towards the rim high above and nods. A young warrior looks the canyon wall up and down then stalks backwards and halts. Taking two loping strides he springs skywards, finding a momentary handhold. He swings sideways, using his momentum to disappear up the rock face. Crowsfoot crawls like a lizard through the silt into the centre of the canyon floor, merging with a cluster of sagebrush to keep close watch. Straight Tree speaks low to those of us remaining.

'They are fewer than we thought. Perhaps thirty. Our numbers are equal. Pale Horse – take ten men, go back along the canyon then cross over and return. Hold to the shadows. The wind blows west, so your scent will not betray you. You will attack from the far side. I will send another man up to the rim. They will push boulders over the edge. That will be the signal.' The War Chief looks once more towards the plateau above and raises his chin.

A second warrior swarms up the rock. It strikes me now, why I feel uneasy. 'They have our women and children, but where is the livestock? They are fewer than we thought – they may have split their camp.'

Straight Tree turns his grizzled head. 'Your caution is wise, but we have seen no signs of more men.'

He does not wish to hear me. I sense disaster closing in with the dusk. I must speak with stillness, respect. 'If there is not one party but two, we may have reckoned half their strength.'

Straight Tree's jaw twitches in and out of shadow before he speaks. 'You have been heard. We attack as planned.' He dwells on each word; his eyes narrow in warning.

I must be in the vanguard. 'If it is permitted, I will ride with Pale Horse and his men.'

'I have given command to Pale Horse, I will not –'

'Pale Horse leads. I ask only to ride with him and the others.'

Straight Tree leans back in his saddle, glaring. I avert my eyes to show respect. Pale Horse looks back and forth between us. The Chief nods once, peering out towards Crowsfoot who pats the air with the palm of his hand, signalling that the Apache remain as before. I join Pale Horse and his men as they trot their ponies back west, crossing the canyon where they will not be seen. It is almost night. The scent from the sagebrush fades as the air cools. An owl screams. I push away my thoughts to rely on my senses. We turn east once more, edging along the far wall. The heat of the day still pulses from the rock, warming my leg. As we draw level with the enemy position, Pale Horse's pony balks and nickers. He reins it in. The other men follow suit, their horses forming a shallow crescent in the moonlight. Where the rock face recedes beyond the raiders, the flames of a second cook fire light a camp with a brush corral behind it, milling with plundered horses. Thirty more Apache warriors feast on venison, talking and laughing as they eat. I watch from the shadows, images forming in my mind of how the battle will unfold. What needs to be done becomes clear.

'Left, or right?' Pale Horse whispers.

'Right, but we are outnumbered two to one – surprise alone will not be enough.'

From high on the north rim, we hear grinding, followed by hollow hammering and the earth shuddering as the first boulder careers down the canyon wall. It fractures as it bounces, showering the Apache in shards of rock. Their screams roil into the darkness. Straight Tree leads the charge at their backs.

I see both camps from here. We have one chance. 'The stolen horses,' I call to Pale Horse and kick my pony into a gallop. He shouts for the men to fan out and ride at the corral. They race towards it whooping and hollering. The penned animals snort and stamp at our voices from the darkness. Their jostling reaches breaking point. I glance across. Pale Horse grins back, pumping the reins as we gallop together towards Death.

The whinnying herd bursts through the far side of the corral, stampeding into the raiders. Then, spooked anew by the canyon wall, they double back, eyes rolling white as they trample the Apache of the second camp. Within moments most are dead or unconscious. The few left upright are taken by our arrows.

Pale Horse calls his men to him and wheels his pony round the outcrop. I follow. The raiders have regrouped and are fighting in a rough line with the rock wall at their backs. Our horsemen shoulder in, firing their bows at will. I scan the field for Straight Tree. He is unhorsed by the cook fire, kneeling on the chest of a prone Apache, knife raised. As he makes the killing stroke, a man close to the fire turns, drops to one knee and looses an arrow through the flames. It takes the chief in the temple. He slumps away, smothering the body beneath. I barge my pony into the bowman from behind, trampling him into the flames. A shower of sparks rises and my horse rears back from the heat.

Crowsfoot is already at Straight Tree's side. He lies dusty and outstretched in the firelight. The sounds of bowstrings thrumming and men shouting diminish. I look for the Akote prisoners. By the alcove, one of the Apache guards lies dead, an arrow in his chest. The other is dragging himself away along the canyon floor. Pale Horse straddles him then folds at the waist, pulling his head back to slash across his throat before striding towards the prisoners. The breeze turns east. The women and children gag at the smoke from the fire, the smell of roasting meat swells, mixed with the bitter tang of burning hair. I return to the flames and jump down from my horse to haul the corpse out by the moccasins. The bodies of Mescalero Apache lie all around.

I join the others dragging the fallen to the second camp. The iron stink of blood rises from the strakes their bodies gouge in the silt. The women and children have been freed, and the casualties are being lined up, side by side, in the shelter of the alcove. A new fire has been built to the west, away from the killing ground where the spirits of the slain will linger like vultures.

*

First light. I stand by the fire with Pale Horse at my shoulder. The two Apache survivors are shoved in front of us. One is cut and bruised down the right side of his face and neck. His arm hangs lifeless, his breathing is rapid, and he sways, struggling to remain upright. The other, taller prisoner has a gash across his forehead. He stares.

Pale Horse speaks. 'You will live. We will give you one horse and you will return to your people. Tell your war chiefs what happened here. The same awaits them if they return.'

The tall Apache spits on the ground in front of me. 'You are a Chigi. A ghost in the darkness screaming death. I curse your bloodline.'

Crowsfoot is behind the prisoners. He kicks into the man's knees, they fold, pulling him backwards. He curses again as he hits the ground. Crowsfoot lifts his foot above the man's face. I stop him, 'Enough. He can do no harm.' Pale Horse leads them out into the canyon, turns the horse east and slaps its rump. It lurches into a trot, its broken riders wincing.

Under Crowsfoot, mounted warriors herd the scattered horses back to camp, to carry the women, the children, the injured, and the dead. In the summer morning, Pale Horse and I lead them west towards their villages, the fresh scent of sagebrush drifting down from above where the air currents from the plateau tumble over the rim into space.

In each settlement we pass through the villagers stand outside their hogans, braced against the news. The day wears on, wives and mothers of the fallen run out with those of the living, their breathing suspended as they crane to look for their own. I see Willow Tree's cousin, a girl of seventeen, spiralling to and fro between her living sister and her dead husband. Her great grandmother, hair white at the temples, corners of her eyes wrinkled like cobwebs, follows the girl back and forth with her shaking hands reached out towards her. My mind turns to Willow Tree, to the terror she will be feeling awaiting my return or the news of my death.

In the next village an old man shuffles forward, his face motionless as the rock, his back stooped. He reaches a gnarled hand up to the saddle of the pony bearing the body of his grandson. Touching the boy's ear long enough to feel the chill of it, he turns and is swallowed by the darkness of his hogan. My fists clench as I picture our unborn child being taken. I feel Pale Horse looking at me; I turn. Our eyes meet in shared fury at our powerlessness.

At last, what remains of the column reaches the final settlement of the canyon, our home. My mouth is lined with grit, my back aching. I dismount. I glimpse Willow Tree through the crowd. She smiles at me, but her eyes are bloodshot and glaring.

Despite the victory, few spoke during the ride. Now Crowsfoot trots his pony forward from the rearguard, 'Hawk, Pale Horse, I will gather the men to choose Straight Tree's successor.' I look at my saddle and nod.

The horses have been led into corrals and women and children dispersed to their hogans. I am with the other men in the lodge, the central fire blasting us with heat. Crowsfoot stands. The voices of the assembled men fade into silence. 'Straight Tree is gone. Who among us will lead?'

Pale Horse rises first, the shadows framing him. I expected him to wait. 'The raiding is worse than ever. We must outthink our enemies to outfight them. As Hawk does. He brought us victory. We are both War Chiefs in this clan, but Hawk should lead, as he did last night.' He sits.

The others speak in succession.

'I will follow Hawk.'

'I too.'

'I will follow him.'

I stare into the fire. I cannot show my fear to my brothers.

*

Autumn 1824 — Canyon de Los Huertos Ocultos

The leaves are falling from the trees. Willow Tree felt the baby's first stirrings and is following Mountain Song's directions. She has stopped drinking milk and working at her loom. She walks in the canyon early, chanting old songs to the new life within her. Songs she has longed to sing. She and the child need fresh meat. Walking towards her, I feel the autumn breeze lift the feathers in my hair and tug the bow in my hand. She looks me up and down, smiling as she ends her song.

I wait for her to finish. 'You never sing to me like that.'

'This is an unborn child. You are a big baby. It's different.'

I recall Pale Horse mocking me when we practised with the bow, 'You too? Where will I get respect in this village?' I turn for the plateau. The fringes of my moccasins jump against my calves. 'We are going to hunt.'

'Hawk,' she calls after me, laughing. I spin round. She admires me again for a moment then, 'Here,' she says touching her heart, 'And here,' she touches her belly. 'Hunt well, War Chief, we are both hungry.'

Coyote

From the rock face, from the orchards, from the cut of the wash, he witnessed them through the months of the small and big winds. He witnessed all things touched by the sky and the earth. They kept the fire in the hogan well fed. The cold outside sucked the smoke up through the chimney. The thaw came in the month of Crusted Snow and in the middle of Squeaky Voice month when the air was sweet with spring, Willow Tree woke at dawn with a start. The child had kicked her hard.

Hawk sprang up as if in battle. 'Is she coming? I'll fetch help.'

She forced calmness into her voice, 'Perhaps, yes. Tell them to come.'

Coyote could feel the panic rising in her body. Her womenfolk gathered round when her waters broke soon after. The pain flooded her in waves. With each push she felt herself stretched beyond breaking point, like a living carcass being butchered. In the brief respite between contractions, she was giddy with the excitement of seeing her long-awaited child. Through the sweat in her eyes, she registered that Mountain Song was chanting, singing out the baby. He paused to instruct her womenfolk. They busied around her, loosened her hair, and told her to squat. She wanted to scream at them to leave, to stay, anything to help her pain. She shook her head in refusal; her sweat-wet hair matted across her face, salting her eyes, and blocking her sight. Mountain Song came close to her. His scent was heightened, overpowering. She felt her throat rising and retched.

He whispered into her ear. 'You must squat now Willow Tree, for your daughter.'

No sooner was she on her haunches than the pain doubled: worse than anything she had ever felt. 'I can't, I can't,' she cried out, clutching the ends of the birthing sash and bracing herself against the wall of the hogan to push again. It was wrong. Something felt very wrong to her. The head would not come through. She braced once more. Mountain Song leant in from her flank and touched his palm to the skin below her belly button. Her guts cramped and she screamed as the pain shot up her spine then dropped away. Her young was out and wailing.

Willow Tree blinked through the sweat as Mountain Song handed the newborn to her, clearing off the muzzle with his thumb. She took the child in her arm and held her tiny hands. Moments before she had thought the agony would break her body, now she felt her heart would rupture with joy. 'The air is good, Daughter,' she whispered. Again, the infant bawled; Willow Tree laughed at the strength of her howling. She looked up at the older women. They nodded as the baby took the teat. Mountain Song swept aside the blanket at the doorway, carrying the afterbirth and cord to bury them beside the loom. Coyote yipped. The new mother called her young cousin. 'Butterfly, run and fetch Hawk.' The beads on the child's dress clicked and rattled as her feet pattered westwards.

Moments later Hawk stooped to enter the hogan.

She had never seen fear in his face until now. He was pale. 'I heard your cries. I feared the worst…' His voice trailed off. He edged towards her and their child as if stalking a mountain lion before dropping to his haunches.

Willow Tree saw his hands tremble. 'Take her!' she laughed. 'She won't break, but she might scream at you!' Hawk rested his young in the crook of his elbow. She opened and closed her hands round his long fingers. Willow Tree saw his struggle. She prompted him again, 'Greet your daughter.' His voice croaked when he tried to speak. Willow Tree stroked his arm with her hot hand. 'Call her by her name,' she encouraged him. 'Bright Flower.'

*

Coyote's delight in the child's Akote spirit made him sing to the moon. She rarely complained, even when she was teething.

By the time she was five, she awoke with her mother to perform the dawn prayer ritual and tidied the hogan as if it was her sacred responsibility, pulling the skins and furs straight and ensuring that the woven baskets of dried food were always replenished. She knew what the infants of the settlement wanted. She could tell between their hunger and needing to be winded; when they were cold or needed attention. She stroked their hair while they were tucked up in their cradle boards, calming them until, breathing deep and regular, they fell asleep.

Coyote knew then, as he had when he carried her unborn spirit to the canyon, that Bright Flower's instinct and alertness were as keen as his own. He witnessed her strengths develop as she weaved cotton and wool, her arms moving with the speed and fluidity of a snake chasing a mouse. She made strong, tight baskets with fingers swift as the wings of a hummingbird. She ground and prepared corn and wheat as well as any grandmother. Coyote could feel the force of her will – as strong as any man or woman's. Summer and winter she would sit outside the lodge, hidden by the night, to listen as her father spoke with Pale Horse and the other men about strategy and tactics. It was clear to her how each of the villagers in the canyon, each of the settlements themselves were essential to the survival of the Akote people. In their arguing the men seemed at times to forget this, raising their voices, losing the vital thread of the discussion. When that happened, Bright Flower lost interest, turning her attention to the call of an owl or the flight patterns of bats.

By Bright Flower's twelfth spring, she had learned and mastered the drying of fruit, skinning and tanning of hides. When cutting, salting, and curing meat, she would take the offcuts and leave them on a rock in the stand of cottonwoods for the ravens and coyotes, 'This is for you brothers and sisters.'

*

In the predawn, Coyote was at the foot of the rock face, pissing on the corpse of a rattlesnake. When he felt Mountain Song's calling chant in his blood, he knew that the child had passed into womanhood.

The villagers were congregated outside Willow Tree's hogan for Bright Flower's corncake ceremony, watching as Mountain Song laid her face down on a blanket, her head at the doorway facing West, her feet pointing away to the East. Bright Flower's hair was loose, her arms outstretched at her sides. She was dressed in fine clothes and new moccasins. The edges of the blanket rose and fell with the spring breeze as if the earth beneath her was breathing. Mountain Song stood by, singing low, rocking. He indicated to Willow Tree to mould her daughter's limbs and muscles into the perfect shape, to represent First Woman. She straightened her daughter's arms and legs, then reached into a deerskin pouch. She drew from it a handful of leather thongs which she used to tie Bright Flower's hair into a knot. Coyote panted, his tail snaking behind him. When she tied in the last thong, Mountain Song cried out, 'Let the children come forward.'

As Bright Flower stood, the village children pressed in on her like a herd of goats each wanting to be fed first. In turn, she placed her hands under their jaws and with the lightest touch, pressed upwards to encourage their growth into adulthood. The last little girl looked up at her with wide eyes, biting her upper lip. Bright Flower whispered reassurance, 'Soon. Soon it will be your turn.' The girl threw her arms around her.

Mountain Song called, 'Run to the East!'

Bright Flower sprinted east along the canyon floor, the children following. The elder boys tried to keep up with her but fell back one by one. Bright Flower was too fast for them. Reaching the edge of an orchard, three hundred paces from Willow Tree's hogan, she turned back the way she had come. Coyote growled and gnawed at the itch in his flank. The gaggle of children were screaming and laughing as she bore down on them coming the other way; they wheeled and ran back with her.

Already the women were busy grinding corn. Bright Flower stepped into the hogan behind Mountain Song and sat on a bench where he indicated. The medicine man started singing then without break. On and on he sang as the sun reached its apex and descended again. It lasted until dusk. When Mountain Song stopped singing, Hawk started, then her mother. Through the night, the villagers added their voices in turn.

Before dawn, Bright Flower fell asleep. Coyote stalked into her dream, sat in front of her and waited. The sun was warming her; she tried to move her limbs, but they were massive and unyielding, stretching left and right without end. And then she grasped it. She was the canyon. The rock itself.

The dream continued. Her attention was caught by a young couple walking away from her towards Mountain Song's hogan. Flame danced between them, a oneness. There was something about the set of the young woman's shoulders, the way she carried her head. What was it? There was an isolation about her, a gnawing grief that set her apart from her Akote sisters. Ah! She was childless. The young man turned back towards the woman. A moment of shock – it was Bright Flower's father. And the woman whose back was so familiar was her mother, but not much older than she was now. In that moment Bright Flower recognised that feeling of isolation in herself, the things Mountain Song had always said, that she would choose her own husband, follow her own path. Her spirit seemed to stretch across time then, united with every Akote woman since First Woman, and with all Akote women to come. She felt their destinies, her own, as a single destiny stretching back into the past and forward into the future.

Mountain Song's voice outside the hogan brought her round. 'Let the children come forward.' It was dawn again. As Bright Flower stepped across the threshold into the cool air, he shouted 'East!'

Without thought, she broke into a run. The number of children was twice what it had been the previous morning. As she sprinted, she noticed that Sky and Bear Cub, two of the tallest, strongest boys in her village, ran with her. Sky kept up with her until she reached the orchard but lagged after the turn. Bear Cub stayed with her until she was halfway back, then with a grunt, also slowed. Once more the women were grinding corn, but some were now digging a shallow pit. Again, Bright Flower followed Mountain Song back inside the hogan for the singing. She had not eaten since the ceremony began, and as the day passed, she started to drift in and out of consciousness.

Mountain Song played a small drum as he sang. The rhythm took her. She dreamt that she was panting, that her back was stretching as her four legs beat the ground fast and even, that she was racing all the warriors of the Akote, that as she outran them all, she could smell the particular scent of each of them, hear their thoughts, their tactics for winning the race. But none had her cunning, nor her wildness – the cunning and wildness of Coyote.

She awoke momentarily as Mountain Song was singing high, piercing notes, then her head nodded forward again. Back in the dream, Mountain Song's voice turned into the sound of villagers running and screaming as horses ridden in anger galloped into the canyon, but Bright Flower was calm, solid. She was the rock. She knew what was happening was part of her purpose.

On the third dawn, her mother woke her by squeezing her hand and whispering in her ear. 'It is time to go outside, Daughter.' Bright Flower stretched, untangling herself from where her calf and foot were hooked around her mother's lower leg.

Mountain Song rose and called the children forward. So many children. This time they had come from the neighbouring villages too, and as Bright Flower stepped out into the thin light, many of them called to her, 'Bright Flower, Bright Flower!'

'East!' Mountain Song commanded. Bright Flower cried out high and clear and was running before he finished the word. She had risen above herself, flying over the earth as the eagle does, taking in the lie of the land with twitches of her head. Her flesh was light, strong, pulsing with the energy of the sun, of the canyon walls, of the water rushing in the wash.

Tears streamed down Willow Tree's cheeks as she watched her daughter speed across the canyon floor, pursued by the multitude of children, 'Look Mountain Song. See how they follow her, how she is already a mother to our people.'

Mountain Song laughed, raised one knee up to his chest and hopped, 'She ensures strength and speed for the Akote.' He started to chant again.

As she ran towards the hogan, Bright Flower slipped back down into her body. It was heavy. She breathed the smoke from the fire that had been lit in the pit. Feeling a deep ache low in her belly, she focused on the flames. In them she saw her own spirit, the spirit of First Woman, now clay, now fire, and in the fire, she saw the flash of eyes. Two green eyes.

The women were making batter now from the ground corn. As Bright Flower followed Mountain Song back inside, Willow Tree pushed a bundle of yucca fibres into her hands. 'You must weave all these into twine.'

Bright Flower sat on the floor and started to plait. Willow Tree sat back to back with her. Mountain Song began to sing. Bright Flower's fingers moved in time with his voice. Plaiting, singing, and breathing, all one in her. When Mountain Song stopped, her mother started up, the soft voice right behind Bright Flower, resonating in her spine. Together they were an eight-limbed creature, and as a spider spins silk, Bright Flower spun the twine without thinking.

She awoke with her head tipped back on her mother's

shoulder, a completed coil of twine on her lap. The smell of the corncake cooking in the pit outside made her mouth water and her stomach ache. Willow Tree caressed her cheek with the back of her hand and helped Bright Flower to her feet.

For the fourth and final time, 'East!' The children swarmed to her as she stepped outside and started to run. The emerging sun warmed her face on the way out, her back as she returned, fuelling her excitement. The women at the pit were clearing the surface now, retrieving the corncake.

Inside, Mountain Song took up the yucca twine, held it above his head as he finished singing. 'The yucca root heals. Its fibres make the twine that binds so securely. Bright Flower is now an Akote woman. It is the Akote woman who binds us together. It is the Akote woman who gives a home to her man, it is she who gives a future to her people.' He turned to the men and boys sitting to one side of the hogan, Sky and Bear Cub two rows behind Hawk who sat in the front. 'She is the soul of the Akote and, as such, is entitled to the help of any Akote man should she need it.'

The women from the pit brought the corncake in, four of them each supporting the edge of the great grey disk. The aroma filled the hogan. Mountain Song broke the edge off, nodded for Bright Flower to follow him outside. The others followed them. He held the piece of cake above his head, 'This we offer you, Great Mother, in thanks for the coming of age of this Akote woman.'

Coyote watched as the huge corncake was shared among the villagers. An early cricket scuttled across the sand. With a forward jerk of the head, the morsel was in his mouth, releasing its grassy flavour with each crunch.

*

At dusk, Bright Flower was working on her mother's loom when she heard shouting and laughter. A boy from the next village was running around two rams, their horns locked together. He darted in and out trying to wrestle them apart while Sky and Bear Cub laughed and jeered at him. The boy was panting hard; blood smeared his forearms. His exhaustion was clear as the animals pushed one way and then the other off their hindlegs, their horns grinding and rattling. The boy had no way out. To give up would ensure mockery and dishonour. Bright Flower saw the fear and hopelessness in his eyes.

When he had a grip on the upper horns of one of the rams, she called out and pointed at the other, 'That's my mother's!' She rushed to straddle the other ram and grasped it by the fleece of its shoulders. Sky and Bear Cub tensed and jumped forward, they crowded round the animal, each gaining a grip on its coat or a leg. Taking advantage of the confusion, Bright Flower held fast with one hand to the horns of the other, until she could see that the younger boy had managed to disentangle them. At that moment she released her grip, and the pair came apart. The young boy waved his ram away, kicking after it. She addressed him, 'Thank you.' She turned to take in the others, 'You saved our animal from injury.'

The boy shook his head, 'But why was your ram grazing near our village?'

'Your village?' She looked the creature up and down. 'Huh! This is not my mother's ram.'

Hawk

The early sky is turquoise, still soft before the sun burns it a harsher blue. The hunt was good this morning, easy and fast. Pale Horse and I each carry an antelope over our shoulders. We reach the canyon's rim and make east for the talus. Far below I see Bright Flower working at the skins with Willow Tree. My heart fills at the sight of them both, but I ache that this fine young woman remains unmarried and childless in her nineteenth summer. She is strong like her mother, perhaps stronger. She has always been. Bright Flower is our daughter and our son, as much Akote as any living or dead, but this otherness she lives being unmarried, waiting, will she be able to bear it any longer?

Life was simpler before she came of age. Before the Mexican soldiers attacked the mouth of the Great Southwest Canyon, killing forty men and taking their women and children for slaves, driving them with sheep and horses across the plateau. Since that time, raiding has increased. We Akote are the main source of slaves. Although our location in this Canyon and richer prizes to the south have protected Los Huertos from the worst attacks, they grow more numerous.

'You look beset with concerns.' Pale Horse smiles at me. 'Tell me, Hawk, what is so serious it can blight the joy of returning from a successful hunt?'

We have reached the talus. I heave the antelope from

my shoulders and cast it down the slope, so its own weight can do the work of descending. I answer him as he does the same. 'The raids. Their boldness grows. We cannot rely solely on the advantageous position of our home.'

'We do not. The alliances we have to the south, north and west have arisen from our success in scouting and in the reprisals we have taken. Our reputation protects us. The reputation you have built for us in the years since becoming War Chief. No one approaches Los Huertos, but we know of it. Even traders avoid our canyon. My friend, I do not think it is this alone that concerns you.'

I cannot help but laugh. 'It is also your vigilance which has kept us safe. I was thinking of Bright Flower. She had another suitor, a man from Great Harvest Canyon. A good, courageous warrior who treated his first wife with respect and kindness until she died. Once again, she shows no interest. She continues with her work and her prayers.'

'She is devout, like her father and her mother. Have you discussed the matter with Mountain Song?'

'He repeats what he told us before she was born, that it is her destiny to choose her husband, and ours to have faith in the wisdom within her. Willow Tree reminds me to be patient as we were when we were childless.'

We have reached the base of the talus. Pale Horse stoops to his antelope. I continue several paces further into the edge of the orchard where mine has come to rest. Flies buzz around its head. In its eye I see the reflection of a single peach tree. First there was one, before there were orchards. Our ancestors waited and hoped. They had faith.

'Are you coming?' Pale Horse prompts me. I hoist the game to my shoulders, and we walk in silence to the settlement. The weight we carry pushes our feet into the earth. Each step raises more dust than when we are unburdened. I turn for my hogan. Pale Horse turns for his. Willow Tree and Bright Flower are outside, waiting, smiling.

*

We sit inside. Bright Flower and Willow Tree have butchered the antelope and are preparing cornbread. Outside, the day burns bright, the canyon shimmering in the heat from the earth. In here it is dark, cool. I fletch an arrow. Turkey feathers cut into shape wait on the stool next to me, ready to form the flight.

Bright Flower looks up at me, then at Willow Tree. 'Father, Mother, will you help me to build my own hogan?'

My breath catches in my chest. Willow Tree stops her kneading. I struggle to find the words, 'Are you? Has someone? Usually you would be –'

Willow Tree is smiling now, 'Of course, Daughter, we will build a beautiful hogan. We shall have it blessed by Mountain Song, and it will be yours. Tell us though, why choose this moment?'

'Because soon I will need it for a husband.'

I make my face unreadable to cover my anger, 'A husband? Who has made themselves known to you?

Why did they not speak with me first?'

'I don't know, I mean no one has. I just feel it's what I'm supposed to do, and this morning when I awoke, I saw that a spider had spun a web in the night between my blanket and the hogan but as I watched she unpicked the silk where it attached to the wall.'

A shadow blocks the light from the doorway. Pale Horse.

'Word from our scouts. Two mounted white men and a mule entered the eastern end of the canyon early this morning.'

*

I watch them from the orchard. They see only what is in front of them. They have not noticed our men to the rear, ready for them. The rocking of their bodies with the motion of their horses is hot and weary. The taller man is loose, open. He listens to the smaller one who is tight and angry. They hear the ponies behind them and turn. I walk out into the canyon. Holding their fear now, they turn forward again and seeing me, halt their horses.

'Why are you here?' They do not respond. Their lips move as they whisper to each other. I ask again, 'What is your purpose?' The taller man coughs, then speaks. His voice is calm, friendly. He indicates himself and the other as he talks. Pale Horse has been watching from among the horses. He comes to stand at my side. The strangers look from his topknot to his moccasins and up again in silence. The smaller one glares at him.

'What do you think, Pale Horse?'

'The one that speaks seems harmless enough, but the small one has the eyes of a snake.' The smell of stew fills the air. The smaller man shifts in his saddle as his stomach growls aloud. Pale Horse snorts, 'One speaks through his mouth like a man, and I understand nothing, while the other speaks through his stomach like an animal and I understand completely.' The women and children tip their heads back and laugh. I use the lightness of the moment to beckon the strangers. They dismount and follow me to our hogan, Pale Horse behind them.

Inside, I invite them to sit. Willow Tree is watching them. She waits for me to explain. 'We believe these men are traders. Let us make them welcome while we find out why they are here, and if there are others.'

She sniffs and looks at me for a long moment then breathes out, her shoulders softening. 'We will show them our best hospitality, even though our husband gave us no time to prepare.' She smiles over her shoulder as she fetches cornbread and piñon nuts.

The smaller man reaches down towards his knife; I feel Pale Horse ready himself to pounce. The stranger does too and shows his hands. With care, he reaches down again, brings out a vessel and drinks from it. He makes a sound to show appreciation, and gestures to Pale Horse to share in it.

'What do you think it is?' he asks me.

Willow Tree interrupts, 'Well if it's poison, he already drank it so you're probably safe, one way or another.'

Pale Horse glances at her then back at the stranger. He takes the vessel and drinks, then throws it down, yelling as he spits the liquid into the fire where it flares. 'They are mad!' He reaches for his knife.

I hold him back, 'Pale Horse, wait. If they were going to poison us, as Willow Tree says, they wouldn't do it like this.' The taller man speaks to his companion and takes the vessel from him. He drinks, makes noises of enjoyment, then gestures us to move backwards as he spits into the fire, causing another flare. He laughs as he speaks to the other man, handing it back to him. The smaller man goes to put it back on his belt but stops and offers it to me. I do not take it.

Pale Horse warns, 'It's filth – it burns your mouth and your throat and makes you cough and spit – although…' he licks his lips, '…it is sweet afterwards, like fruit, but warm.'

We stay like this, I unwilling to take the vessel, the stranger not wishing to withdraw his offer. Willow Tree saves further tension, offering a basket of food to her guests, 'These are corn cakes. Please, eat.' He puts the liquid back on his belt and takes one. The taller man does the same, humming his thanks while holding the corncake up as if it is a rare gem to be examined in the light.

Pale Horse is rubbing his mouth with his hand, 'They have had too much sun.'

Willow Tree chides him, 'Pale Horse, these are guests in my hogan. Show them respect as you should.'

He looks towards me, but I avoid the contact. The taller man is admiring the empty basket. He reaches into his shoulder bag and produces a Spanish coin and two small pieces of silver. He mimes a trade, the silver for the basket.

Bright Flower comes in, bringing peaches. 'Mother, I thought you might want fruit for our guests.'

'Thank you, Bright Flower. This basket holding the peaches, would you trade it with these white men for silver?'

'What's mine is yours, Mother. Do what you will with it.' Willow Tree takes it, tips the peaches in to the corncake basket then offers the empty one instead. 'This one, not the other,' she explains.

The smaller man speaks, but his friend does not respond. Instead, he chooses a tiny piece of silver to offer. We do not want these men to undervalue our goods. 'Willow Tree let us not sell our wares too cheaply.'

Willow Tree shakes her head and indicates two with her fingers. The man nods, his voice low, friendly. He positions two silver ornaments before her. She offers the basket. He reaches out to take it but stops and looks at me.

'He wants your approval for the trade,' Pale Horse mutters. I nod and he takes it. He does not confer with his friend.

Bright Flower watches from the doorway. The sun bathes her in gold, heightening her radiance. The taller man glances towards her and is momentarily unable to look away. Bright Flower smiles and casts her eyes downwards.

'Daughter, thank you for your basket. Do not let us keep you from your work.' She leaves.

'You don't trust them, neither do I,' Pale Horse says. 'Especially the small one.'

'I do not know whether to trust these men or not. They want to trade with us, let them do so. If you and your family wish to barter with them next, they will learn that we do not give away our skilled work cheaply. If you are satisfied with the bargains, we will let them trade with others in the settlement.'

The strangers whisper to each other as Pale Horse rises, stooping to avoid the ceiling of the hogan. 'Visitors, come to my hogan and we will trade.' He gestures for them to follow. They stand.

The taller one turns back and speaks. Again, the words are peaceful in his voice. He indicates his companion, 'Abraham Knox,' then touches his own chest, 'Francis Meavy.'

I acknowledge the man's friendliness. 'Hawk,' I say, omitting to list the ancestry customary in Akote introductions. Willow Tree looks at me, surprised.

The trader speaks my name, 'Hawk?'

She smiles, repeating it and nodding.

*

They trade with Pale Horse. When they have finished, he takes them over to the cottonwoods and addresses the village, 'These traders come here for baskets and blankets and other items. If you wish to trade with them, do so, but remember we do not know these men.'

We watch them bargain until their purchases form a mound beside them. They load them on to the mule, surrounded by children, marvelling at their clothes, the colour of their skin, the greenness of Francis Meavy's eyes. They are at the point of leaving when he turns, holding out a heavy buckskin parcel. As they approach, he calls my name. He stops in front of me, the smaller man in front of Pale Horse. He speaks again as they offer us the packages. I take it and unwrap it. Inside is a fine steel knife, weighty and long. Pale Horse admires his. They mount up and leave, back the way they came. As I watch, Francis Meavy looks over his shoulder and waves.

'Do you think they will come back here?' Pale Horse asks me.

I look down at the knife. 'They will.'

*

Autumn 1843 — Canyon de Los Huertos Ocultos

The aspens are turning to gold. I stand watching their dance in the breeze. The scout has told me that the traders are returning. As they approach the settlement, I seek Pale Horse and we ride out together. We canter up to the pair, reining in ten paces off, the horses facing each other.

Pale Horse hails them, 'Francis Meavy and your small friend. Here you are. We thought you would return. The harvest has been gathered since you left, what does your stomach have to say about that?' He laughs aloud.

I warn him, 'Your mocking is wasted, and if Willow Tree catches you she'll chide you like last time.'

'I'm enjoying myself,' he grins. I see that Francis Meavy is also smiling. His friend is still, and stone faced.

I sit with Pale Horse in the village, observing the traders at work again by the cottonwoods. This time, as well as blankets and baskets, they are shown skins. They bargain for them along with turquoise. They have a particular appetite for that stone. Abraham Knox remains expressionless and contained in his dealings, while Francis Meavy is warm and animated. I invite them to share food, gesturing for them to follow me.

Once in the hogan, it seems that Francis Meavy is missing something. Every time Willow Tree comes and goes he looks at the doorway. I have asked Bright Flower to check the sheep on the plateau, preventing contact between them, cautious of what passed between her and Francis Meavy last time. She is vulnerable despite having inherited her mother's wilfulness. We sit eating corncakes. The traders carry knives that match, along with their ammunition pouches and powder horns.

'You're looking at their weapons,' Pale Horse says, always vigilant.

'I am. You have noticed.'

'I have. Shall I fetch the medicine man Shadow Bloom from the next village? He speaks Spanish. We could question them.'

I nod. Pale Horse rises and leaves. Willow Tree brings more food. Francis Meavy is appreciative. He nods, smiles, and speaks softly in what I assume to be thanks. By the time the guests have finished eating, Pale Horse returns. He lets the medicine man enter the hogan first.

'The air is good, Shadow Bloom.'

'The air is good, Hawk.' He stares at the traders, Abraham Knox in particular.

Pale Horse addresses him, 'Shadow Bloom, you know Spanish. Will you speak with these men?'

'What do you wish to say?' His voice is as cold as always.

Pale Horse points his nose towards Knox. 'Ask this, but ensure it is clear that it is the smaller man you are addressing. Are they warriors of their country? Have they been sent here as scouts? Are there more of them coming? Do they trade with our enemies?'

I watch the traders as Shadow Bloom translates the questions. Abraham Knox turns towards Pale Horse with sharp words. Shadow Bloom translates. 'They were soldiers. They left the Army three years ago. That is all he says.'

Pale Horse glances at me, irritated. Before he can talk, Francis Meavy continues. He speaks several sentences, his demeanour open, friendly. He finishes and leans forward, hands on his thighs, to listen to Shadow Bloom's translation. A man who wants to learn.

'He says he and the smaller man, whom he calls Abraham Knox, are partners in trading only, not scouts. They come from far to the east. They report to no one. They sell goods in Corazon and Santa Fe and have traded with the Ute, the Pueblo, and with the Apache. They say their intentions are peaceful. They acknowledge the quality of goods here and say they would not betray the Akote to their enemies.'

I watch Francis Meavy. 'Will he promise this?'

Shadow Bloom translates the question and the reply. 'He gives his word of honour.'

'Abraham Knox?' He listens but hesitates before he nods.

I look out through the doorway. It is late afternoon, and the sun is low. Francis Meavy stops Shadow Bloom as he leaves the hogan.

'They ask to make camp in the canyon, away from your homes.'

'Beyond the cottonwoods? I will show them.' Pale Horse offers. I look at Francis Meavy and nod. Shadow Bloom explains. Francis Meavy thanks him. They leave. I stand alone in the firelight, breathing the scent of burning juniper. My spirit is uneasy. Away to the North, Coyote howls.

*

It is after dawn but still early, the morning slow in its awakening. We watch them on the far side of the canyon. Abraham Knox prepares to ride out. He readies his horse, straps their goods to the mule and makes east. Francis Meavy walks towards us. As he approaches, he is surprised to see us and removes his hat, raising it towards the sun. Smiling, he speaks, then seems to await an answer.

Pale Horse shakes his head, 'We cannot understand you.' Francis Meavy walks towards the horse pen, pointing at the animals. He speaks again and limps back to us before he kicks out with one leg, jumps to one side, and rubs his other leg, limping again.

Pale Horse's frown clears. 'It is a ceremonial dance. Or his companion has been kicked by one of their animals in which case he seems untroubled. Either that or he wants us to sell him an injured horse –'

'His animal is lame, Pale Horse.'

Pale Horse points at Francis Meavy then at himself. He mimes stroking the neck of a horse then kicks out. He sways to show the animal is unsound. Francis Meavy throws his hat on the ground, speaking and nodding. Again, he indicates the sun and draws the path it will take across the sky until dusk. He shuts his eyes as if sleeping but flashes the fingers on both hands showing eight of them.

'Eight nights he wants to remain,' Pale Horse interprets.

'It is safe to let him stay until his horse is sound, but will Abraham Knox return?' He hears the name and points to the east. He indicates the sun moving backwards through the sky and acts riding east with his reins in one hand and a halter in the other. Now he counts sixteen with his fingers and mimes a horse limping less and less, then departing.

'Back in sixteen days if Francis Meavy doesn't leave in eight?' Pale Horse guesses, turning to me for confirmation. 'If we let him stay and trade he could be of use. He might have information about the Ute and the Anaii, perhaps the Mexicans.'

We nod our permission. He thanks us and returns to the alcove. I watch him go. He is respectful, always respectful.

Pale Horse grunts, 'An honourable man, I'd say.'

*

Pale Horse seeks me out in the hogan, his head appearing in the doorway. 'No word from our scouts on the northern plateau.'

Something is amiss. I step out into the canyon. The sky is clear, taut. Towards the east the wind spirals the dust into a funnel the height of a man, twisting counter sunwise then dropping. 'Gather the men.'

We ride west then turn north up on to the plateau. The birds are silent. The air hangs sullen. In the distance a lone horse stands on a mound. Dust rises in clouds from its fore-hoof as it paws the ground. Its rider lies forward along its neck. He sits up in the saddle then slides off, falling onto the earth. The sound of his cry reaches us and his pony bolts towards ours. I lean over him. Flies busy around the gunshot wound in his shoulder. The blood soaks his shirt and breeches. Burning rises in my gut. I vault onto my horse and kick on towards the canyon rim.

Far below, two raiders gallop into our village. Movement at the base of the southern talus. Francis Meavy is sprinting across the canyon floor. I search for Willow Tree and Bright Flower. Bright Flower comes out of the hogan and starts to run. They see her and turn their ponies in pursuit. We are too far off to get down in time. One comes up alongside her and tries to lift her onto his horse. She fights him off, but the other is on her blindside. He strikes her with his rifle. She falls limp. My heart beats with half its strength then stutters and beats hard again. She lives.

I call out to my Ancestors, to the Holy People, to the spirit of my horse and drive him over the canyon's edge.

I lean back until my head touches his spine. I call to Mother Earth, to Father Sky, and I am no longer Hawk. I am the rock pushing up beneath my horse's feet, I am the air slowing our descent, I am the heat rising from the canyon floor. The high notes of our cries rise as we slide and tack down the sheer slope. Now we near the base of the wall, moments from the silt and I am the man standing alone in the canyon, blood drumming; the fear in my guts, clenching and unclenching, is enough to overpower any warrior, but the courage in my heart is greater yet. Burning, stabbing pain but I stand. I am honour, I am sacrifice.

I am Francis Meavy, and I stare down Death.

Part Two

Francis Meavy

I squint to see through the heat haze. The reins in my right hand are swollen with sweat, the palm of my left is wet where it rests on my thigh.

My partner, Abe Knox, speaks as we ride, the words rasp in his throat. His eyes are blue-grey, same as the storm sky over the Ute mountains behind us. As he talks, they pan across the canyon, up the rock wall to the rim and back down across the wash. 'Baskets and blankets. And turquoise. Good fur, but nothing we can't get elsewhere. They don't have firearms yet, but they make their bows with oak and deer sinew, so they're better than we've come across before. They're good with horses, too, I heard. Very good.'

The motion of my mare rocks me from side to side, lulling me. I glance across as I listen. Abe is always observing, assessing, ever since we were boys. He's leading our mule, its bundles cinched with straps. Its tail swishes at flies and the leather creaks as it flexes in the afternoon sun. We walk our animals further into the canyon close to the dry bed of the wash. I look down, entranced by the rhythm of the hooves flicking up sprays of sand. A tugging at the back of my head breaks the spell. I slip my hand beneath my hat and free my hair from the collar of my buckskin jacket. It's wet in my hand.

A light breeze comes through from the west. I breathe in the coolness while I can. The sound of bleating and laughter over to the right. Children driving goats through an orchard of fruit trees at the foot of the canyon wall. They stop and stare. I laugh. Children are the same wherever you go. I smile, wave, and look across at Abe who is staring back at them. The breeze lifts again, picking up the scent of the trees. I draw the air in through my nose then sigh it out again.

'Smell those peaches, Abe?'

Abe smirks as women come out to join the children. 'I do, and I'm hungry. Where are the menfolk?'

A horse whinnies behind us. My gut tightens as I turn in my saddle. Ten mounted Akote warriors, line abreast, match the walking pace of our horses a hundred feet behind us. Their lances are upright and faces impassive beneath their pale headbands and red topknots. I turn forward again and we rein in. Twenty paces ahead a tall, broad-shouldered man stands in our path. We are trapped. The man speaks, his voice carrying clearly to us, neither friendly nor aggressive.

Abe whispers, barely audible, 'Why can't they learn English? What the hell do you think he's saying?'

The warrior repeats himself.

'Same as usual, I guess – who are we?' I whisper back, then clear my throat. 'I am Francis Meavy.' I say it slowly, touching my left hand to my breastbone. 'This is Abraham Knox.' I indicate Abe. 'We have come here to make your acquaintance. To see if we can trade with your people.' My words echo back at me from the rock. Another warrior strides out from behind a corral of horses and stands beside the first. He's huge, a head taller and a handspan wider at the shoulder.

Silence. I try again, 'We hope that you will find value in the goods we have brought. We would like to discuss your basketwork and weaving if you are amenable.' My voice trails off, and I see the first warrior speak under his breath to the second. They are looking me up and down. I make myself smile and nod. They turn their attention to Abe. I glance over, he's staring back. 'Nice and friendly now, Abe.' The sweat crawls down my backbone.

A goat bleats. The cottonwood trees shush as another breeze comes in, catches the smoke from the nearest chimney and casts the rich aroma of mutton stew out into the canyon. The silence is broken by Abe's stomach rumbling like a dog yawning. The larger warrior snorts and speaks loudly. The women and children laugh. I sense Abe tensing and calm him with a hand on his arm.

The first warrior steps forward and gestures for us to come with him. A boy takes the reins of my animal as we dismount. We follow on to one of the mud and timber dwellings, the huge man falling in behind. He ducks through the entrance past the blankets hitched to one side and motions for us to sit on low stools covered with buffalo hide. His woman is there, she stares at us. I smile, remove my hat, and sit. I nod at Abe to do the same. It is cool and smells of old smoke and corn. Homey.

The man says something to his wife. She sniffs and stares at him for a long moment then breathes out, her shoulders softening. She smiles over her shoulder as she fetches baskets of food. The men sit opposite us.

I'll start up the conversation again. Goddammit, Abe's reaching for the whiskey flask he keeps on his hip above his bayonet. The larger man tenses. Abe holds his hands up, fingers spread, palms visible. Slowly, he moves his left hand down to his belt, points at the flask, brings it out and unscrews the stopper. He takes a slug then lowers it with an 'Ahh.' He offers the flask to the large warrior whose face is stony. 'It's good!' he says nudging it towards him. The man takes it, his eyes never shifting from Abe.

He speaks sidelong to his comrade. My breathing stretches my chest. The woman cuts in, speaking quickly. I brace myself. The large warrior glances at the woman then back at Abe. He raises the neck to his lips and tilts his head back. There is a moment's stillness in the hogan as everyone watches, then an explosion as he spits, coughs and shouts, jumping backwards as the liquor hits the fire and ignites. Abe grabs up the flask from the floor to stem the spillage. Lord preserve us. The man shouts and reaches for his knife. The other blocks his arm, speaking as he does so.

This is the tipping point. 'Abe, give it to me. Give me your damn flask.'

The large warrior scowls as Abe passes it across. I know what to do. I take a nip from the flask, roll it round my mouth and swallow. I exaggerate an 'Ahh!' and tell them, 'Watch.' I take a mouthful, gesture for them to move back a little, and blow the lot into the fire, matching the theatrical flame with theatrical coughing. I thump my chest with the top of my fist like a buffoon and shake my head at Abe. 'Are you sure that isn't poison?' I make my voice warm and jovial, laughing. I hand it back to Abe. He stoppers it and is putting it away but pauses and holds the vessel towards the other warrior who looks down at it then back into his eyes. 'What the hell, Abe?' I force a smile.

The woman catches my eye for a moment before she grabs a small basket and steps into the space, offering corncakes to us both. Grateful for the distraction, I take the cue, and reach across Abe to pluck a cake from the basket, 'Thank you, ma'am.' I raise it as if making a toast and bite into it. Abe puts the flask back in his belt and does the same. I nod and make appreciative humming sounds, holding the corncake up to admire it. The woman gives me the slightest of nods. An ally.

The larger man starts to make a remark but is cut off by her. He looks to his friend who avoids the contact. A woman to be reckoned with. I examine the empty basket. The work is fine, the colours rich. 'We would like to trade with you for these baskets and ones of other sizes and designs,' I put it back in front of the woman. 'We have silver with which to bargain.' I shrug around the small leather satchel I keep hung across my shoulder and open the flap. I feel inside for a Spanish coin and two small silver spirals that could be used for ornamentation on clothing or a bridle. With one hand, I offer a spiral to our hosts and with the other, I mime drawing the basket towards my chest.

A young woman ducks through the entrance of the hogan, a basket of peaches in her hands. She closely resembles the older woman. She gives the fruit to her mother. While they exchange words, the sun edges west. Rays stream through the chimney hole and bathe the girl in light. Her skin is amber brown and her teeth bright white in her broad smile. She feels my gaze and looks up. I look away. Her father has noticed the exchange. Quietly, he says something to her, and she leaves.

Abe's voice breaks through my thoughts, 'Be careful they don't expect too much silver for one small basket, or else they'll want the same each time.' It's what he always says, and every time I pretend not to hear it.

The warrior speaks. His wife shakes her head and closes her fist except for the index and middle fingers. She's bargaining. I nod. 'Good. Yes. That's a bargain, ma'am. Two of these for your basket.' I take the spirals from my right palm and place them on the earth in front of her. She holds out the basket. I reach out to take it but stop to seek the approval of the warriors to the trade. I look to them for their blessing, my hand extended. Our host has not taken his eyes off me and nods slowly. I take the basket.

Abe whispers to me. 'Don't agree to prices we'll regret later.' Again, I ignore him.

The men confer for a moment then the larger one rises, stooping to avoid the ceiling of the hogan. He gestures for us to follow. We stand and I turn back towards the other man and his woman. 'Thank you for your hospitality.' I point towards Abe, 'Abraham Knox,' then place my open hand on my breastbone. 'Francis Meavy.'

The man mirrors the gesture, 'Hawk,' he says. The wife is watching us closely. I say the name, 'Hawk?' The woman repeats it and nods. Hawk indicates the larger man, 'Pale Horse.'

I duck out of the hogan after the others. The sunlight in the canyon is blinding. I narrow my eyes against the glare and hear the swell of Akote voices. Mingled with that sound are others: sheep bleating; a dog barking in response; the rhythmic scraping as hide is worked; the long cluck-cluck of a turkey; and on the breeze, once again, a smell of fruit – peaches or melons. I pause to close my eyes completely, turning my face to the sun for a moment.

Warmth and peace fill my head and percolate down through my body. I reopen my eyes. The others are watching me. I follow as they move off, the tall warrior leading. The same trading sequence unfolds at his hogan, but this time we bargain for fine blankets and buy two. Once we have conducted our business, he leads us to one side of the canyon where low rocks in a cottonwood stand provide shade and seating. He turns towards the villagers and addresses them, indicating to us as he does so. We trade for silver and blankets, baskets, and cotton goods. I'm always inclined to greater generosity than Abe in these first dealings. Our prices are flattering to the Akote at the outset since the intention is to open up future trades. Got to be careful though, our growing pile of bargains risks being too much for the mule. We draw our dealings to a close, stand and carry our purchases over to where the animals have been tethered to the fence of the corral. We load up. Children jostle around us, chattering and smiling. Such beautiful children. Hawk and his giant friend are watching us.

I put a hand on Abe's shoulder, he's not going to like this. 'We are going to make an investment.' I go to the back of the mule and rummage inside the pack. I find what I'm looking for and search for a second one. 'You present this to Pale Horse and I will give this one to Hawk.' I hand one of the buckskin parcels to Abe. He hesitates before taking it, but I push it on him and approach the Akote men. I slow my pace and hold the package out on the fingertips of both hands.

When I'm ten paces away I call out, 'Hawk,' then walk up holding the parcel towards him. He takes it. I smile at him, 'Please. Unwrap it.' Hawk unfolds it. The steel knife is two spans long with a horn handle. He turns it over, feeling its heft.

Abe says, 'This is yours,' making the same presentation to Pale Horse who looks down the straight edge of his gift.

That should do some good; they're strong, heavy knives. I touch my hat, 'Thank you for the hospitality and the opportunity to trade.' We mount up and ride back up the canyon. It's a shame we can't communicate better. 'Abe, I thought the Akote spoke Spanish?'

'Not these. The Anaii Akote, south of here. Used to be part of the same tribe, now they raid Akote territory and sell the women and children they take to the Mexicans. They hate each other.' Abe's eyes narrow. 'We should use that.'

I feel his mood souring. 'What's with you?'

'They laughed at us. Giving them the good knives was a mistake.'

We ride level at the walk. I check the sky. There's still some light to be had before dusk. I feel his eyes on me. See if I can jolly him out of it, 'That was a tight moment back there with the riders behind us.'

He's slow to answer. 'Did you notice what I did? We didn't hear them.'

'How do you mean?'

'No silver. None of the mounted Akote wear silver on their bridles or clothing. They don't jangle.' He leans over and spits onto the canyon floor, squirting a lizard on a rock with tobacco juice. The liquid stains the rock the colour of molasses. The lizard bolts. He continues. 'I heard from the Ute that this is the last Akote place they raid because of the warriors here. We best watch ourselves.'

I can't help baiting him, 'I like it here. The smell of juniper smoke and mutton stew, the sounds of sheep and goats, the way the men wear a stony mask while the women smile, and the children bustle in like feeding fish.'

We continue eastwards. There is an old man observing our progress from a cave high in the rock face. He sways in the breeze, the currents carrying his soft chanting out into the chasm. I wonder if he's been there all along.

*

A light wind funnels down the canyon from behind us, fanning the back of my neck and stirring the trees. It is so much cooler since we were last here. Our bargains fetched good prices in Corazon, as we thought they would.

This time we see the scout galloping back to warn Hawk and Pale Horse of our coming. They ride up to us, Pale Horse calling out as they approach. I hear my name before he starts laughing. They seem to be bantering between them, a good sign. I smile back and look across at Abe, his face is expressionless, he isn't feeling the humour of the situation. They lead us back to the settlement and show us to the same spot by the cottonwoods. We've mainly come for turquoise, but the skins and woven goods they tender are exceptional, so we buy in as much as the mule will allow. The villagers are more friendly this time and the bargaining relaxed.

Once again Hawk invites us to eat with them. My pulse quickens as I think of the girl from last time. I hope that she will join us. I watch the doorway, but she never comes. Hawk and Pale Horse have noticed our army-issue powder horns and are speaking among themselves. Pale Horse stands and leaves as Hawk's wife offers us smoked meat.

'Thank you, ma'am, for your trouble and hospitality, much appreciated.' I hope she'll understand my sentiments if not my words.

As we finish up, a man enters the hogan. He is bare-chested with necklaces hanging against his mahogany skin and pouches at his waist, but the thing is his eyes. Black and gleaming like a raven's. Hawk greets him.

The man returns the greeting. His voice is harsh, monotonous. Pale Horse speaks to him, and he stares at Abe. He starts to question us in Spanish – Are we army scouts? Where do we trade? With whom? Abe answers, but he's peeved, telling him we left the dragoons three years ago and that we are from back east, but he doesn't provide the assurances they clearly seek. I step in, giving them my word that all we want is to trade, that we would never betray them to their enemies. They insist that Abe gives his word too, which he does resentfully.

By the time the discussion ends it is nearly dusk. I stop the translator as he leaves and ask him to seek permission for us to camp somewhere in the canyon. Pale Horse answers him and he tells us to follow him. As we leave, I inhale the scent from the fire. It is fragrant, comforting – juniper wood, I think.

*

I lean back in the saddle to take the place in. The alcove is the height of a man on a horse and kicked upwards at the junction of its ceiling and the canyon wall. Judging by the scorch marks on the lip, I'd say it's long been used for shelter. It'll do us well.

Pale Horse turns his pony for home and calls to us over his shoulder. He uses my name again. 'Meavy' sounds strange in his voice but it's good to hear him use it. He says 'Abraham Knox' too, but Abe looks sour. Whatever Pale Horse is saying, there's humour in it. He throws his head back and laughs. He lopes his horse back to the settlement, its hooves kicking silt towards us.

I start to pile firewood in a corner at the mouth of the alcove, 'They know both our names now, Abe, and let us camp in the canyon. That's progress.' Abe mutters something in reply, but I go on, 'The back of the cave's good and dry for the guns and powder overnight.'

I've been coaxing him out of his bad moods since we were boys. Busyness helps. I start to untack the animals. He joins me. We make ourselves comfortable by the fire using the packs from the mule and blankets from the horses as bedding. I look around the cave. Images are painted and scratched into the walls. Strange animals with sharp teeth and long bodies, others with short legs and ears like a hare. Elsewhere there are pictures of men on horses: red, white, black, and even a life-sized antelope. They still my mind and fill me with awe. We both stare at the nightscape on the ceiling, the stars precise and regular in their depiction. I breathe in, deep and slow. There is great peace here.

'Who were they, do you think, Abe?'

He shrugs and rolls over.

*

It's dawn and the sky is already clear, the dew sparkling on the arrow weed by the cottonwoods. I go to check the animals sheltered under the overhang of the rock which forms a natural corral. Whistling, I grab the feed bag and unhitch the deadwood barrier. A crow caws. It drops from the trees and flies under the shelter, landing on the rump of Abe's horse. I can see what's coming and try to shoo it. Too late. The horse swishes its tail and kicks out, catching the knee of my mare. She squeals and leaps sideways. I run my hand over the leg. The skin twitches and the joint swells as I watch. She limps away from my touch. Damn it.

Abe is at my side, 'I heard the horses. How bad?'

'Lame. A week's rest I'd say, maybe longer.' I replace the barrier and we return to the fire. 'Looks like we'll have to separate, Abe.'

He spits into the embers. They bubble and hiss. 'You think the Indians will let you stay here?'

Hawk and Pale Horse were more wary of him than they were of me. 'I figure if you're gone and I have a lame horse, they'll understand.'

A smoking stump falls from the flames and rolls towards Abe. He kicks it back with his boot heel, 'I'll take the mule and head to Corazon to sell out the bargains. Same route as before. If you don't catch up by the time I'm finished, I'll bring the next load back with me. Whichever. We can bargain with some of the other settlements before winter. I'll be on my way.' He turns his back on me, tacks up, loads the gear, and rides off without another word.

I inventory my supplies. I saw a stream in the next side canyon with a shallow pool at the foot of the rock where it forms a shelf, so I'm set for water, but I'll need more food and wood. The smell of bread cooking wafts over from the far side of the canyon. I set out on foot towards the settlement. As I draw nearer Hawk and Pale Horse appear as if they're expecting me. I'm glad to see them.

I use my hat to point to the sky and smile, 'Beautiful morning. My horse has been kicked lame and can't be ridden. I need to rest her for a few days. May I camp in the cave until she's sound again?' They stare at me. Pale Horse shakes his head. I've already run over in my mind how best to convey my meaning to them. I hold up a finger and walk towards the corral, pointing. 'My. Horse. Is. Lame.' I walk back to them, limping. Hawk frowns. I mime Knox's horse kicking mine, then rub my leg and wince as I imitate my own horse again. Pale Horse's frown clears. He points at me then at himself. He pretends to stroke the neck of a horse then kicks out. He sways to show the animal is unsound.

'Yes. Yes,' I tear my hat from my head and throw it on the ground. 'That's exactly it. My horse has been kicked lame. She's unrideable. May I stay longer in the cave?' I point at the sun and trace its path from its current position to where it will disappear at night, close my eyes and rest my head on my palm, then show eight fingers.

Pale Horse interprets, turning to speak with Hawk. I hear them say 'Abraham Knox.' I gesture away towards the eastern end of the canyon.

'Abraham Knox left this morning.' I retrace the path of the sun and pretend to be Knox riding east with his reins in one hand and the lead rope of the mule in the other. I point at my own chest and show eight fingers again. They nod their agreement. Good. I thank them and set off back to my camp.

I gather kindling and fallen branches from around the cottonwoods and notice aspen further east that could provide fuel later. I restock the log pile by dragging limbs which score tracks into the dirt outside the cave; I heave them up and over the rock lip, so they topple inside.

At first light I wake up hungry and smell meat cooking in the settlement. There is game up on the plateau. To the east of the cave is a talus climbing to a ledge, rising from there the rock splits into blocks like piles of books. The formation is a staircase to the canyon rim. I slide my bayonet into its sheath, attach the powder horn and ammunition pouch to my belt, sling the better of the two rifles onto my back and set out. It's a fine morning, and I thank the Lord for it. I hum as I climb, using the rhythm of my steps as drumbeats. By the time I reach the lip I'm singing full-voiced to the endless turquoise sky. Emerging onto the plateau, I spook a herd of deer which could have fed a man for weeks. I laugh at my foolishness. I hunt well, taking four rabbits with five shots. Upwind I spot antelope. Next time, maybe.

I turn for home and stand, stilled by the majesty of God's creation. The landscape is vast, the sagebrush like countless herds stretching to the horizon. I crest the rim. Far below, ten or fifteen mounted warriors head east from the next village along. I descend the rock and peer more closely. Something isn't right. Two gallop their horses past my cave, the silver on their clothes and bridles catching the sun.

I start down the canyon wall.

The riders veer right, towards the settlement. There's a large party of warriors on the opposite rim of the canyon. They turn their horses and kick hard. Hawk and Pale Horse are among them. I drop the rabbits and run down the talus, heels first for traction.

Shards of rock skitter before me. I fight to keep my balance and hit the canyon floor at a sprint, snatching my hat from my head and tossing it away. The pair of riders on the far side race into the settlement, thrusting left and right with their lances, shrieking war cries. My gut twists with fear. The leader seizes a young woman as she runs from his horse. She thrashes back at him, struggling to break free. The second man comes up on her blindside pulling a musket from behind his saddle and clubbing her with the butt. His partner forces his arm under the girl's shoulders, hauling her slack body on to the back of the horse. The raiders whoop, turn their ponies east and kick them into a gallop.

I reach the middle of the canyon and stop, facing west. I plant my feet to gauge distance and wind direction. Hawk is a quarter mile off leading his party over the rim of the canyon where it ramps most. Like mountain goats, they drop the full height of a man to the talus. The slope is suicide. The Akote gallop down it in clouds of dust and scree. The raiders charge me.

I drop the butt of my rifle to the dirt, snatch the horn from my belt and pour powder into the measure. My hand is shaking. 'Calm and fast,' I say aloud and take a breath. The tang of corn cooking on a fire fills my nose. I replace the horn – the horses now at two hundred paces and bearing down. There's no cover, nowhere to run if I miss. This is as good a place as any. I repent of my sins, Almighty. One way or another I won't die alone here. Father, forgive me for not being there when you passed, if I could change anything it would be that. I reach into my pouch for a wad. I pull it out, forcing my hand to move with care and accuracy. I tease it into the muzzle, feeling for the metal rim with my thumbnail.

How close? One hundred paces. The thundering of hooves drums up through my boots. Into the pouch again for a ball. I fumble and lose it to the canyon floor. 'Calm, for God's sake.' Another ball, this time slower, into the cupped wad. I rip the rod from the barrel and ram down. Seventy paces now – I lift the gun to my waist, cocking the hammer, fingers trembling a percussion cap onto the nipple.

Fifty paces. I shoulder the weapon.

The rider with the girl on his horse pulls his gun from its saddle sleeve and aims it. I see the smoke then hear the shot. It's like a horse has kicked me in the thigh. The pain spikes up into my back and down my leg which buckles under me. I roar the wound away, forcing the leg straight.

Now. Slow my breathing. The barrel rises and falls as I look along it, synchronising the movement to the rhythm of the galloping hooves, watching for the moment when the bottom of my breath matches the point in the horse's stride when all four legs tuck underneath. I sight its chest and when my breath is empty, squeeze the trigger. I'm deaf in my right ear, and smoke blind, but through my feet I feel the horse crash into the dust. The raider yells as he flies from the saddle. I twist to avoid him as he shoots past, hitting the canyon floor headfirst with a crack of the neck. He's done. The animal, killed instantly, ploughs on in the sand coming to rest a few paces away, pitching the young woman's unconscious body into me, taking me off my feet and knocking the breath from my lungs.

The second raider pulls up just east of us. He's reloading. He has the rod halfway down the barrel. Once he's loaded, we're finished. One slim chance. I struggle to breathe. I reach for my bayonet, wrench it from its sheath and twist myself to hurl it backhanded. It's a wild throw, wide of its mark even as it leaves my hand. It spins through the air high and left of his heart. He's pushing a cap onto the mechanism, blind to what's coming. The handle hammers into the socket of his right eye with the noise of an egg falling onto rock. He screams and drops his rifle, clutching his face. Wheeling his pony eastwards, he kicks it into a gallop. Safe. We're safe.

My vision is darkening now. Hawk and his warriors are jumping from their horses.

*

My eyes flicker open in the gloom. Light pierces the roof in shafts here and there. I look around the hogan, then at the floor, trying to judge distance but failing, giddy. The girl is here, above me. And an ancient medicine man. She smiles, just as the pain hits me. My back arches and I double over, retching. She holds a bowl in front of me, speaking soft Akote words. I slump back onto the bed, I'm trembling. Trembling so much I can't still myself. She shakes her head. The medicine man comes closer, standing over me. The noise, his voice, chanting, it vibrates in my ribs. I try to blink my eyes into focus. He's rocking back and forth and it's making me feel sick. I push myself up onto my elbows. 'How long has it been? Please stop, stop the rocking.' He speaks, sounds like a question, then continues with his rocking and chanting. I lie back on the soft skins and close my eyes.

*

She stands, with her father and the medicine man, next to the fire crackling in the centre of the floor. The doorway is open. It's dusk. So hot in here. The medicine man nods towards me, he's speaking to her. Hawk interrupts. The mother comes in. The daughter smiles at her. They leave. Voices outside. The medicine man, shouting.

*

I touch the wound. My buckskin pants, pierced by the gunshot, are stiff with dried blood and cut open to reveal the injury while preserving my modesty. The medicine man comes daily to check the wound, chant, and perform rituals of healing.

She's here constantly. Her name is Bright Flower. She fetches in water for me to drink and wash. She ensures I am warm enough and feeds me. Mutton stew with chilies, squashes, melon, cornbread, wheat bread, beans, fruit; the peaches – they remind me of the first time I saw her. I speak to her in English as I eat, humming my appreciation of the food as she sits on the edge of the bed. 'This is very good, thank you.' She smiles but shakes her head to show she doesn't understand. I raise a hand to mime an explanation but misjudge the movement and touch her arm. Her eyes move to the contact, then to mine before finding the floor and staying there.

She starts to teach me Akote, and I teach her words of English. The wound was clean, the shot passed through the muscle and out the other side. Within a fortnight I can explain to her my yearning to walk in fragments of Akote, English, and mime. Our communication is like a private joke to be enjoyed only by us, the ambiguity of it causing wild misunderstanding sometimes. I ask her for cornbread, and she laughs till she weeps. She informs Willow Tree and Hawk of my progress during the day. When I sat up unaided, she told them, and again now when I manage to raise myself up to hop a few paces. She fetches Hawk back with her. He carries a bundle of clothing and a length of oak. As they duck inside, I sit up.

Hawk says something, gesturing me to be at ease. Bright Flower translates in our private pidgin. 'He says stay, don't stand for him.' He looks from her to me and back again on hearing our mixture of languages. He puts the oak staff on the floor, takes the bundle in both hands and holds it towards me. I need no translation to understand this expression of gratitude. The bundle consists of a pair of buckskin trousers, exquisitely stitched, a rough cotton shirt and a buffalo hide. I look at the gifts, but I cannot think of what to say.

Hawk reaches down for the piece of oak and shows

how the spur towards the top can be used as a handgrip to lean on. He says something to me. Bright Flower translates, 'You stood like the forest stands, resisting all comers. Father has made this staff for you to stand again until you heal.'

Hawk is bestowing an honour on me, with these gifts. I laugh with pleasure at my new clothing and start to rise from the low bed. Hawk steps forward and slips his muscled arm beneath mine, squatting and lifting from the legs in an elastic thrust, raising me to my feet. I wince at the pain. Bright Flower hands me the staff. I take a few steps and smile at them both.

'Thank you,' I say in Akote.

She hovers at my elbow as I edge to the doorway, holding the crutch on my injured side, steadying myself with the other hand on the timbers of the hogan. She ducks in front of me to hold aside the blanket, watching each tottering step. I shuffle towards her, eventually hopping clear of the threshold and standing once more in the open. I breathe the air in deep, turn and smile at her. My heart lifts at the joy glittering in her eyes. God, but it's good to stand in the open. The villagers close by grin and nod encouragement. I take a few steps towards the far side of the canyon, but stumble. Bright Flower jumps forward but Hawk is here already. He speaks low as he grabs my shoulder.

'Father says you don't win the war in one battle,' Bright Flower translates. 'Back in the hogan, more walking tomorrow,' she chides me. I recall her mother talking to her father in their hogan when we arrived here. How long ago was that?

I struggle to reckon the time since I was shot. Those first days are mixed up – the darkness of the hogan, the sound of Mountain Song's chanting, the smell of smoke and bitter herbs – but two constants: Bright Flower, always tending me, and the pain whenever I moved, stabbing up my back and down to my foot. It still aches now but at least I can move without retching. It's been a month judging by the weather and the shorter days. Where has Abe got to? I want to know he's safe, but in truth I also want this time with Bright Flower to last. Each day on waking I yearn for the moment when she comes smiling through the doorway, for the smell of her. When Abe returns it will be the beginning of the end, the calling back. I am free here. I have never felt as free, but what life could I hope for among these people? They aren't Christian, they can't read. I am an outsider. I'd always be the outsider.

Late morning, I sit with Bright Flower as she checks my wound. 'It is good, but more rest is needed.'

I make my face serious, 'Not only rest.'

She tilts her head in earnest concern. I glance up at her. 'Mutton stew also.' We are laughing as Pale Horse leads Abe through the doorway.

He nods at my garments, 'Looks like you're assimilating.'

I'm pleased to see him despite my concerns. I push up off the low seat and hop across. 'Abe! I was beginning to worry!'

'I heard you had trouble, how's the leg?'

'Better than it was, thanks to a lot of nursing from –' something stops me talking about Bright Flower. 'How did you hear?'

'The medicine man from the next settlement. The

translator. He told me about the raid and you getting shot. Looks like you're set up fine here though.' He looks at Bright Flower. The corner of his mouth puckers into a leer.

She gets up to leave. My heart sinks, 'Bright Flower –' but she's gone.

Pale Horse claps a hand onto Abe's shoulder, 'Abraham Knox must have eaten today. His stomach did not warn you of his approach!' He throws his head back and laughs.

Abe hears his name and scowls, 'You understand them?' It's an accusation.

'What do you expect? I've been alone here for weeks.'

I see Bright Flower less. She avoids me when I'm with Abe. I feel my resentment growing. Abe makes camp in the cave as before and spends the time trading. I sit outside on a cottonwood trunk carried here for me by Pale Horse. I watch and join the negotiations from time to time to translate. Since the Anaii raid, the bartering is more relaxed.

The wound is healing fast, but still, I rely heavily on Hawk's oak staff and am unfit to ride. I agree with Abe that he'll take some of the stock and trade with the other settlements in the canyon. I ask permission of Hawk and Pale Horse. They say that Crowsfoot will accompany Abe to vouch for him. They set out east this morning leaving me here to convalesce. Now Bright Flower busies over me as before and we speak for long hours. She tells me the traditions of the Akote, how the First People came up through the darkness and the water to this chosen earth. She describes the farming of pumpkin and corn, the harvesting and drying of peaches, the rearing of sheep and goats.

I tell her about my people, that Father was an Englishman, an army officer who served far to the east in India. There he met and married Mother, a woman from a high caste family, who died giving birth to me. On bringing his mixed blood son home to the Dartmoor Manor House of our ancestors, Father realised that I had no future there despite my green eyes – the mark of my bloodline. He agreed to forego his inheritance and any further claim on the Meavy wealth in return for the family's New World estates and brought me to Maryland to start a new life. I grew up in the plantations where I befriended Abe Knox, the son of Father's steward. He was older than me, but we were schooled together and ranged the tobacco fields as brothers until, seeking adventure, we joined the dragoons. I've never told the story before. Bright Flower listens without interruption. She seems amazed that people and places so different exist. She says she would never have taken me for a mixed blood and asks after my father. I tell her the truth.

While I was away in the army, bad debt had ruined Father's business and his health. His decline was brutal and by the time I returned home, he had died alone and been buried by strangers. I promised him he wouldn't. That he would never die alone. But he did. Because I was not there. I show her the silver watch from my pocket, 'All that's left to me of him is here –' I touch it to my chest. 'And here. I will never again permit anyone I love to die alone.'

*

I breathe deep the cool ripeness of the autumn afternoon. I lean on the staff Hawk gave me, having set up three pumpkins on poles in the sand. Bright Flower, Hawk and Pale Horse stand with me, our backs to the wash, facing the canyon wall twenty paces ahead. I show the warriors how to hold the rifles, how to slow the breath, letting the barrel rise and fall, and how to squeeze the trigger on the bottom of exhalation, when movement is minimal. Bright Flower watches every detail. I demonstrate how to measure the powder, put a wad and ball in the muzzle, use the rod to push it home and place a percussion cap in the mechanism before shouldering the weapon and firing. I feel stronger doing this. My former authority asserting itself through the drill. Bright Flower looks gladdened to see me at work. I explain windage and elevation over distance – how these adjustments are similar to those made with the bow.

At last, it is time. Hawk first. The shot goes high and left of the target, scarring the rock behind it with a shriek. I reload and pass the rifle to Pale Horse. He raises it easily and fires, jerking his right elbow as he squeezes, as if releasing a bowstring. The round strikes low and to the right.

'Watch now.' I reload. 'I am still, very still. When my breath is gone,' I look at the trigger, 'I squeeze. Very soft, like touching your finger on a blade so as not to cut the skin.' The report of the rifle cracks back and forth across the canyon. The smoke clears revealing a hole the size of a man's eye socket in the centre of the second pumpkin. Around the pockmark in the stone, the canyon wall is stained orange. Bright Flower smiles at me, pleased with my skill. 'Hawk, you again. Make your feet as I showed you. Remember the breath. First without firing. That's it. Now, aim bottom right of the target.'

Hawk looks along the barrel of the rifle. He slows his breath and fires. Left and high of centre, the pumpkin gains a second puncture.

'Good. Pale Horse, like before but touch the trigger like a knife.'

'I will shoot next,' Bright Flower declares.

I look to Hawk. He starts to speak but checks himself. Pale Horse laughs aloud. 'Did Mountain Song take your tongue?'

Hawk turns to Bright Flower. 'My daughter, watch Pale Horse first, see his mistakes, show him how it should be done.' She starts to load the second gun.

Pale Horse snorts and grins. He takes the stance I have shown them, slows his breath, locks his right elbow tight and squeezes the trigger. A nick appears at the bottom right edge. He coughs the smoke out of his lungs, 'Ha! Hawk, for once you spoke too soon. She may be your daughter but even that won't be enough to –' He's cut off by the report of the rifle. She loaded fast, fired, and is admiring her work. I stare at the target. Pale Horse turns, 'You see, not a scratch on it. I acknowledge your spirit Bright Flower, but –'

Bright Flower points at the pumpkin on the left of the group, pierced dead centre. The men stand in silence. I can't help it. I throw back my head and roar with laughter. Without thinking, I wink at her. She looks anxious, 'Do you have powder in your eye, Francis Meavy?'

Pale Horse turns and stalks off, 'We are better off with our bows, Hawk, they are simpler and more accurate.'

*

Abe and Crowsfoot return. I have practised limping around without my crutch and am capable of mounting up. I'll manage. Abe shows me the remaining stock of silver, knives, and other goods. 'Seems a shame not to bargain these out, but the cold's coming in.'

We agree to trade for two or three weeks more in the untested settlements to the west before returning to town for the winter. We'll return to Los Huertos on our way back through to reequip for the final leg south and east to Corazon. I ready myself and the animals in silence. My mood is sour at the prospect of leaving.

We set out at first light. Hawk and a handful of Akote men ride with us. Where the wash broadens and the walls of the canyon slope down towards the earth, they halt their horses.

'Francis Meavy, there are raiders in the Akote country who do not venture into our canyon. Be wary. We will feast together when you return.' Hawk turns his pony, and his men follow. I'm sad to wave them off. I realise I have a growing respect and affection for him.

The Akote we meet heading west tell us stories of

raids by Mexicans, Anaii, and Ute. Once they hear me speak snatches of their language, they welcome us but watch us closely and are slow to reveal the goods they have to exchange.

The days grow shorter and the nights colder. We bargain out the remainder of the stock. The mule is laden with turquoise, blankets, and baskets when we turn for Los Huertos after two weeks. I have not spoken much during this time but come evening when we sight the end of the canyon in the distance and start to make camp, I feel the urge to talk.

'They are different out there, aren't they?'

'Hm?'

'The Akote on the plateau. They're different to the people in Los Huertos. Less outgoing, I'd say. And the colours in the weaving are different, the reds and blacks.'

'More raiding. Makes them wary.'

'Food's still good though.'

'If you like Indian food.' Abe pulls a blanket round his neck as the howls of the coyotes wrestle with the autumn winds. Sometimes he just needs to disagree, whatever you say.

Excitement wakes me before dawn. I contain myself until daybreak then rise and pack up the animals ready to move out once breakfast is done. I start to cook. Abe stirs, stands, and spits in the dirt. He readies himself without a word of good morning. I look up at the sky. Although colder, it's dry and the distance we need to cover to reach Los Huertos before nightfall can be ridden comfortably. Nevertheless, I set a pace fit to race for shelter in bad weather. We approach the canyon towards noon. The horses' sweat pipes the edges of the saddles with foam and my mount fidgets with my impatience.

Abe glances over. 'Let's water the horses and rest awhile.'

'Sure,' I agree uneasily. I dismount and lead my animal to a shallow stream in a side canyon. While the horse sucks up water, I look up at the sun, around the rock walls, down at the silt underfoot, then again at the position of the sun, the arrow weed, Abe, the horses at the water and finally the sun once more. I take my silver watch from its pocket, open it, close it, and put it away again.

'I still want to buy that watch from you,' Abe says.

My mind is elsewhere. I'm thinking of the welcome Father's family gave him. Because of me. The anger rises in my gullet. I register Abe's words and shake my head in irritation, 'You know it was Father's. It doesn't even work.'

'I'd fix it.' Before I can reply, he tilts his head towards the horses, 'That's enough watering. Let's walk them a while and let it settle.'

*

They must have known we were coming. A crowd awaits us at the settlement. I scan it for Bright Flower, my head light. Instead, I find Hawk at the front. He's looking at Abe. I look over too and follow Abe's stare to Bright Flower who is biting her lip. She is looking at me. We make eye contact, she beams a smile, then looks away. We dismount and walk towards Hawk. I make the Akote greeting to him, Pale Horse and Willow Tree. 'The air is good,' then turn to Bright Flower, and do the same.

It is a welcome feast for us, but I'm not hungry. I eat a few morsels to avoid causing offence and force myself to smile and talk. Afterwards, when the settlement sleeps, I stand mid canyon staring at the glittering sky. Behind me, I hear feet scuff. I turn, knowing already who it will be, 'The air is good, Hawk.'

'The air is good. You choose not to sleep? Perhaps you cannot.'

'I was thinking of home.'

'Where is that?'

The truth is I don't know. I shrug and look up again at the stars.

'You have a home here.'

*

Abe is readying the animals while I look for Hawk. Instead, I find Bright Flower outside the hogan wearing a blanket skirt and shawl, examining the loom on which Willow Tree has started to weave another. She does not notice me watching. Her eyes stray beyond the hogans to the toddlers teetering around their mothers, scraping deer skins near the aspen. Hawk and Pale Horse approach.

'Abe and I would like to thank you for your hospitality and the provisions.' I want to say more, to find other words, to delay leaving. I cannot. Abe mounts up, I follow suit, hauling myself onto my horse slowly like a man twice my weight. Then, before we set off, I speak again. 'Please thank Willow Tree also. And Bright Flower.' Abe kicks his horse on. I look back over my shoulder. As we leave, Pale Horse is standing next to Hawk, talking to him. He jerks his chin towards us and waves at me.

Coyote

Early Winter 1843

He bridled his fur against the chill. The late piñon nuts had long been harvested. From the trees he observed Bright Flower. She toiled with the others, enjoying the work, each task a prayer: cooking, weaving, preparing skins from game. She loved the company of her Akote sisters, the belonging, the purpose it bought her, but she longed for more now. He felt her longing, knew it – the fire of First Woman. But she had enough faith for all the Akote.

From time to time, she stopped in her tracks to look east along the canyon or into the sky, before returning to her labour with a quiet smile. It was three weeks since the traders had left. She milled corn with her mother.

'You miss him, don't you? You were bound to become attached to him. Who knows what Spider Woman has woven into her web?'

'We will be married.'

The older woman's hands stilled. 'When did he?'

'He didn't. We didn't. I'm not sure he knows yet, but I think he does and anyway, he will soon.'

Sundown. Bright Flower was eating with her parents in their hogan. Her father spoke. 'Daughter, it is right that you helped Francis Meavy to recover from the wounds he suffered saving you, but marrying a man so –'

'Father. Francis Meavy is brave, honourable, and respectful, and he has wealth from his trading.'

'Do you feel this out of obligation? You have repaid your debt, and, in any case, we will not see him again for many months, if at all.'

'He will be back, you will see.'

'No, Daughter, you –'

Bright Flower's arguments were strong, but she had kept one back. Now she used it. 'Father, we could ask for Mountain Song's guidance?'

Willow Tree dropped her head and smiled. Hawk sighed. Coyote panted his pleasure.

*

Mid-morning the next day, Bright Flower was covering the loom. Snow flurried in the canyon. Coyote watched a lone rider to the east, leading a mule packed high with bundles, fighting through the whirling flakes. The man headed towards the settlement, wearing buckskin trousers, boots and a buffalo skin over his coat, rifles jutting up from the leather slips either side of the saddle. His hair lay on his shoulders beneath his hat, tipped forward to shelter his green eyes from the brightness. The flame of First Man heated his blood. Francis Meavy was returning to her.

She saw him. He did not see her, but rode on into the settlement and dismounted, tethering his animals at the corral. Neither of them saw Coyote watching from the rock face. Brushing the snow from the hide on his shoulders, Meavy walked towards the hogan of her parents. She had left her father sitting by the fire, planing a shaft of arrow weed with the knife the traders had given him. The door was hitched open.

Hawk called out, 'I did not expect to see you.'

Still limping, he slowed his pace. Bright Flower ran to catch up, following him as he stepped inside.

Her father was speaking, 'My daughter told me you would come.'

Meavy hesitated. Becoming aware of Bright Flower behind him, he turned to her. She stared at her feet, unable to contain her smile.

Willow Tree came. 'Francis Meavy, the air is good.'

'The air is good, Willow Tree.'

Bright Flower looked at her father. He was preparing to speak. The feathers in his hair jostled in the draft from the doorway. The sinews of his forearms rose and fell as he put the arrow weed shaft and the knife on the floor beside him. When he drew breath, his chest muscles twitched under his cotton shirt.

Willow Tree cut in. 'You do know, Francis Meavy, that it is Akote custom for the son-in-law never to look directly at the mother of his wife? So, if you wish to see what Bright Flower will look like when she's older you must take a good look now.'

Bright Flower clapped her hand over her mouth.

'I... I –' Meavy shook his head.

Outflanked, Hawk sat in silence.

'Anyway,' Willow Tree continued, tossing another juniper log on to the fire, 'You have travelled far, and it is time to eat.' She gestured towards the stools. 'Sit and we will talk about the future.' She turned and started to busy around the food baskets to the side of the hogan. At a loss what to do, Bright Flower joined her mother in the preparation of food.

Hawk was seated opposite Meavy, arms crossed. He glanced over at his daughter. She frowned and pointed towards Meavy with her nose. Hawk unfolded his arms. 'Francis Meavy, this matter is not simple. Where would you and Bright Flower live? If you have children, will they be raised as Akote or in your ways?'

'Here.' Bright Flower interrupted. 'Francis Meavy loves Los Huertos, I have seen it, and our children will be raised in the tradition of the Akote and of Meavy's people.'

Meavy smiled at her. 'Yes, both. We will make our home here. Our children will not be Akote, they will not be American. They will be both.'

Willow Tree's back was turned. She disguised her sob with a cough.

Hawk handed Meavy a beaker, 'You need tea to chase the cold from your bones.' Bright Flower watched her father assess him. The questioning was not yet over.

Meavy broke the silence, 'Bright Flower told me the Akote tradition. The marriage bargain between the father of the woman and the new husband. I have two good buffalo skins and silver.'

Hawk shook his head. 'I have seen you breathe deep the air of Los Huertos and turn your face to the sun in stillness. Do you love this place because of what it is, or because of what it is not?'

Willow Tree joined them by the fire. Bright Flower followed close.

'I feel peace here. You honoured me with gifts. I love Bright Flower.' He shrugged.

The emotion rose up in Bright Flower. She looked at her feet again.

Willow Tree rested her hand gently on her daughter's arm, 'We know how you feel about our daughter, Francis Meavy, and how she feels about you has been clear to me from the beginning, but we are deciding the paths of lifetimes. Yours, hers, children unborn.'

Hawk leant forward to prod the fire. 'It will not be easy for you leaving your own people. Nor for Bright Flower that you have done this.'

Meavy nodded, 'My own father and mother –'

'Bright Flower has told us. And so, I ask you again, this 'love' you speak of, is it love of our daughter, our life here, or is it your heart seeking to heal your past?'

'All I know is I have to be with Bright Flower, to be here with her as my wife.'

Bright Flower looked at her father, motionless at what Francis Meavy had said. At last, he spoke, 'There will be no negotiation.'

Bright Flower gasped.

Her mother intervened. 'Husband, remember Mountain Song's words –'

'I remember, but no bargain can match Bright Flower's worth. The skins and silver are acceptable.'

*

At dawn four days later, the girl waited for Pale Horse to bring Francis Meavy on horseback to her hogan. When he arrived, she could not wait to be alone with him. The ceremony seemed unending to them. At last,

Mountain Song raised his arms in a sweeping motion, indicating to all but Bright Flower and Meavy that they should leave the hogan.

In the morning, in their bed of soft deerskin, he stroked her face. 'You are my heart, Bright Flower, my wife.'

'You are my blood, Francis Meavy.' She rolled onto her side and rested her head in her hand, knowing there was one last thing in the way of their happiness. 'My husband, it is not enough for us to have had the Akote ceremony. We must have a ceremony in your tradition as well.'

He shook his head. 'My priests will not marry a woman of your people and a man of mine. They will make you forego your Akote traditions before they consider it. There are few who will credit what we are. I will tell you all I know about my religion. Then we will visit one man I know who might understand.'

During the winter months, by the light of the hogan fire he instructed her in his Christianity. When the snow covered the canyon floor in the darkness outside, she heard about their Holy Land, its Roman occupiers, the enslavement of the Jewish people, the flight from Egypt, the parting of the Red Sea, how Jesus Christ walked on water, turned water to wine and few fish and loaves into many. Her eyes filled with tears as her husband described the young man crucified and pierced with a lance – betrayed by his own people. Francis Meavy sang songs to her he called hymns. She smiled and rocked with love at the strange discordant noise. She accepted that the man Jesus was the son of God since she believed that all men and women were the creation of the Divine.

Coyote watched on, proud once more of the spirit he had brought to this place.

In the spring, once the snow had thawed, she said it was time. Francis Meavy saddled his horse and one of her father's ponies. She packed smoked elk meat, cornbread, and dried peaches together with piñon nuts wrapped in buckskin. They filled their water skins in the wash and made for Corazon.

She was anxious about the return to his people, whether it would change how he felt – the reality of being with her. She also knew they were at risk on the open plateau. More Akote women were taken as slaves than from any other tribe. Francis Meavy scanned the landscape without rest, travelling with a pistol against his ribs beneath his buckskin jacket. As they threaded through the sagebrush, the earth was still hard underneath from the winter, and the sky bright cobalt. Bluebirds sang, countless high chirps, one after the other, piercing through her ears into her chest. She imagined the hundreds and thousands of days like these they might spend together and, if they were blessed, with their children – children of a marriage recognised by the Akote and by their father's people.

She knew Francis Meavy loved the red grandeur of the canyon, the infinite sky with its herds of flat-bottomed clouds casting shadows the size of lakes over the desert beneath. These things gave him a sense of freedom and contentment he found only with her people. But now, although there were no secrets between them, he struggled to look her in the eyes as they travelled. He was nervous, quiet.

Francis Meavy

Spring 1844 – Corazon

Finally, we are here. This was a bad plan. I turn over and over in my mind the differences between Corazon and the canyon, the Akote and the townsfolk. Bright Flower doesn't belong in this place. How the hell did I agree to bring her here? I turn to check her horse is close behind. She sits upright to show her status as my woman. My woman. She has met so few white men, what if she sees one here that she prefers? The smell of ripe excrement – animal and human – hangs in the air. Mexican faces watch us, they assume that she is my property. I told her. They are used to the sight of white owners with Akote slaves.

I dismount in front of the Corazon Hotel and lead my mare to the rail. I help Bright Flower to the ground and tie her horse for her, my damn fingers unable to work fast enough. 'Stay close to me. There's a good chance we'll find Abe here.' I put my hand on the small of her back and guide her up the steps, checking left and right along the street.

I hold open the door of the building with one arm and enter first, looking over my shoulder to see she's still close behind. The room has windows on two sides and is populated by wooden tables and chairs and people speaking Spanish and English. She hesitates at the smell of whiskey and the noises of the piano, glasses clinking, and patrons talking over each other. The hubbub hushes, all eyes are on us. Bright Flower stares back. I search for Maggie, the landlady. She's behind the counter looking us up and down, a lopsided smile on her face. She wears a blood red dress with cream lace edging cut low at the bust. The skin of her breast and her face are like milk but her cheeks blush chili-red. Her eyes are large and blue with thick dark lines on the lids. Bright Flower stares at her in fascination.

I touch my hat. 'Hello, Maggie.'

She shakes her head. 'Same rules as ever. No slaves.'

Bright Flower takes in a breath as I cringe. 'This is my wife, Bright Flower.'

Maggie raises her eyebrows. A bulge appears in her left cheek where she prods it with her tongue. 'Well, well.' She surveys Bright Flower again. 'She's a pretty young thing all right but – ah, never mind. Have a drink on the house to celebrate.'

'I appreciate it, Maggie, but we're looking for Abe.'

Maggie starts to buff the countertop with a check cloth. She nods towards the rear of the building and smiles to herself. 'You'll find him in there.'

I take Bright Flower towards the parlour, open the door, and lead the way in. It's half the size of the main room. Drab rugs cover the pine floor. The sweet stink of stale tobacco. I scan the room and cringe again. Abe is reclined with a half-smoked cigar in one hand, in the other a heavy glass with a remainder of caramel liquid in its base. A girl half his age sits on his lap, cheekbones high and broad, eyes dark, hair black and straight.

Bright Flower's brow tightens, she addresses the girl in Akote. 'Sister, what are you doing here? Is this man your husband?'

The girl glares. 'No. I was taken from my husband and family by raiders and brought here to be passed among these men. Perhaps you will end the same.'

Bright Flower turns towards me, 'We must free this girl, Francis Meavy, and take her back to her family.'

'My family are dead. I'm here now. I have nowhere else, I don't need your –'

Abe interrupts, 'Francis Meavy, Francis Meavy.' He waves the glass in his hand. 'You're back. Welcome back, Francis Meavy. How was the tribe? Did you do good for us?' He squints at Bright Flower and grins.

'Well, Abe, I've traded through the winter as we said.'

'What did she just say to this girl?'

'She asked what she was doing here. She's Akote.'

Abe speaks slowly with the rhythm of a lame horse. 'A-ko-te.'

'Abe, Bright Flower and I are hoping to be married. I want you to witness for us.'

'As God is my witness, I'll be your witness.'

'Best lay off the liquor.'

'My fitness to witness. My fit-mess to wit-less.'

'Listen, Abe. I'm going to find Patrick Monaghan and see if he will marry us this afternoon, so your fitness to witness is required. Shall I fetch you coffee?'

'Yup, yup, yup.' He nods three times, 'I can do that. I can do that. You give me half – maybe an hour. I'll be there.'

'You know where to come?'

'I do, I do. No. Tell me.'

'I'll tell you what we're going to do. You stay here. I'll come and get you if Monaghan can accommodate us.'

'I'll stay here.'

I guide Bright Flower back through. 'Maggie?' She looks up at me in the mirror behind the bar. 'No more liquor for Abe and make him drink some coffee, will you? I need him sober in an hour to see Father Monaghan. I'll be back.'

'Sober in an hour? You'll need a miracle not a priest.'

We leave the hotel and turn left along Main Street. On foot we will be less conspicuous, but I keep one hand on my pistol as I guide Bright Flower to the priest's house. I try to ease the tension by talking, 'Patrick Monaghan was a soldier before he became a priest. He does right and he talks true. We became friends when he arrived in Corazon a year or two ago.' The path of our friendship was lubricated by Irish whiskey. I rarely drink these days, but when I do, it is with the blessing of the Lord.

I knock at the plain wooden house. No reply. I take Bright Flower through the doors of the stone church, kneel, and cross myself. Monaghan is a ruddy man with rolling shoulders and the hands of a giant. He's brushing the floor with delicate sweeps. He moves on the balls of his feet and wears all black but for a white collarless shirt under his full-length coat. His auburn hair forms a cropped rim around the back of his pink scalp then peters into a neck like a bull's. He looks like he's waltzing a stick woman. He hears the door and swivels his head round to see who it is. His pale blue eyes gleam and he opens his arms wide, his dance partner clattering onto the stone tiles.

'Frankie Meavy, you've been sorely missed.' My smile stretches my face and for a moment I forget Bright Flower. 'Where are my manners, Frankie? Who is this grand young lady you've brought with you?'

'Patrick, this is Bright Flower Tseyi'nii. We want you to marry us in your church.'

He raises his eyebrows high on his freckled brow. 'I see, I see. What does she know of the Christian faith, Francis?'

Bright Flower cuts him off. 'She knows about the birth of a child from a virgin to the Spirit of God. The teachings of that child, of his twelve followers. That he was nailed to wood and killed when his own people could have saved him. She knows about Moses, John the Baptist, the Old and the New Testaments, and that God is everywhere and everything. She also knows certain hymns, and some prayers in the language of the Romans.'

He leans towards Bright Flower, half closing his eyes. 'I was talking about you as if you weren't here, wasn't I?' She smiles at him. I can tell she approves. 'I shall not make that mistake again. Frankie, when did you want me to carry out this ceremony? I'd like to talk to the intended a while first.'

'Wife. Not intended.'

'We have been married already in the Akote ceremony,' Bright Flower adds.

'You need a witness, who do you want to stand with you?'

'Abe is in the hotel. I can fetch him when we are ready. You'll do it then, Father?'

'As well as I can see, the Lord Christ made a point of breaking the rules on a regular basis. Who am I but his poor servant wishing to follow his example? You fetch Knox and we will stay here and talk while you do.'

I hesitate. This is a church but the risk of bringing Bright Flower to Corazon has gnawed at me since we left Los Huertos. In this place of slaves and their owners, she is gold. I am also shamed by another concern. What if the town changes her?

Monaghan sees my reticence. 'If I'm not mistaken you have a pistol under that coat. If it makes you happier to leave that here, in case we need it, then that's fine. The Lord helps those who help themselves and you know I can handle a firearm.'

I put the gun on the pew where they are standing and touch Bright Flower's arm. 'I will be right back.' I nod at Monaghan.

As I leave, he turns to Bright Flower. 'Now, what I'd really like is for you to tell me about where you are from.'

I head back to the hotel. As I tramp through the dirt, I look across the street. In the window of the store a smooth-faced mannequin wears a muted version of Maggie's dress. In its wooden fingers a cream silk rose. I walk over, avoiding the fresh pile of dung left by a high stepping horse ridden by a straight-backed Mexican. I buy the rose with a piece of silver and cross back to the hotel. As I walk through to the parlour, I look towards Maggie bantering with a table of well-dressed landowners by the bar. She glances back and shrugs.

Coyote

He watched as Francis Meavy emerged through the heavy doors, closed them behind him and turned towards the hotel. But he was not the only one watching. Coyote's throat vibrated with a low, long growl. Two off-duty soldiers, barely men, sat against the building opposite. Passing a bottle of whiskey between them, they had noticed the trader escort a fine Indian woman into the church and now, drunk as they were, registered that he had left alone.

Bright Flower held Monaghan's gaze as he sat still, looking at her. At last, he glanced down, saw a cobweb on the pew next to him and brushed it away with the back of his hand. 'You know, Bright Flower, in our society, marriage is a holy union, made for life, never to be entered into lightly.' He looked up at her. She tilted her head, her eyes smiling. He coughed into his hand, 'And, well, we need to be absolutely certain that both parties understand that before entering into what is a sacred contract, in the correct spirit. You're, well, you're young, Bright Flower and you know you're – you're both from such different...' he hesitated, searching for the word to rescue him, 'places. Such different places.'

She straightened her back. He shuffled, turning towards her a little. He opened his hands and made to speak again but no words came.

Bright Flower spoke first, 'You love him too, don't you?'

Monaghan's reply was immediate, 'He's a grand man with a generous heart. I'm pleased to call him a friend. But, you know, there are things – blows he's suffered in the past – I'm concerned for him, for you both. There is the need to wander, to search in his spirit.' Monaghan was blushing from the neck up. He looked towards the altar, 'In your place I'd want to know he had made peace with that aspect of himself. Enough to settle, anyway. Some men take local wives, but...' Now he was speaking low, head bowed as if examining the flagstones at his feet.

Bright Flower leant forward, put her hand on his arm. 'I saw the searching in him when I first cast eyes on him. I recognised it. He seeks a home. A place to belong, a family to belong to. We Akote women live out our lives in the place we are born, generation after generation. Our husbands come to us, to live with their wives' families. So it is for Francis Meavy. I am his home. My family is his family. However anyone else feels about it, however he feels about it, he will be Akote now until the end. And he is my husband – he is one spirit with me and I with him, each of us the balm that soothes and the fire that heats the other. We are destined. I knew he would come.'

Monaghan looked her in the eye once more, his eyes wetter than before, 'You do really understand him, don't you?'

Bright Flower grinned back, 'I do. But he is also brave, and beautiful, which are good things in a husband.'

They both laughed. The doors creaked open. Monaghan and Bright Flower turned to see if it was

Francis Meavy returning. The two soldiers stepped into the pool of light at the entrance of the church. One held a bottle, the sun catching the copper liquid in the bottom of it and making it glow.

'Stand behind me,' Monaghan whispered as he rose to his feet. 'Gentlemen, welcome. What can I do for you today?' He held his arms wide in invitation.

The men looked him up and down, taking in his height and span. They swivelled their eyes from one to the other, before replying. 'We wanted to see what was going on in here. What with the traders and Indian women and all.' The man speaking leaned to the side to try to get a better view of Bright Flower.

Monaghan reached for the heavy broom, propped against a pew. 'Well now, I have been sweeping the place clean.' He held the broomstick in one hand at its end and lifted it as if it were a leaf. He made a couple of quick powerful sweeps towards the men, they staggered back a step. 'I don't suppose you'd like to help?' He gestured around the church with his free hand. 'It's a lot of floor to clean. I'd certainly be singing your praises to your commanding officer.'

Still trying to get a better view of Bright Flower, the men shook their heads slowly and backed out the way they had come. Monaghan closed the doors behind them, turned back towards Bright Flower and stopped as he noticed the cocked pistol in her steady hand.

'I needn't have worried about you then?'

'A show of force is often effective, but readiness is everything.' She covered the hammer with her thumb and gently released the trigger.

Francis Meavy

Abe has discarded his cigar butt into his whiskey glass and the Akote girl is gone. The room smells of coffee, thank God.

'You set, Abe?' He grunts. This return to his saturnine self is encouraging. 'Well then, Monaghan is waiting with Bright Flower, let's go.'

As we leave the hotel, Abe grabs the handrail on the stairs. He steadies himself then nods. He's clenching his teeth, no doubt against the exertion and the rising mixture of whiskey, tobacco, and coffee. When we reach the church, I remove my hat. Abe does the same with a shaking hand.

Monaghan and Bright Flower are sat in a pew up front. He's laughing and repeating 'Ts-eyi-nii. Tseyi'nii.'

She nods. 'Better.'

'And it means canyon dweller?'

'Yes. It's my clan name.'

Monaghan turns towards us and nods to Abe. 'Abraham.'

'Father.'

'And Francis has returned too. I'd say that Bright Flower knows more about the Christian faith than many that were born to it. You here as witness, Abraham?' He looks Abe up and down.

Abe croaks, 'Uh-huh.'

'Good, but Bright Flower needs to be baptised before you can be married. We have discussed it and

I rejoice that she wants to go ahead. Let's get started.'
Monaghan ushers my wife to the font.

What other priest would baptise an Akote woman and marry her on a morning's notice?

After the ceremony Monaghan takes me aside. 'Francis, you're a good man and you know what you're doing, so all I will say is that if you ever need me, I'm your man. I might visit you both out there. I've a mind to start a mission in the desert. This place of whores and cutthroats has had attention enough. Would you be agreeable to me coming out to see you?'

'Patrick, it would be a pleasure, but I make no promises that your preaching will be heard. The Akote are devout in their faith, practising it every day from dawn onwards. You might find you're converted yourself.'

'Well, if I am, so be it. There are several paths to the mountaintop as some wise man said. Good luck to you both and God be with you as I know He is already.' We shake hands, and I see Monaghan's mouth set as tight as my own.

*

We put Corazon behind us. I can hold off no longer, 'Well, what did you think of the town, the church, Monaghan?'

'I am relieved to be married to you in the way of your people. Your friend the priest is a kind, wise man, but the town is a place where the evil inside men takes hold of them. I have no wish to go there again.'

My frustration wells up. 'But you wanted to go there to be married, Bright Flower, you wanted –'

'No. Not for me. For you. And for our children. If we are to raise them in the ways of both people, this is needed. There would always be a voice whispering in your ear that we were not truly married if we did not have the ceremony in your church as well, and perhaps in theirs.' Her shoulders and hips rock from side to side with the rhythm of the horse.

I look to the horizon for guidance. I can't fault Bright Flower's farsightedness. I turn to her. 'Thank you.'

She smiles. 'Thank you, Francis Meavy.'

'You don't need to thank me for doing what's right.'

'I'm not. I'm thanking you for the child I carry.'

I pull my horse up hard. 'Are you sure? I mean, how long?'

She's grinning. 'I am sure,' she leans across and puts her hand on my arm. I look down at it, cover it with my own, and look up at her again, unable to stem my tears.

*

Bright Flower is watching Mountain Song's hand hovering over her belly. His eyes are closed. The tension leaves his arm. He moves his palm away, blinks his eyes open and takes a deep breath through his nose, the nostrils pinching together. We wait, my heart beats in my ears like Akote drums. I reach for Bright Flower's hand. It's clammy. She's pale.

'The child has already been ensouled with a Holy

Wind Spirit. It is rooted firmly and that is good. He will need to hold fast to himself since he will have to endure. Bright Flower, the struggles you feel while the child is unborn will prepare him for those he will face in the world. You must provide a calm and peaceful home to this spirit despite the discomfort.'

Bright Flower frowns. 'What are these struggles?'

'I cannot say. But I have sensed them. His destiny is the destiny of all Akote.'

I need to know. 'You are sure it is a boy?'

'Yes, it is a male spirit.'

'How can we avoid –'

Mountain Song shakes his head, his wrinkled mouth turns down at the corners. 'We cannot avoid. We can only listen to the winds as they speak to us and honour the Holy Ones in what we do. The web the Spider Woman weaves is beyond our understanding.' He laughs to himself and smiles at Bright Flower, his teeth broad and white as if he were a lifetime younger. 'I would like to see the man this child will become. He must be allowed to choose for himself, as his mother was...' His voice trails off, but before we can question him further, he claps his bony hands together as if struck by lightning. He shoots a glance at me and speaks to Bright Flower again. 'In addition to the offering you have brought,' he gestures towards the goat she holds by a yucca cord, 'I will require mutton stew, cornbread, perhaps dried peaches, piñon nuts.'

She takes the hint. 'Mountain Song, will you eat with us later?'

He encircles his chin with the thumb and index

finger of his right hand and looks up at the spring sky. An eagle soars high above the canyon. He lifts his right foot and with the tip of the moccasin scratches his left calf. 'I accept your invitation. Thank you.' He throws cornmeal from his pouch over her abdomen, leans forward to take the yucca cord from her hand and leads the goat off beyond his hogan. As he walks away, he raises his hand in an unseeing wave.

The nights are still cold. Bright Flower asks her parents to share the meal and witness whatever Mountain Song has to say. Hawk wears buckskin from neck to foot. Willow Tree is wrapped in a woollen blanket dress. I wear the trousers Hawk gave me and a flannel shirt with a blanket around my shoulders. Mountain Song is bare-chested, wearing cotton leggings and high moccasins. Under the necklaces his ribs are visible, the skin stretched across them like ancient hide. We watch him devour the meal like a colony of ants. When the spring winds blow the smoke back into the hogan, concealing him in a pale grey cloud, he does not cough nor do his eyes water.

Mountain Song addresses Hawk. 'You have been busy these past years, maintaining the defences of this canyon against raiders. It becomes more difficult, does it not?'

Hawk looks at the medicine man, then towards the doorway. 'The Mexicans take women and children from our Akote lands. The Anaii and the Ute trade for guns. The Americans come in greater numbers this last year.' He looks sad, weighed down.

Mountain Song concentrates on his piece of

cornbread like he's listening to it. When the conversation has slowed and the embers cast a glow up the walls, he speaks again. 'There is suffering to come. You and I must ride together, Hawk. There is something of great importance to the Akote which you must safeguard. Tomorrow we will travel out onto the plateau. We will be gone several nights. When we return, I will prepare for a pilgrimage to the sacred mountains to listen to the spirit of each.'

'But Mountain Song,' Bright Flower starts, 'before you leave, the blessing of our baby –'

He cuts her off. 'One of the most important things in life is this: do not run out of cornbread.' She passes the basket across. 'Things are much more straightforward than people dream up.'

*

Nine days have passed. It is dusk and I am talking with Bright Flower outside our hogan when Hawk and Mountain Song return, their ponies blowing and sweating. As Hawk dismounts, Mountain Song calls across to him, 'Remember, Hawk, only you until the time comes, and the chant – use it only once.' He waves a hand and trots his pony east. Hawk nods his agreement.

Later, by the hogan fire, Bright Flower asks him, 'Father, you have been quieter than usual since you returned. What happened?'

He prods the flames with a stick. The glow rises to bathe his face. 'He showed me the Akote's past – and our future.'

*

The baby fights inside Bright Flower, shifting, waking her often. I think of my mother. I wish I had known her. I wish I had given her the chance to know me. Now I will cost Bright Flower her life with the child I have given her. She lies in our bed, unable to sleep. I pace the gloom of the canyon, wearing tracks into the silt with my fear. And my shame. Can I ever be forgiven?

Mountain Song attends her on those mornings when her rest has been most disrupted or in the late afternoons which prove particularly testing. He chants, burns herbs and prescribes teas to relax the child and bring on sleep. Mostly though, he reminds Bright Flower to maintain her peace and resolve to remain calm. How can these prescriptions benefit her? He even suggested she help with the harvest and continue with the duties of cooking and milling.

'Mountain Song, among my people these activities are avoided in pregnancy, for fear of risking the mother and the infant.'

'The spirits have spoken. This child must learn that life continues whatever the circumstances. Bright Flower is an Akote woman. This is the way of our people. We are your people now.'

*

Bright Flower's time has come. Snow covers the canyon floor. The baby is the wrong way round in her womb and so it will kill her, I know this. I beg Mountain Song to purge her of the unborn child so at least she will survive.

Shortly before birth it turns. Willow Tree orders me out of the hogan. I run through the snow to the alcove by the cottonwood trees. I hoist myself over the lip and scrabble in the dirt for a pointed shard of rock. I scour a crucifix into the wall and drop to my knees. I cross myself, clench my hands together and bow my head. 'Deliver her, Lord. Deliver her. Deliver Her. Deliver Her, Lord Christ. Deliver Her. Take my life, Lord, take mine. Deliver her. Lord Christ. I beg you. I beg you,' I have no control now. I scream at the symbol I have drawn, 'I BEG YOU.'

The wailing of a baby reaches me from the far side of the canyon. My heart rises, then drops into blackness. She's gone. I haul myself to my feet and trudge back through the snow. Ahead, Willow Tree emerges from the hogan and looks around. She beckons me then disappears inside. I start to run. As I reach the doorway, Mountain Song comes out bearing the cord and afterbirth. He nods back over his shoulder. I swat aside the blanket at the door.

Bright Flower is alive and smiling, holding the newborn. She looks up at me, her hair plastered round her shining face. 'I waited for you before greeting him. Come and hold his hand.'

I stumble towards her, unable to believe, repeating 'Thank you, Lord. Thank you, Lord. Thank you, Lord.' I kneel beside them and take the baby's hand. It's tiny, warm, and soft, and powerful. Powerful beyond anything. My heart fills the canyon. I am overcome. I cannot speak.

Bright Flower's voice is low, 'Welcome Raven Francis Meavy Tseyi'nii. This is your father.' She hands my swaddled son to me. He is wrinkled and almost weightless. Green eyes and a head of black Akote hair, but wavy like mine with two whorls at the crown. My eyes fill with tears, I cannot help but sob as the baby wails at being separated from his mother.

Coyote

He observed Knox and Monaghan as they set out from Corazon in the thaw. Knox's mule was laden with trading goods. Monaghan, in black, dwarfed his horse. As they rode out of town, Monaghan started to hum. Coyote felt the irritation in Knox, the desire to punish. They rode hard without rest until darkness stopped them.

First light lit the brush askance. He basked in the glow, waiting for the men to stir. Monaghan rose first and left Knox asleep by the embers. He tramped over the ridge to the east and dropped his pants to relieve himself. The inside of his knees and thighs glistened raw from the long ride. He took a flask from his coat, unstoppered it and poured it onto a kerchief. He dabbed the abrasions, hissing through set teeth. Coyote inhaled the waft of whiskey and licked his muzzle.

The sky was breaking pink and blue when Knox awoke. The air was alive with the cracking of burning wood and the aroma of coffee. The priest was on his haunches by the flames. He nodded at the pot. 'Drink up, Abraham.'

Knox smirked, 'How are your legs holding out? You sure about coming out to Los Huertos? You'll be missing the comfort of your bed and a roof.'

The priest laughed, holding up his tin cup. 'We'll go even longer today with this in our blood,' he winked, 'I've slept in the open often enough. Don't assume I've gone soft yet, Abraham.'

They settled into a fast pace early and Monaghan kept up all morning. Coyote loped alongside, invisible, listening. As the sun reached its high point, Monaghan asked, 'So you and Francis have known each other a long time, I'd say?'

Knox looked straight ahead. 'Since we were boys.'

'You grew up together! Well, that would account for it then. And where was home to you both?'

'Maryland.'

'Your people grew tobacco?'

'Mine did.'

'Not Meavy's?'

Knox snorted. 'The Meavys owned people who grew tobacco.' Monaghan looked across, waiting. Knox at last relented. 'Francis' father had estates in Maryland. My father was his foreman. Until he was killed.' He looked into Monaghan's face. 'A slave spooked his horse. His neck was broken.'

'God bless him.'

'God might, but I never will. Took his hand to me every day of his life till he died.'

'I'm sorry to hear that, Abraham. What became of your family?'

'It was me and my mother. Meavy took her in as housekeeper.'

'And you?'

'Schooled with Francis, though I'm the elder.'

'So, he treated you like a son?'

'He treated my mother like his woman.' They came to a wash, swollen and fast with the thaw. Coyote laughed at their predicament. Knox handed the lead for the mule to Monaghan. 'Hold this. I'll look upstream.' He cantered off northeast, the vapour of his breath hanging in the air for a moment as he urged his horse up the bank. When he returned, he shook his head. 'We'll follow it down as far as needs be.'

An hour later the water flattened to a broad grey ribbon. Their animals high stepped through the shallows. The far side, Monaghan spoke again. 'I'm right in thinking that you and Francis were soldiers together?'

'We were.'

'As was I. Before all this.' He took in the plateau. 'If a man does not worship in the sunlight of the spirit, he will worship the darkness.' Knox rode on in silence, the shadow of a cloud tearing the colour from him and his horse for a moment. 'What will you do now he's settled out here? Will you go on trading together?'

'He'll start farming, living the way they do.'

'The Akote?' Knox nodded. 'And you?'

'I have pots on the stove. Trading further south, investing in Maggie's place in Corazon.'

'It's a land of plenty, that's for sure.'

It is, Coyote thought. A land of plenty to be shared. He followed them to Los Huertos, where the wash of the canyon was still running with the melt from the Ute Mountains in the east.

Francis Meavy

My heart is as swollen as the freezing flow as I watch Patrick wade in with Raven in his arms. My son. The family looks on. Hawk frowns at the spectacle of the big priest rolling up his black trousers and taking his grandson into the icy water.

'Francis Meavy, he does not expect the child to swim?'

'No. He will be put under for a moment, then Father Monaghan will draw the symbol of Christ on his forehead.'

Hawk turns back to watch them in the current. I wish Father was here to see his grandson baptised, to see me the father of a son at the beginning of his life. Once more the grief of being absent at his death stabs at me.

'He knows not to touch where it is soft at the back of the baby's head?' Willow Tree asks.

I nod. 'He has done this many times, he is careful.'

'Strong too, by the look of him.' Pale Horse adds, 'Although not in the head since he chooses to swim in his clothes in the snow water.'

Willow Tree starts to chide him, but is cut off by Raven's wailing, filling the canyon. On the edge of our group, Abe turns his head away and spits into the dirt.

*

I sit with Patrick in Bright Flower's hogan after a long day on horseback exploring the plateau to the south of the canyon. I enjoy sharing the landscape with him. His company lifts my spirits.

'Francis, someday I would like to establish a mission out here, preferably up top where it will be visible to all. This place seems to me to be at the heart of the country and with you in the canyon I'd be near friends. What do you think? Would the headmen agree?'

I know they will not and shake my head. 'Why would you want to leave Corazon, surely you have your work cut out there?'

'Swindlers and whores – and that's just the officials. I could do with a clean page to work with for a while. I know it seems like my challenges will be great out here but that's not how I see it. Good people are good people and I think there are those here who will be ready to hear the word of Jesus Christ and feel the joy of loving Him and the Lord, His father, as I do.'

'Listen Patrick, these are good, devout, people but you must understand that the way the Mexicans have treated them means that they are not going to want your brand of God. Particularly if you say you are right, and they are wrong. These Akote live well, eat well, care for each other and fight together to repel and avenge raids. They don't need us, and they certainly don't need our religion.'

'Would you speak with the headmen for me?'

How to tell him it's pointless without offending him? 'I'll speak with Hawk and Pale Horse, but you must also realise that they do not speak for the Akote as a whole. They lead for as long as they are followed, for as long as they bring success. Their approval is necessary for you to start a mission here, but it doesn't guarantee you anything more. You are my friend, and they understand that you are a holy man, and it is their culture to be helpful and welcoming, but I fear that if you try to push our ways on them, your welcome will be short-lived.'

*

We sit around the hogan fire. Patrick to my right, Pale Horse and Hawk facing us.

'What does your friend wish to discuss?' Hawk asks.

I turn to Patrick. 'Now's your chance.'

He coughs into his big fist then runs his hand up and down the back of his neck. 'Thank you for meeting with me, and congratulations on a fine grandson. It was my honour to baptise him. I am a servant of God, I carry out ceremonies of adoration, prayer, marriage, funeral rites and, as you saw with Raven, baptisms. I respect your people and I have come to ask if I could build a mission not far from here, so that I may bring, to all those who are interested, the word of God and His son Jesus Christ. This is my venture to which I seek your approval.'

I translate, Hawk and Pale Horse stare at the priest. Pale Horse speaks first. 'He is not like any medicine man I ever met. More like a bear.'

I translate again. Patrick throws his head back and laughs from deep in his belly. 'Tell them I haven't always been a priest, that I was a soldier, and that I am not a medicine man. I have no knowledge of herbs or cures, only prayer and rites.'

'A medicine man who has no medicine and was once a warrior. These are strange people you come from, Francis Meavy. You should show him our Mountain Song, then he'd know how much unlike a medicine man he is.'

Hawk speaks for the first time. 'Does he wish to persuade our people that his God is more powerful than ours are, as the Spanish did two generations ago? They turned the Anaii Akote against their own. There is no good in this. But he is a friend to you, Francis Meavy, and to Bright Flower, and my grandson. If he wishes to build a house on the plateau I will not object. He may not preach; if he does, he will no longer be welcome.'

Pale Horse agrees, 'Your friend seems to be an honest man, but we know what the Mexicans do to those Akote enslaved to them. They separate them from our gods, enforcing their own. We cannot tolerate this here in our home. He may settle if he lives here in peace and gives his promise not to confuse our people.'

I sense Patrick's disappointment as I explain. He smiles at Pale Horse and Hawk. 'I understand the chiefs' reluctance and I appreciate the permission to settle. Someday I hope to do that, but I do not wish to force myself upon these good people and now does not seem like the time.'

Pale Horse bends from the waist, reaching for another log. He tosses it into the fire, putting me in mind of our first meeting. 'We will not mark our agreement with the burning poison Abraham Knox gave us.'

I clear my throat against the smoke and tell Patrick the story of the hip flask. He guffaws, 'Well then, it's a good job we met after I left soldiering.'

*

Abe is finishing up a trade with Crowsfoot. I stand with Patrick, watching him make ready for the ride back to Corazon. When he has strapped the last bundle to his horse, he turns and nods.

'These are good people, Francis, I'm happy for you.'

'Thank you. I'll see you in Corazon.'

'Will you join me in prayer?' He takes off his hat and holds it to his chest, tipping his head forward. 'Lord, may these people continue in peace and prosperity, may they be spared evil to live in your bounty. May we assist their harmony and be of service, to the glory of our Lord Jesus Christ, Amen.' He gathers the reins like threads in his fist, leans on the pommel of the saddle, steps into the stirrup, and with a creaking from his trousers, hauls his frame over the animal's back. It flattens its ears.

I reach my hand up to him. 'Safe trip, Father.' He grasps it hard, then heels his horse into a trot, bouncing as he waves. I flex my hand to ease the pain of Patrick's crushing grip.

Walking back, I meet Pale Horse striding through the settlement with a broad smile. 'The air is good, Francis

Meavy! I am a grandfather! My daughter Aspen Leaf just gave birth to a son, long-limbed and with a voice to scare the darkness. He has the mark of an arrowhead next to his heart – a good omen!'

*

It is perhaps vanity, but I stop to admire our boy in the cradle board whenever I pass. Always nestled next to Arrowhead. I hope his first memories will be of Bright Flower's soft voice singing and chanting as she labours side by side with Aspen Leaf at the loom, making baskets or tending crops. I want Raven to live with the warmth of his mother in his life, even when she's gone. If I could give myself anything it would be that, and I want it for my son.

Sometimes the loud cluck of a turkey or the sudden bleat of sheep or goat startles the child to tears, but Arrowhead laughs in his swaddling and shifts to look for the origin of the noise. I am ashamed of the disappointment I feel in those moments. At night in the hogan, I play with Raven, swinging Father's silver watch like a pendulum above him, we laugh aloud as he grasps for it again and again.

Coyote

He breathed in the perfume of cedar wood from the fire as he watched Hawk stand with the villagers gathering outside Mountain Song's hogan. The chief looked up at the sky. It was still pale pink from the dawn. Mountain Song's small herd of goats bleated in their pen as he fed them, speaking to them and laughing from time to time as they answered him. For as long as any of them could remember Mountain Song had been an old man. Yes, Akote, he thought, the Sacred endures, and brother Mountain Song is a sacred spirit.

Mountain Song turned back to where the people awaited him, asking aloud as he walked, 'Who would want goats?' He stopped to look at his neighbours with their questioning faces. 'Never mind, we can deal with that later. Over eighty summers I have lived with you in this place and now I leave to make a pilgrimage. I will go to each of the four sacred mountains. I have no apprentice so you must call on Shadow Bloom or other medicine men from nearby settlements until I return. Always remember to honour the dawn and to listen to the voice of good carried on the wind. Turn away from thoughts and activities that will attract evil winds which will ruin your life. Now, these animals will need tending while I am gone, so who wants goats?'

Hawk anticipated the competition between his neighbours. Mountain Song's herd was made up from gifts brought to him by the villagers. They chose the best animals to give in payment, so these goats were of the highest quality, the use of them a great benefit. Several men and women stepped forward. Mountain Song smiled and waved his hands. 'No need to panic, there's the sheep and the other horses as well.'

Later, Hawk sought him out and presented him with two large pouches of silver and turquoise as a gift for his journey.

'Very good,' he nodded. 'Remember, Bright Flower will choose her own way and you must accept that in her and her children. Her blood will return to the rock.'

Out of respect, Hawk said nothing, suppressing his irritation at the stipulations for his own daughter.

*

Before dawn the next day, Coyote followed Mountain Song as he left his hogan to head west in the darkness. That first night he made camp at the cusp of the canyon where the wash gathered itself before rushing south. He chanted over his fire at first light, rocking back and forth. The aroma of the herbs he burned carried on the breeze over a low ridge to the north, where, waiting on the skyline, Coyote filled his lungs.

Late in the morning, up on the plateau, Mountain Song turned at the clacking of hooves on the rocky ground behind him. As he did so, smoke covered two riders to the east and a musket ball threw him sideways out of the saddle. His foot snagged in its stirrup as he fell. His pony bolted at the noise of the shot. By the time his killers caught the spooked horse, the body of the old man was flayed beyond recognition. He had been dragged to the edge of a deep fissure in the rock.

They dismounted. One untangled Mountain Song's lifeless leg while the other cut the pouches of silver and turquoise from his belt. He spat on the corpse, then barrelled it over the lip of the ravine. The other, a man with one eye, led Mountain Song's horse to the edge of the drop, its eyes rolling white. Holding its bridle with one hand, he punched his knife into its spine above the withers. It fell sideways after its master. They strapped their new wealth to the back of One Eye's saddle, remounted and kicked on. Coyote threw his head back and howled.

Francis Meavy

1851 – Canyon de Los Huertos Ocultos

Raven's sixth year. Time to read and write. He's enthusiastic. It's a special thing, I suppose, being taught something none of the other children can learn from their parents. In the evenings I encourage him to trace letters on rough paper, and to compare them with the same ones in our family Bible. Before long the letters make words, then sentences, each advance more satisfying than the last. During the cold months we study together by firelight in the hogan; and when the weather grows warmer and the days longer, by the cottonwood stand or in the alcove – the place I had first stayed on coming to Los Huertos. We go over and over the story of Jonah.

'But why didn't he drown?'

'When Abe and I were boys, we asked the same question. We figured that Jonah must have taken the biggest breath of his life and held it until he was safe inside.' Each time, Raven inhales and holds it until my laughter forces him to breathe again.

*

He's ten now. Bright Flower has been teaching him how to tend the crops and detect the ripeness of melons and pumpkins by the colour of their skin and by feeling around the stems. He has learned how to check the peaches by sniffing them and twisting them on the branch without bruising them. Bright Flower and Aspen Leaf take him and Arrowhead out with the flocks of sheep and herds of goat when they move them to graze on the plateau above, calling after them to stop skipping and whirling sticks so they don't excite the animals.

I watch them, lean and sun browned, as they climb the talus to the canyon rim. Arrowhead races ahead, clambering over larger and larger boulders before jumping back onto the crumbling path, challenging Raven to join him. The boy's fast and strong, but hesitates, observing, calculating the drop, or the run-up required to jump for a handhold. His caution vexes me. While my son looks to his mother, Arrowhead is called back by his.

Hawk, Pale Horse and Crowsfoot take Raven with the other boys of the settlement to hunt, to learn their sacred chants for the pursuit of each prey, the differences between tracks and their meaning.

He comes back and tells me, 'When the soil is soft, the visibility of the dew claws in elk or deer prints or splaying in the marks of the bighorn sheep mean that it's running. Antelope don't leave dew claw marks, but an indentation wider at the base than deer. On the lower parts of trees, where they're bald, it's where deer rub but the higher stripped patches are where bears have fed on sap. Where the bark's chewed it's porcupines.'

The boy knows to watch for signs of the coyote since to follow a path crossed by one can bring ill fortune. If the claws are not visible in the prints, then it's a bobcat instead. Sometimes when Hawk or Pale Horse set out on foot to track, the boys race the men to the rim by climbing the rock, swinging, and hauling themselves from handhold to toehold to ledge using fissures and ridges invisible from the canyon floor.

*

Hunting with me is different to the hunt with Raven's Akote menfolk, I know. There's no chanting, no speaking to the land or to the spirit of the animal pursued. Just calm preparation. We go out with the rifles. Raven has grasped that the powder is precious and needs to be borne in mind constantly so it stays dry, and that the mechanism on the side of the firearm must be protected from impact.

I whisper instructions while preparing for a killing shot. It's something private, to be shared by us alone. I've taught Raven to clean the gun long before I'll let him use it. He's physically cautious, and if he's shocked by the explosion and the recoil on his first shot, he'll fear the gun and tense at the crucial moment, blighting his aim thenceforth. I delay letting him discharge the rifle as long as I can. Only after three hunting seasons, during which I have tried to accustom Raven to the noise and smell and to teach him respect for the weapon rather than fear, have I decided to let him fire it.

It's his twelfth autumn and, following the harvest, the winter is coming in fast. We climb up to the plateau. The wind is from the east. We skirt the canyon rim to the west and circle towards an area of crisscrossing arroyos and trees, many with the bark rubbed off, where deer herds graze. Raven's teeth are chattering with the cold. No matter, the boy will have to toughen up. Approaching a gully from the west, we spot two does wandering in and out of sight and stalk closer to them. Four others appear then, silhouetted against the rock. Raven squeezes my arm and points. Ahead, a stag grazes. It's heavy with muscle and armed with a forest of gouged and broken antlers.

We are downwind, thirty paces off. The breeze rattles the sagebrush, carrying the musk of the animal to us. I weigh it up. It's a trophy beast to set up Raven's confidence for life, but thirty paces on his first shot is long and the massive male will need to take a round in the heart to go down clean. The does wander off into the brush. The stag lifts its head from the grass, ears flicking. I drop to my belly to peer over a boulder, gesturing for Raven to do the same. It stares straight at us. We neither blink, nor breathe. It looks over its shoulder, ears flicking again as it stands motionless. Moments later it drops its head once more, taking half a step into the sagebrush. Its black-tipped tail twitches.

I creep back into the arroyo and prop the gun against the rock, motioning for Raven to load. I slip the powder horn from my belt and fumble it. It falls from my hand. Raven catches it. I smile at him, nodding my approval, then take the rifle and pass it across in silence. The boy taps powder into the measure, then pours it into the muzzle. I pass him the wad and ball which he presses into the tube with his thumb. I remove the rod from beneath the barrel and, looking upwards to ensure that the end is not visible above the rock, ram home. Slowly, I take a firing cap from the pouch and hand it to him. He places it on the cock. I mime for him to stay still. I crawl ahead, raising my head to see over the boulder.

The stag still grazes. I put my index finger to my lips for silence and gesture Raven forward with the other hand. He inches up against the rock, slides the barrel forward on a cushion of air, then rests its weight in the palm of his upturned hand.

I whisper into his ear, 'Remember. The heart. Get the aim rising and falling with your breath and adjust so it's right when the breath is empty.' He is shaking. 'Hold the stock deep into your shoulder, right in the crease. Squeeze gently like you're holding a turkey chick.'

The boy is forgetting to blink, his eyes are watering. He is trying too hard, waiting too long. The gun is growing heavy for him, even supported by the boulder, soon his trembling will guarantee failure. The barrel rises and falls. Raven exhales, closes his right hand, meets the pressure of the trigger. Just as I feared, he anticipates the recoil and the noise, and snatches, spoiling the aim as he fires. A moment's heat and we're blinded by smoke, coughing in the sulphur stink of the powder. I jump up, breaking cover, reaching for my bayonet. The stag has straightened and stares at us now as the ball hits him low and to the side, smashing the left foreleg below the chest. It bellows and rears, flailing its ruined limb before crashing down on it, collapsing as it buckles under the weight.

I'm up over the boulder and sprinting, knife drawn.

As I reach the stricken creature it rakes the air and the ground with its antlers. I come along the back of it, raising my arm above my head and stab downwards into the side of its chest. It spasms. I pull out the knife and, in the moment of shock, slam it into the top of the creature's neck where it meets the skull. I wrench my shoulders, twisting the bayonet two handed to sever the spine. The danger of it hits me, my adrenaline giving way to fear, then rage.

Raven calls me in that moment. 'Father?' I turn, my face burning with the fury of survival. He stammers, 'I'm-I-I'm sorry, Father.'

My glare scorches the boy and I make myself look away. 'Well, we got him anyway. Remember that for next time, squeeze don't snatch. That's what brought the shot across, so it wasn't clean.'

'I'm sorry, Father. I meant to do as you said I –'

'Enough!' I'm shouting. Disappointment bloodies us both. No words come, just taut silence. I rope the stag to the travois behind my horse and we make for the settlement. Raven traipses alongside, sullen. We draw near the hogan. Bright Flower emerges, sees us and waves. I look away to the side, Raven stares at the ground in front of him.

She sees the stag as we approach. 'You had a good morning! Whose kill?'

'Raven saw him first and he took the shot. It is his kill.'

Bright Flower reaches her hand out to Raven with a smile. The boy twists away. 'Leave me alone,' he shouts and runs to the canyon wall, jumping for a handhold, his legs pushing him upwards. Within moments he rolls onto a high ledge and is invisible from beneath.

Bright Flower turns to me. 'What happened?'

I'm exhausted. 'I need to sort this out,' I wave towards the horse and the carcass behind it.

She makes a feast of the stag, sharing it with Aspen Leaf and her family. It is butchered and cooked over a fire in the early evening while there's still light and the warmth of the flames is enough to keep off the cold. I praise Raven for bringing the great animal down, but my words feel empty as I say them and Raven neither smiles nor looks up.

When Arrowhead and his father join the meal, Bright Flower greets them, 'Come and eat this proud stag my son hunted.'

'You weren't there,' Raven shouts.

I snap, yell at him, 'Raven –' The boy runs into the hogan without waiting for me to finish. There's a moment's silence around the fire.

Aspen Leaf breaks it. 'May this be the first of many.'

Bright Flower leans towards me as the others talk, puts her open palm on my cheek. 'Tell me what happened on the plateau.'

I stand. 'I'm leaving for Corazon at first light. I must prepare.'

*

Bright Flower shakes her head at me. 'Francis Meavy, you know it is long past time. I should have insisted before. He is already in his fifteenth year, and you have not yet taken him.'

I have tried to avoid this argument for months, but now it seems there is no escaping it. 'What's to be gained? He's fine here, what's in Corazon that he needs?'

'It is what we agreed before he was born, and yet you have not taken him. What is he to understand by that? Both traditions, we said.'

'Alright, alright. I'll take him with me.'

I set out for Corazon two days later with Raven, the boy wearing one of my hats over his topknot. As we approach the town, I become stiff in the saddle and quick with my horse.

'Remember what I said. Don't talk unless I say. Apart from that, do as I do. Don't stare at the men. Or the women. Keep your eyes low.'

We dismount, Raven mirrors my actions. Two richly dressed young Mexican women walk past arm in arm. I touch the brim of my hat. Raven does the same. They look him up and down, giggling as they continue on their way. I watch him for a moment then nod towards the doors of the hotel. A storey has been added since my last visit and a new sign outside, squeaking as the wind swings it. I enter first, take a few paces then stop and remove my hat. I realise my mistake as soon I make it – Raven goes to remove his – I block his arm and replace my own. 'We'll keep these on for the time being.' We cross to the counter. He's gawping at her blue eyes and low-cut dress. She looks up, holds Raven's gaze and smiles.

'Maggie!'

'Francis Meavy! It's been too long.' She tips her head towards Raven. 'Where have you been hiding this fine young colt? Since you're two green-eyed peas in a pod, this must be your son?'

'This is Raven.'

She turns back to the boy. 'Well, it's a pleasure to meet you, but haven't you been taught to take off your hat when speaking with a lady?' He turns to me for help. Ashamed, I look away. He removes the hat and holds it to his chest. Maggie puts her hands on her hips and looks at his topknot. 'That's a pretty red ribbon.'

The patrons at the table closest are looking across, whispering. 'Alright, put it back on.' Raven does it too fast; it goes on askew, damn it. 'Straighten it, boy.'

Maggie smirks, 'So how do you like the place now, Francis?'

I look around. Maggie's husband died of a fever years ago. At nearly thirty she warded off suitors by saying she was too old to land another man to her liking. How wrong she was, the most handsome woman in Corazon and for miles around. But Abe suggested a business partnership to her. He'd traded hard in the lower Akote lands after we parted and proposed investing some of the profits into expanding and improving her Corazon Hotel. Back then everyone knew that certain customers were happy enough to take advantage of the widow. No doubt the prospect of Abe's presence in the hotel, along with the pistols strapped to his waist, appealed to her. There's an additional floor now and much improved furnishings, but also a more civilised atmosphere in the place and the outward signs of respect in the customers. Abe bargains hard. Too hard sometimes. I hope Maggie's still getting all she should from the deal. I liked the place better before.

'Maggie, it's grander each time I come back. I hope your hard work is being duly rewarded?'

She doesn't answer my question, looking instead towards the door of the parlour. 'Here's Abe, now.' She heads off along the counter.

Abe long ago discarded his buckskins in favour of tailored pants and a long jacket with fine boots. He emerges now from the back of the hotel and pauses to light the cigar of the Mexican army captain he accompanies before touching the match to his own. He's seen us. He claps the officer on his back and shakes his hand.

*

We sit in the parlour. Abe turns to Raven, 'You look like your father, boy.' He does. I cannot help but smile. 'What brings you to Corazon, Francis?'

'I heard that Mexico was signing over the territory to the United States.'

'Not all of it. Just as far north as Corazon and fifty miles west of here.'

'So, it's true then?'

'That's what I'm told by the military. They've asked me to be the agent for the Southern Akote. They expect

Mexico to give up the rest of their territories in a year or two, then they'll need an agent for the Northern Akote. I've said you're the man for that job.'

I push down my rage. 'We're happy as we are, Abe.' Raven knocks back the last of the whiskey Abe gave us. 'I wouldn't –'

'Listen. When it happens, your Indians will need someone out there to represent them. The army and the government will want a man who knows the territory and the Akote. It won't happen overnight, but if you don't want it to be an unknown or maybe hostile person, then you need to tell me now, so I can line it up.' The noise of a glass falling onto the floorboards cuts him short. It smashes, sending shards skittering.

'Goddammit, Raven.' The boy jumps to his feet, sways, then slumps back into the armchair. 'Help me here will you, Abe?'

We manoeuvre him back through the main room. Maggie looks over and wags a finger. I curse again. Raven snatches the hat from his head and holds it against his chest. I try to force it back on, but he resists. Seeing the struggle and the boy's topknot, the men at the bar turn and straighten, hands hovering over knives and pistols.

Maggie heads off the trouble. 'Just a young man and the drink having their first tiff,' she hollers. 'Nothing to be vexed about, gentlemen.'

We reach the door, 'When the time comes, tell them I'll do it, Abe. I'll be the agent for the Northern Akote.'

*

I sit with Hawk and Raven, planing arrow weed shafts, wearing buckskin against the turning of the season. My misgivings rise as Abe approaches the settlement with a troop of cavalry. I cross the canyon floor towards them, wondering whether the soldiers are aware of the Akote warriors surrounding them.

'Abe! This is unexpected.' I reach up to shake his hand.

He takes it and looks down at me from his horse, 'Francis.' He nods towards Hawk.

Hawk replies, unblinking, 'Abraham Knox.'

I see the surprise of the officer next to Abe. Abe turns towards Raven. 'More and more like your father.' He gestures to his right, 'This is Captain Cross.'

The man is slight and sallow, his eyes like a crow's. He shifts in his saddle. 'Captain Meavy,' he nods. 'A pleasure.'

'No one calls me captain anymore, not in a long time. What brings you here? Will you come in for refreshment? Do your horses need water?'

In the hogan, Cross removes his hat revealing long dark hair. I offer him a stool. He brushes it with his gloves, then sits and looks around, barely disguising his revulsion. At last, his gaze settles on me with a slight smile, but it's Abe who speaks.

'You are aware that the US Army occupied a good part of the territory south and east of here when Mexico signed over its territories round Corazon to the United States five years ago. A treaty was drawn up with the

Southern Akote swapping land rights for supplies and provisions. Now this land and the territory to the west of here are to be ceded by Mexico to the US as well. As I have been the agent for the Southern Akote, ever since Mexico signed that land over, the Captain here asked me to bring him to Los Huertos. He has been visiting with Mexican and Indian headmen further south and knew of your circumstances here among the Northern Akote.'

Cross clears his throat. 'The United States will shortly gain sovereignty over all the former northern Mexican lands including the lands occupied by these Indians. We are introducing a major military presence and will be building forts throughout the territory. Soon an agent will be appointed to these Northern Akote. They must learn that we are their masters, the owners of the land they enjoy.'

My irritation flares as he speaks. 'Captain, these people have lived here for generations. To arrive and say you own the land will make no sense to them. Their use of the land is a holy gift from the gods.'

'Mr Meavy, I had hoped to find you less – how shall I say – wedded to these Indians. We are present because Mr Knox proposed that you become the agent here. However, I detect that your loyalties lie elsewhere.'

'Captain, I assume that –'

Cross interrupts, 'Mr Meavy, *I* assume that you are not a headman here since you are white?' He does not wait for a response. 'I would be grateful for you to introduce me to the headmen so that I may convey to them the situation.'

'Hawk and Pale Horse are the chiefs here, but you should understand that they do not speak for all the settlements in this area.'

'I shall choose what I should understand.'

I storm from the hogan, barely able to contain my rage. Abe follows me. 'Francis, hold up. Go easy on Cross, he lost his daughter and his wife to Indians in Pennsylvania. Murdered and burned before he could get there.'

I'm shaking my head, unable to find words worthy of the information. 'That. Is.' I give up. 'Abe. You haven't been out here in years and now you come for – what, exactly?'

He looks down before he answers. 'The territory has changed. Trade in the hotel is up fourfold. I've bought property in Corazon and mines in Argento and Nebraska territory. With the land to the west opening up, there will be travellers and profit. The government needs grazing and minerals and to bring people and troops across country. Before long the army will be everywhere. With you as agent, requisitioning supplies through me for these Akote, there's real money to be made.' He takes in the settlement with a gesture of his hand, 'No more scratching a living, Francis. No more huts.'

'What's happened to you, Abe? You've been the agent for the Southern Akote all this time, but when I go down there all I see is thin horses and hungry people. Cross despises us and now I know why. I've a notion the treatment these Akote will receive will not be to their advantage, and when that happens, I don't want my family harmed. I can't be their agent, Cross knows that, and you know it.'

Abe turns back towards the hogan. 'We'll wait while you bring Hawk.'

The war chiefs sit while Cross speaks, and I translate. When I describe the government ownership of land, Pale Horse laughs.

'What does he find amusing?' Cross asks, glaring at him.

I explain the question to Pale Horse. 'Francis Meavy, whoever heard of owning the land? Can they own the air, the sky? Perhaps the wind will carry provisions for them! This is nonsense the small man speaks.'

I translate for Cross, 'The concept of land ownership is alien to these people.'

'Well then, that is convenient. If they do not conceive of ownership, then it will not vex them that the land they inhabit will very soon belong to the United States government.'

'How can we reason with this man who has lost his wits?' Pale Horse asks. 'Better that we take him to see Shadow Bloom to remove his confusion.'

Hawk is looking at the pistol at Cross's waist. 'Ask where the soldiers will be based and how many they will be.'

Cross straightens. 'For the time being Corazon is our headquarters. As to how many – our numbers will be more than adequate.'

*

The outsiders mount up. We stand watching them, my hand on Raven's shoulder. Cross turns his horse towards us, looks at the boy then back at me.

'I will see you again soon, Captain Meavy.'

Over the next week I discuss the exchange at length with Hawk and Pale Horse. We agree that I will head to Corazon to gauge how many troops have already been stationed there and what other changes are taking place. I set out, riding between islands of bright copper aspen turning for the season, overnighting in Akote settlements. The feeling of belonging swells in me day by day as my Akote hosts greet me and ask after Bright Flower and Raven.

*

My horse fidgets. Corazon feels alien to me. I knock at Patrick Monaghan's door, but there's no reply. I make my way to the hotel. It's grander yet, painted red and white, over three storeys now and dominating the street. Maggie's behind the bar as if she hasn't moved since last time, save that her dress is brown, and her face is bloated. The counter is longer, polished mahogany with a brass foot rail.

'Francis Meavy,' she sighs, 'still walking as straight as ever. The Akote life agrees with you. The Corazon Hotel welcomes back its old friend. What will you drink? Whiskey?'

The place is full. I have never seen it so busy. 'Plenty of custom, Maggie.'

'The town is growing fast since the army came.

Traders, officials, all sorts. Some pass through, some stay.'

'What are they saying about the tribes?'

'The country is on the move. The soldiers say they're here to ensure peace, or at least safety for the people moving in. There's talk of cattle grazing and timber and minerals. The world is coming Francis, there's going to be a tide of folk looking to settle.' She pauses. 'Abe has been up and down the territory buying into land and trading opportunities. He says there are fortunes to be made – he should know.' She wipes the counter harder, looking away.

'Is he around?'

She nods towards the back. 'Another meeting with the military.'

The parlour door opens to the sound of a man's laughter. Cross ambles out and half turns towards Abe, a thick cigar stub in his fingers. Abe holds his cigar up. 'Good?'

Cross draws on his, the tip glows. He blows a smoke ring. 'Excellent as ever, Abraham.' Abe stares through the haze and sees me at the bar. Cross turns too then strides towards me. 'Mr Meavy, good to see you again. Thank you for your help in Los Huertos. It seems that in the heat of the situation we got off on the wrong foot. A pure misunderstanding, no doubt.'

I see from his uniform that Cross now holds the rank of Major. God help us all.

'I would stay and buy you a whiskey but, alas, duty calls.' He holds his right hand out. I take it slowly and we shake. 'I shall leave you in the dangerous company of Mr Knox. Until next time.' He nods at me, smiles at Abe, then swaggers out of the saloon as if he were a taller man.

Maggie picks up a towel and starts wiping clean glasses cleaner.

'Come with me.' Abe leads the way to the parlour. The old furniture is gone. A table and four chairs are surrounded by unpacked crates.

'Cross is more jovial than the last time I saw him.'

'He's second in command of the garrison now and in charge of procurement. He's doing well. I'm sourcing the supplies. What brings you to town?'

'I want to find out what plans there are for the Akote land, what we can expect.'

'Like I said before, the army is coming in numbers your Akote can't imagine. You and I always said that we left our family behind, that we were alone. These Indians are not your people. Bright Flower and Francis Junior, you can take with you and head west or north. There's silver and copper that way. But here the army and the settlers will catch up with you. You need to understand that the tribe will not have the freedom they have taken for granted. Sooner or later, Washington will enforce the treaty with the Southern Akote across the whole territory. More troops will come, and they will not show much favour. You could have been the Indian agent, that was your chance to make things easier for them, but at Los Huertos, Cross saw you as one of them.'

'Thanks for the drink.' I knock back the whiskey; it's as good as I've tasted. I look over at the bottle, it's the same brand Father drank.

I head up Main Street, images of Akote villages being overrun in my mind, the rage building. I near Monaghan's house. He's coming fast from the other direction, frowning. Seeing me, he smiles with unmistakable warmth, lifting my spirits.

'Francis!' He smothers my hand with his gigantic paw. 'Come in, come in.' He gestures for me to take a seat at the plain wooden table in the middle of the room. Monaghan removes his cassock, takes a log from the stack next to the iron stove in the corner and tosses it into the embers before closing the door with the toe of his boot. He rolls up the sleeves of his undershirt. 'What can I get you? I have some fine Irish tea just in – the goods in the store are improving.'

'No thanks, Patrick. I was just with Abe Knox.'

His eyes fix on the floorboards before moving back to me. 'And how's Maggie?'

'Maggie seemed distracted. Abe was telling me how things have been changing here, how many troops they expect to come into the territory to assert sovereignty on Akote land.'

He shakes his head, 'You know they will want forts and possibly a mission in the heart of the territory, don't you? It's the formula. You get the wrong commanders out there and it will work out badly all round.'

I turn it over in my mind. Under the Mexicans the Akote were raided, but it had been out of the question that their land would be invaded and taken. Los Huertos is the most home I've ever had.

'Patrick you've been out and met the people, would

you build a mission now?'

'Francis, I believe that the Lord Jesus Christ is the way to forgiveness of our sins, to salvation and eternal life, and I also believe in plain good when I see it. Those people are living God in their own way and frankly are a lot more Christian in their dealings with each other than many of my flock, so no, I wouldn't interfere –'

'You misunderstand, I meant would *you* come out and run a mission? God knows we could do with a good man out there, and there was a time when you asked Hawk and Pale Horse if you could do just that.'

He hesitates. 'I'm an older man now, Francis. Let me consider it and talk to those above.'

I leave him and walk east, the length of Main Street, to where the garrison has swallowed one end of the town. It mills with horses and men. I turn back towards the hotel and look up at the autumn sun. If I'm quick I can be out of Corazon and make it to Hole Rock before nightfall. I cross the street to the general store. It's packed with townsfolk and transients, the shopkeeper and his clerks shuttling back and forth, reaching for boxes on the shelves behind the counter, weighing flour, wrapping soap and small items in paper which they tie with twine. There's no room to move. I wait. My trance is broken by the storekeeper himself.

'Mr Meavy?' Bronze is just over six foot, with a pale complexion, and a wet, rosebud mouth. He oozes affability, but I know his reputation for young girls and old wine from years ago. Somehow, he got the funds together to take over the store in time for this boom.

'Bronze.'

'Sorry for the wait, Mr Meavy, you can see how busy we are. Things have changed so much since the garrison has grown. People want things they never asked for before and more of what they already had. We struggle to keep up with demand. But we can't complain, can we? It's progress and we all make from it, don't we? Now, how can I help you?' He leans across the counter, lowering his voice. 'Friends of Mr Knox are afforded special prices in this store.' His breath is like a latrine. He leans back to his own side of the counter, his mouth slick.

'Gunpowder, Bronze, packed to travel.'

*

I step out of the store, the parcel heavy under my arm. Two riders approach at the walk. Cross and a colleague, an older man in the uniform of a colonel. They draw level with me and rein in.

'Good day again, Mr Meavy.' I nod. 'Colonel Waldron let me introduce Mr Francis Meavy.'

The man's hair curls white underneath his hat. He inspects me with his pale blue eyes, his head tilted back slightly so he appears to sniff the air with his long, hooked nose. 'Captain Meavy, no less.' He looks at Cross then turns back to me. 'You know the territory intimately I hear, as well as its inhabitants.' A smirk kicks up the corner of his mouth. 'A man with your experience and military pedigree could be of great service to his country. We should talk at an early opportunity. I currently command here in Corazon but will be departing to take up the governorship in Santa Fe in the coming weeks.'

He notices an offending speck on his britches and brushes it off with the back of his glove. The silence between us is broken only by the sounds of passing horses and Cross' saddle creaking as he shifts.

At last Waldron reins his mount left and heels it on. 'Good day, Captain Meavy.'

They walk their horses back down Main Street. Waldron's gelding lifts its tail and empties itself. Feeling eyes on me, I look back towards the store. Bronze is in the window, observing, his assistants scurrying like ants back and forth around the customers. He turns and disappears into shadow. I want to get out of Corazon, to leave it behind. I kick the horse into a canter. On the porch of the hotel an Anaii man follows me with his one good eye as I ride out of town.

*

Canyon de Los Huertos Ocultos

'They will force on us the treaty they have with the Southern Akote. It will make you give up land in return for protection and supplies. But how much land? What conditions? When I go south the people and their animals are thin. If the terms they offer are fair, will they honour them? The garrison is already heavily swollen, a sure sign they plan to use force.'

Pale Horse grasps what I am saying, 'We have lived here for generations. Why should they want to interfere with us? At least we knew where we stood with the Mexicans when they were Mexicans.'

Hawk nods. 'Their animals will need grazing and their people will want land. Francis Meavy, you know these people. Can they be trusted?'

My shoulders drop. 'I'm sorry, Hawk, there were officers, years ago in the dragoons, but now? These are the sort of commanders who do not consider our people to be men and women in the same way they are. The agreements they make in their language on their own terms will last only for as long as they are useful to them. I warn you. I do not believe they will hold for long. They want this land: to settle, to travel across, to graze, and to mine.'

Pale Horse rises, uncrossing his arms. 'Then we must attack first and kill so many of them that they will know to come here will mean only death.' He looks to Hawk, then to me.

'They all have guns, Pale Horse, not just a few like the Ute and the Pueblo.'

Hawk examines the back of his right hand and starts to rub it with his left thumb, speaking as he thinks. 'If it is as you say, they will send soldiers until they are too many for us. Most Akote will not wish to believe this. It is our way to be hospitable. Our people will need to see for themselves. Other settlements will not wish to fight these soldiers without trying to make peace first. We will call a council and tell the war chiefs what we know. Once they know the strength of the army it will be clear how many of our sons and brothers would die in a war with this opponent. Many will wish to make a treaty. If they consider us less than men, they will not stop until they have taken everything from us. We must prepare. I will send messengers out to the other Akote war chiefs to meet in the Great Harvest Canyon before the snows come to hinder travel.'

*

We ride out. Hawk at the head of the party with Pale Horse by his side. I ride behind them with Crowsfoot, followed by Arrowhead and Raven, then the rearguard. High on Bear Rock, Shadow Bloom watches us go. Pale Horse has seen him too and nods towards the rim. He pulls tight the neck of his buckskin shirt and adjusts the blanket wrapped around his shoulders.

Hawk calls the younger warriors forward and looks towards the horizon. 'Tell me.'

Raven and Arrowhead have been brought up with this ritual during the hunt with their Akote menfolk. They are expected to list the lie of the landscape: rock; slopes; blind spots; stands of trees; potential hiding places; areas where the ground would be softer and therefore slower for the horses, but still able to hold clear tracks. They listen to the birds, feel the direction of the wind. Circling vultures can indicate the presence of carrion. The presence of carrion could mean a bear or mountain lion. The disturbance of birds might signify an enemy in hiding. They describe all this to him, together with the scents in the air, the condition of the clouds and the light where we are and in the distance. From this they predict the changes in the weather. They speak these things without hesitation. Hawk and Pale Horse have instructed them on how to take these factors into account in the use of the bow. Only Raven assesses the effect of windage on an arrow and the necessary adjustments for a rifle.

The second day. Horses and men breathing vapour in the afternoon chill. We penetrate the western end of the Great Harvest Canyon. Raven is craning his head further and further back to take in the full height of the towering walls. Stone buildings like wasps' nests cling to high shelves, similar to the few in Los Huertos, but paler against the red of the rock and with no visible approach except for those where a talus has formed. The number of warriors increases as we progress through the canyon. Hawk and Pale Horse are acknowledged by each of them, but only a few of the most important men look directly at them for more than a moment. Many shout greetings to me, warm but with less formality.

Pale Horse leans across. 'Look at Raven and Arrowhead, they have never seen so many Akote in one place!'

I take another glimpse. They turn their heads this way and that, struggling to take in the sheer activity.

*

Night has fallen and the war chiefs meet in the great cavern formed by the partial collapse of a side canyon. Fires blaze round the edges of the vault and in its centre. Hawk seems to be contemplating the paintings on the walls. The shadows cast by the warriors give life to deer darting across red landscapes as stick men with box bodies chase them – their ancestors, who enjoyed this land since emerging from the darkness. Raven's ancestors.

Juanito, the greatest of the Akote war chiefs, rises to speak first. Of average height, he's as lean and muscular as a man twenty years younger. His hair is thick with feathers. There is no grey. Only the wrinkles lacing his broad face betray his age.

'This is a simple matter. The soldiers who have come to Corazon are warriors. Warriors fight either to protect or to conquer. Since they have no land nor people here, it is clear they come to conquer. They made a treaty with an Akote headman to the south. Why do we need treaties? This is where we live, where we have our homes, our crops, our stock. This land provides for us. What can they offer in their treaty that we do not already have? Nothing. And so, they will seek to take from us if we let them. It can only be this way. Before more of the soldiers come, we must attack in great number and make them understand that they would be better to keep to their own places.' Juanito sits. So far so good.

Cloud Shadow struggles to his feet; white hair, arms and legs stick thin. He's from the southwest of the Akote lands and has fought the Anaii, the Mexicans, and before them, the Spanish. His voice is high and nasal. 'These soldiers and their people are powerful beyond any enemy we have faced. Few of us have guns. We know, from fighting the Mexicans and the Spanish before them, that these guns give great advantage. And now the Anaii and the Ute have guns from the white soldiers since they serve them as scouts and guides. The soldiers took the land to the south and to the east from the Mexicans whom we have fought for long years and who have caused us great losses. They say that the Mexicans are now under their protection. They cannot protect and be an enemy at the same time. If we accept their terms, they will protect us. Perhaps we will no longer have to fight off Mexican raids and attacks from other tribes? If that is so then many lives will be saved, our women and children will no longer suffer enslavement. We should listen to what they propose. If they wish to use our land for grazing and passage in return for protection, should we not agree to save the lives of our people?'

Hawk rises. 'Cloud Shadow's reasoning is just. It would be fair for the soldiers to protect us. But we know that they do not consider us the same as the Mexicans. They believe we are not men as they are, that we are less than them. Who would protect the interests of a goat or a dog against those of another man? They will not honour an agreement with us, nor respect our customs or possessions. This should guide us in our dealings with them. In our tribe we have one who was born among them and lived as one of them before marrying into the Tseyi'nii clan of Los Huertos. Francis Meavy, tell us how do these people see us?'

It's been two decades since I came to Los Huertos. Each time I return I look down on the settlement from the rim of the canyon and marvel at the contentment and peace I've found among a people whose way of life is so different from what I knew before. There, I am at home. But here, now, standing in the firelight with the flames and shadows playing across the broad faces and dark eyes of those born Akote, I am other. The outsider I was twenty years ago. I remember being a boy in Maryland, running through the tobacco with Abe, but even with him there was something missing – a closeness we should have felt as near brothers which never came. And Father, who so rarely said an unkind word to me – in his presence, I always felt the guilt of my mother's death, the sacrifice of name and home he made for me. Bright Flower. It has only ever been with Bright Flower that I have belonged, felt at home, felt no more the outsider. Although she is far off in Los Huertos, my wife gives me the courage to speak.

'I am Francis Meavy of the Tseyi'nii clan in the canyon of Los Huertos. My wife is Bright Flower Tseyi'nii, daughter of Willow Tree and Hawk. My father was Francis Farrer Meavy born in the county of Devon in England across the great Atlantic Sea, then of Maryland many weeks east of here. My father's family were English, the fathers and forefathers of many of the people we call Americans.

The reason I am here and not in the land of my ancestors is that my mother was not like them. She was the daughter of a headman, but of a race with dark skin and dark eyes whose lands came to be controlled by the English soldiers and officials. She died giving birth to me. My father's family would not accept a child of mixed blood, so he brought me here to this land where people of many different origins live together. But still there are those considered to be less by many men because their skin is darker. I have always been accepted as white. My skin is paler than my mother's and I have my father's green eyes. If I were darker, it would be different. The soldiers who have come here and the people who follow them will not believe that the Akote are men and women as they are. I know this from my life with them. I was one of their soldiers myself before I became a trader. They will use the treaty they made with the headman in the south to bind all Akote. When it is broken, as they will ensure that it is, they will say that we have chosen to break it and use that as their reason to take land, food, and livestock.'

Cloud Shadow hauls himself to his feet once more, as Hawk warned me he would. 'Francis Meavy, these people, surely, they must have good men and women among them. They cannot all be as you say. We are told that they are countless. Can it be that you are the only one among them who is willing to understand and respect us? I cannot believe it.'

'There are good men, but not in positions of power here in our land. I have met the soldiers' war chief at Corazon. His name is Waldron. I know this type of man. He will be obeyed, or destroy us.'

I look towards Hawk. He stands. There is silence as all eyes turn to him. 'Time will reveal the truth. If we agree to the treaty and the soldiers do not honour it, we will know that it is as my son-in-law says. If the treaty is honoured, we will live at peace with these people. It is for them to decide how we shall react. Let us hope for peace and await their treaty but prepare to defend ourselves.'

*

It's late. Under the waxing moon Hawk, Pale Horse, Crowsfoot and I walk beneath the walls of the Great Canyon.

I have a plan. 'We need firearms, so our warriors can defend themselves against the soldiers and the enemy tribes who are arming themselves. If the army has decided to take these lands, then no dealer will be able to sell guns to us. If it becomes known that the Akote are acquiring them in quantity, they will use it as proof of our hostility to justify attacking us. We must find a way of buying them without it being known.'

'Where?' Pale Horse asks.

'Corazon. We could suggest to Cloud Shadow that he comes with me to see the garrison for himself?'

Hawk agrees. 'We will speak with Juanito, then we will travel to Corazon with Cloud Shadow. Pale Horse, will you stay to lead should we not return?'

*

Early snow flurries without settling. I hold in my mind the Great Harvest Canyon as we left: Raven standing shoulder to shoulder with Pale Horse, and Arrowhead who ran to the canyon wall and scaled it like a spider to reach a ledge from which he could watch us leave.

Thirteen. It's not enough. Hawk, Cloud Shadow, five warriors each, and me. We run the risk of meeting a superior raiding party. Only three of us in buffalo skins to protect us against the cold. The remaining men have woollen blankets over their buckskins. The steam comes in geysers from the nostrils of the ponies as we canter across the plateau towards Corazon.

We ride in silence. The warriors scan the landscape with the tension of men sensing an untouchable enemy. We make camp in a settlement set in a large hollow on the southern plateau. As we crest the dip, I'm glad for the sudden shelter from the cold wind, but neither this nor the welcome we receive is enough to change our dark mood. When we set out at dawn, we leave our hosts newly sombre. At Hole Rock, the last Akote village before Corazon, we stop to discuss our plan for entering the town. I am to go ahead, to talk with Abe and arrange a meeting with Waldron.

I arrive in Corazon in the early afternoon, tie my horse to the rail of the hotel and climb new stone steps to the freshly painted door. Opening it, the hot stink of liquor and men hits me in the face. Maggie's tending bar. Her face is taut and she's wearing little makeup. Every chair is occupied as I thread my way through, and the odours of cheap tobaccos struggle for dominance until I reach the table closest to the centre of the room, where the rich aroma of a fine cigar crushes its common rivals.

Abe is playing cards with a handful of other men and from the way he's sitting – easy and quiet – I can tell that the stiff-backed adversaries surrounding him are coming off worse. He looks up. 'Gentleman, since this is an opportune time and I have a visitor, I'll thank you for your company.' He places his cards face down on the table, pushes his chair back and nods for me to follow him to the parlour. As Abe rises, a ruddy-faced player in an expensive coat reaches across and grasps his elbow.

'You will continue to play. I must have fair chance to win back my property.'

He looks at the man's hand on his arm, then into his face. 'You've had two hours of fair chance. I don't know how it works in Germany, Herr Hirsch, but here, you just lost your hotel.' He stares the man down until he withdraws his hand and looks away. He walks towards the parlour, I follow.

'You always this busy now, Abe?'

'Yes,' he's smirking, 'and getting busier, I just acquired an inn in Nebraska Territory.' The door to the back room is heavy with mirrors. Inside, the glittering opulence of chandeliers and rich fabric on French couches. I wonder. The steward's son risen above the landowner's. Is he taking pleasure in being the richer of the two of us?

He sees me taking it in and interrupts my thoughts. 'What brings you back to Corazon at the start of the cold season?'

'I need to talk. Hawk and Cloud Shadow are coming into town tomorrow morning to see the troop movements for themselves. I met Waldron with Cross last time I was here. We all know what's coming. I wanted our chiefs to meet him, to see what sort of man he is.'

'They're appointing the new agent for the Northern Akote, to offer peace in return for compliance with the Southern Treaty.'

'Who is it?'

'They wanted someone experienced, who knows the country. As agent for the Southern Akote, they've asked me.'

'What did you say?'

'It's good you coming here like this. You and I have more experience of the Akote than other traders. You get a man out there in the pocket of some officer with political connections, it could go badly for the Indians. On the other hand, the incentives that agents can offer for peace are valuable. That's a lot of goods from Washington making their way here: flour, tools. Most of that will go amiss before it ever reaches the tribe unless the agent is well disposed towards them.'

'What have you got in mind?'

'If I took on the responsibility, I could look out for you and your wife's people. Of course, there would be compensations, the post is poorly paid.'

'We need guns.'

'Waldron won't allow the Akote to buy guns.'

'Could you arrange it? You have interests now in Argento and further north, couldn't you bring them through there?'

'I have a hotel there and mining but it's a long way up. In any case I can't supply them with guns. What would Waldron make of that? I know him well, Francis, we have common interests but don't forget he's the new governor of the territory.'

'You know Cross. Could you organise for us to meet with Waldron through him?'

'Cross is in Corazon, but I don't know if Waldron

is back yet from Santa Fe. I'll find out. I could help you with the guns indirectly – a man who owes me. You'd have to keep it quiet and arrange for the trade to take place well away from here. I'm guessing you know already that they'll be expensive. If you can swallow that, then I might be able to set it up.'

I have no other choice but to agree. 'Yes.'

'I'll let you know.' He leads the way back through to the main room. The noise of voices and glasses clinking fills the parlour as he opens the door. I wrap my arms around myself in a bear hug, exhale and straighten my back. It cracks, relief. I need to find Monaghan.

The door to the church house is unlocked but no one's in. From out back the rhythmic sound of knocking. I go through. Despite the cold, Monaghan is in his shirt sleeves, braces stretched across his rolling shoulders as he brings the axe down on the firewood with savage force. It splits in two. The smaller piece shoots across the yard and strikes the side of the house just below the window. He tugs at the undershirt rucking beneath his shoulder blades, the veins in his forearms swollen. He holds the axe lightly in his right hand, and encircles the shaft as if it were a pencil.

'Francis!' He places the head on the block, wipes his hands in a cloth from his waistband and strides across the yard, shaking my hand as if to remove the arm. 'What brings you to this den of vice and avarice? Let's go inside.'

The tea is good and strong. I describe the Akote war council, tell him that Hawk and I have brought Cloud Shadow to Corazon to see for himself the strength of the garrison, and to meet with Waldron.

'Your chiefs won't get much courtesy there, Francis, but maybe that's your plan?'

'You know how it works, Patrick, and so do I. We all know what comes next except the Akote. I want to give them the opportunity to understand what we are facing, to be ready before they regret not grasping what they're up against.'

'No one's against anyone yet, Francis.'

'Someone wants your land, they want to limit your freedom, they consider you to be something less than human, I'd say that's an adversary.'

He sighs, rubbing his face with the flat of his hand.

'Patrick, we could do with you out there with us. Have you thought about it?'

'I have. As far as I'm concerned, it's time for me to leave behind the dog-eared pages of so-called civilisation and concentrate my efforts on the blank ledger of the plateaus and canyons, but I haven't yet heard from the bishop. Listen, where will you be later? I have to visit Mrs Bronze.'

'Mrs Bronze? Trouble with her husband I'm guessing?'

He wipes his forehead with the cloth and pulls his coat back on. 'Not the wife, the mother. I visit her two or three times a week. She has a growth in her gut, the doctor says she has months to live at best.'

'A growth in the gut and a wayward son, that's a lot of bad luck for one woman.'

'The Lord works in mysterious ways, Francis. She's a good, good woman. She worked much of her life helping her husband build a general store in Boston, raised the children while the business became established and they set aside savings, then watched him and their daughter die from tuberculosis.'

'Poor soul. How did she end up here?'

'By the time the husband died, the son had learnt much of the work and had his own dreams of moving out west to supply the tide of settlement and discovery with goods and provisions at, no doubt, great profit. He persuaded his mother to sell their store and brought her and his long-suffering wife Jane to Santa Fe. I'm sad to say it didn't take long for the man's desires to get the better of his sense. The prices he charged increased month on month to fund his drinking and a taste for young women. Jane Bronze knew about his vices – everyone did – but she kept house and tended to her husband and her mother-in-law. I heard he took his hand to her on his sprees so the customers in the shop could hear the cries coming through the ceiling. You can imagine, his trade dwindled quickly. It put him out of business.'

'But the store in Corazon?'

'Mrs Bronze says he fell on his feet; he was bankrolled to start a new general store here in town.'

'By whom?'

'I don't know. She doesn't know herself, but he seems to make good money.'

'And the vices?'

He sighs. 'You've heard the gossip when you come into town; he's succumbed to his old patterns of women, liquor, and expensive tobacco. Jane Bronze is pitied by folk, but he doesn't raise his hand to her anymore, and nor should he unless he wants me to reckon with. Old Mrs Bronze always asks me to pray for his release from carnal desires and to treat his wife with respect. She asks me to try to influence him for the better once she's gone, but you know how it is, he has to want to change. Anyway Francis, I've said too much. Mrs Bronze will be expecting me.' I walk with him as far as the store. He knocks at the side door, straightening himself as he waits.

'Patrick, I'll be at the hotel when you've finished.' I move off and he crosses himself. We are both laughing as the door opens and the storekeeper's wife appears dressed in black, her face drawn. I walk past the shop and glance in. Bronze is emerging from the door at the back with an Anaii scout.

*

The three of us sit in red velvet armchairs in the parlour of the hotel – Abe, Cross, and me.

Cross moves the conversation on. 'So, Abraham informs me that you would like to arrange a meeting between yourself, Colonel Waldron, and some of the Indian headmen arriving tomorrow, is that it?'

'Yes. These are some of the most senior Akote war chiefs. It would be useful to establish dialogue at this point ahead of discussions about the Southern Treaty.'

'Well, indeed, that is helpful of you, Mr Meavy. Colonel Waldron has only just returned from meeting with the outgoing governor in Santa Fe. He is, as you can imagine, pressed with matters which have accrued in his absence. If, however, your, ah, friends would like to attend the garrison just before lunch tomorrow, I will try to engineer the opportunity for you all to come to the Colonel's attention for a few minutes. Convenient also that your companions will be able to meet their new agent.' Cross turns towards Abe. 'I'm sure Mr Knox will hold the position to the advantage of all.'

Abe suggests moving into the saloon for a drink. I'm first through the door, glad of the opportunity to dilute Cross' company. Patrick Monaghan enters the hotel. It's teeming with patrons so that even a large man in black pushing through the crowd goes unnoticed. Maggie leans over the counter and taps Abe on the shoulder. He turns. She shakes her head and points. I follow the line of her arm. She's indicating a man with his back to us, sat with a group at a table next to the window. He has a young Akote girl on his lap and his companions are laughing and raising their glasses. Abe looks towards the table then at Maggie again. Her head is tipped back, her hands on her hips.

He crosses to the window; the men at the table hush, the laughter slipping from their faces. He stops ten feet from them. The man becomes aware of him and stands. It's Bronze. He lets go of the girl. She runs to the door beside the bar. Abe turns on his heel and strides back towards us. The others at the table snigger.

The small sombre figure of a woman pushes past Patrick. She winds her way between the tables to the window. Something makes me watch her. She reaches the table. It's Jane Bronze. Her husband's companions nod towards her, alerting him. He jumps to his feet, knocking the chair over behind him, glaring. She starts to speak. Patrick closes in as Bronze spews spittle from his twisted mouth, his eyes feral. I put my hand on my pistol. As the priest draws alongside, Bronze raises his right arm – the elbow scissoring back to strike. He hasn't registered Patrick beside him. He brings the open hand round, but Patrick's arm shoots out, his grip closes on the wrist, stopping the blow dead. Bronze rotates, scowling, looking first at his arm and then into Monaghan's eyes. The place hushes.

'You let go of my arm, Priest. I've business with my wife.'

Jane Bronze hides her face in her hands, shoulders hunched. Monaghan's massive shoulders twitch. Bronze's knees buckle as his wrist twists down and against itself. He yelps. With his free hand he rifles the table, snatches up a knife with trembling fingers and reaches under his captive arm so the point is hard against Patrick's ribs. The place is silent now save for the noise of Bronze panting through clenched teeth and the soft unnoticed click as I cock my pistol under my coat.

'You want to strike her, Bronze, you'll have to use that knife first.'

Abe is back at the table. 'Put it down, Bronze.' The shopkeeper releases his fingers, dropping the knife to clatter between Patrick's feet. He watches his wrist as the priest relaxes his grip. Abe turns to Monaghan and nods towards me. 'If you're looking for Francis, he's at the counter with Major Cross. I'll tell him to come over to the church house when they're done.'

Patrick walks to the door, onlookers moving aside as he crosses the room. Abe steps in close to Bronze and whispers something. Bronze looks round the room as if becoming aware of it for the first time. He sways, turns, and stumbles. Jane is at his side in a moment, guiding him out of the place, his arm across her small shoulders as they sidestep tables and chairs.

*

The frost is melting when I ride out with Abe to meet Hawk and Cloud Shadow. We sight them and their warriors within the hour. Our two groups halt, facing each other, breath steaming. I greet them, 'The air is good.'

Hawk and Cloud Shadow reply in unison. 'The air is good, Francis Meavy.' Hawk looks across at Abe and nods.

I make the introductions, 'Cloud Shadow, this is Abraham Knox. We have known each other since we were boys together. He has helped arrange for us to meet with Colonel Waldron, war chief of the soldiers here. He is also to be the agent dealing with the Northern Akote for the government in Washington.' Cloud Shadow's horse whinnies. 'Our meeting will enable us to see the soldiers and their numbers close up.' I turn my horse and lead the way to Corazon.

As we reach the town, Abe breaks into a trot and heads off to inform Cross that we are on our way. I ride level with Hawk and Cloud Shadow as they walk their horses slowly along Main Street. Two Ute men in

Mexican jackets watch us from the boardwalk, pistols at their waists. Bronze is in the window of the general store. He smiles a wet smile and turns away.

The garrison has absorbed the blacksmiths and livery with its large corral and barns. The headquarters are in a run of wooden buildings making up the easternmost part of Corazon. Abe and Cross stand waiting as we approach. I dismount and tie my horse to the rail. The others follow suit. They're nervous, looking around as I lead them towards the steps. The troop traffic is incessant. On the flat ground, west of the buildings, at least a hundred and fifty men are drilling. Riders come back and forth. A squadron of cavalry return from the south, horses' heads low, their movements laboured. Hawk catches my eye and looks towards Cloud Shadow, scrutinising each group of soldiers in turn.

Cross hails us. 'Mr Meavy, welcome to you and your, ah, party of visitors. I hope that we will be able to introduce them to Colonel Waldron for a few moments at least. Please ask them to follow us.' He turns and walks towards the stairs, Abe with him. I gesture that we should all follow.

The air bursts and the ground shakes. The warriors duck, forming a circle. Cross shakes his head and walks back towards them. 'Howitzer practice. We become accustomed to it.' He pauses, 'Here, let me show you.' He leads us to the back of the building where three field guns and their crews stand abreast. The last smoke curls from the barrel of the furthest. 'I suggest you cover your ears,' he yells as he put his hands to the sides of his head.

A gunner steps forward. Flame spurts from the mouth of the weapon. The shockwave hits just ahead of the noise. Out on the flatland south of the town, an old wagon erupts into splinters and the ground beyond it kicks up into a storm of dirt. The Akote stand in silence, staring at the carnage. Cloud Shadow looks across at Hawk and shakes his head slowly.

'We mustn't keep Colonel Waldron waiting.' Cross leads us back to the front of the building. As we enter, eight armed soldiers fall in behind us marking time on the wooden floor until their sergeant orders them to stand. Cross and Abe lead the way to a room laid out with desks and chairs in rows with soldiers sitting at them working at papers. As Cross enters, they rise to their feet. 'At ease,' he calls.

We walk over to a large door with an unmanned desk to one side of it. Cross knocks. After two or three seconds a voice shouts, 'Come,' from inside.

Cross steps in first. 'Colonel Waldron, sir, I have with me Mr Knox, Mr Meavy, and a group of his Indians who wish to make your acquaintance. Mr Meavy informs me that among them are headmen of high standing.'

Waldron sits in a leather armchair behind a broad desk. A soldier stands behind him to one side, bare headed with a white towel hanging from his folded arm. Waldron remains seated, raises his chin, and examines the Akote in silence for a long moment before speaking. 'You are fortunate indeed to find me here. I have but very recently returned to Corazon. I am pressed from all sides with matters requiring my attention, so we will be brief in our discussion.' He stares at Cross who takes his cue.

'Mr Meavy, perhaps you could make the introductions.'

I open my hand towards Cloud Shadow. 'This is Cloud Shadow, War Chief of the Akote, from the settlement of Broad Rock.' Waldron examines Cloud Shadow but says nothing. 'This is Hawk from Los Huertos –'

'Major Cross?' Waldron interrupts. 'Are we at war with these Indians?'

Cross hesitates. 'No, sir.'

'Then, Mr Meavy, we shall hear no more of war chiefs since there is no war. Indeed, please explain to them that dispute over this territory is an impossibility since we already have sovereignty of their lands by treaty with the Mexicans, yielding it to the United States some years ago. They may be headmen in some tribal capacity, but they occupy their homes and graze their livestock on our land and only for as long as we choose to allow it.

'The fact is, Mr Meavy, that you bring these Indians here today as if they are some form of delegation, meeting us on equal terms. We are not equal. As the strong arm of the government in this territory, I am the power in this land. These –' he gestures backhanded, 'live in huts with no sense of discipline nor organisation. I do them a courtesy, sir, by permitting them into my headquarters.'

The rage settles in my body, calm and cold. 'Is that what you wish me to translate?'

'It is the truth in any language and must therefore be understood.'

I turn my back on Waldron to face the Akote. When I've finished talking Hawk's eyes are fixed on the Colonel and Cloud Shadow is shaking his head. The younger warriors start to yell. Hawk raises his hand to still them.

Cloud Shadow implores, 'Will he not protect us as he has said he will protect the Mexicans? Will he not show us the favour shown the Anaii and the Ute? Are we not chiefs like him? Ask this.'

I translate.

'I am glad you have raised the question of the New Mexicans.' Waldron leans forward onto his desk. 'I understand that you have taken livestock from them – horses and so on. These must be returned. You must desist from raiding them or you will face the consequences.'

Enough now. I cut him off before he can continue. 'Hundreds of Akote women and children have been taken and sold into slavery with these New Mexicans by tribes now enjoying your favour. Will you demand these women and children are also returned?'

'It is clear to me that the women and children of which you speak have found civilised occupation in the houses of New Mexicans so they may avoid a life of unpalatable savagery. I will certainly not require them to return to that against their will.'

Again, Hawk has to silence his warriors.

Waldron withdraws the watch from his coat, clicks it open, snaps it shut, and replaces it. 'I am empowered to extend and enforce the existing treaty with the Southern Akote regarding the provision of certain goods and supplies in return for undertakings. These undertakings require the return of New Mexican chattels and a commitment that no further raiding will take place. The details can be discussed with the good Mr Knox here whose agency will now include the Northern Akote. I had anticipated the enforcement of the treaty over the course of the next year once we had established military communications across the territory, but since the mountain has made itself known to Mohammed, it is convenient for me to tell you this now. I expect the treaty to be honoured. To break it would be an act of aggression involving the nullification of the rights and privileges it seeks to grant.'

'Colonel Waldron, your information concerning Akote enslavement, and the redress taken for the theft of their own livestock is incorrect. Embodied in any sort of treaty, it would also be unjust. I know these people –'

'Mr Meavy, it is well known that you have a particularly intimate knowledge of these Indians. That is not in question. What is in question is what you will do for them? Change is here for all of us, particularly for these tribesmen. If they do not choose to understand that, and to obey, then they will be broken. It is indeed as simple as that.' He leans back, chair creaking, and touches the fingertips of his left hand to those of his right as if in prayer. 'You may translate in those terms.'

Hawk speaks, 'Francis Meavy, ask this man how long his people have lived here with the blessing of the

Holy Ones. Our people have lived here generation on generation. Roots that deep cannot be torn out.'

Waldron tuts, waving his hand in dismissal. Hawk turns, leading the Akote out of the office, I'm still translating as we leave. Waldron calls after us. 'You have been warned, I have warned you – Major Cross, escort the visitors out.'

I close the door behind us, beating Cross to the task. I expect to see disappointment and concern on his face. Instead, his features are untroubled, amused. When we're back outside, he speaks. 'I shouldn't worry about all that, Mr Meavy, the real work will take place through Mr Knox and myself. Mr Knox has certain business interests in common with Colonel Waldron and since you and he are childhood friends, well...'

We ride back through Corazon in silence. Abe peels off at his hotel, wishing us safe road. Once we are clear of the town Hawk surveys the skies.

'We will talk tomorrow.'

'I will meet you at the settlement as early as I can.' I canter back.

Abe is waiting for me in the parlour, the thick heels of his boots resting on a gilded footstool, a fresh cigar just starting to glow at the tip as he draws on it. How different life is for us both since we traded together, making camp in the open. Me without the responsibility of family, Abe without the burden of wealth.

He smiles a sour smile and rises to close the door. 'Waldron is a piece of work.'

'What hope can there be when a man like that commands here? You and I have seen his like before

– happy enough to get others killed to satisfy their own sense of power. How can war be avoided if he thinks like that?' I remember Cross' parting words, 'What business interests do you share?'

'He won't be here much longer. He's going to be the new governor of the territory based in Santa Fe.'

'For God's sake –'

Abe cuts me off. 'Go see Bronze in the store this afternoon. He will talk with you in private about guns, payment, and delivery. I'm not involved. Don't give me any of the details.'

'I appreciate it, but how are you going to show the Akote any kind of fairness with Waldron at your shoulder?'

Abe sucks on his cigar, tilts his head back and blows a thick cloud at the ceiling.

*

My boots knock on the floorboards as I walk into the store. Bronze is serving a middle-aged woman in a velvet dress. He nods and smiles, jowls swaying. He looks me up and down, recruits an assistant to complete the transaction and makes his excuses. He speaks too loudly, ensuring everyone knows our business.

'Mr Meavy, I've been expecting you. Please come into my office to discuss those agricultural supplies.'

We enter his office where piles of goods line the shelves like a paperless library. By the window, overlooking the bare earth at the rear of the building, is a broad desk. The top is claret leather, the handles polished brass. Between the desk and the window is a matching carver. Bronze slides into his throne.

'I understand from our friend that you want firearms. What exactly did you have in mind? It goes without saying that due to the nature of our customer here, providing the latest models or a competitive price will be difficult.'

I sit down and observe him. His rosebud mouth gleams wet. Unable to hold my stare, he lowers his eyes to the top of the desk, looks up again, meets my stare for an instant then looks away. The man's a coward.

'Also, I will be taking considerable personal risk, it would have to be worthwhile. Last time you were here, I noticed your watch –'

'Fifty Spencer repeaters and ammunition in quantity. The watch is not for sale.'

Bronze raises his eyebrows. 'Spencer repeaters?'

'Yes, Bronze. I was told you could source what we need, but perhaps your connections would find the order too demanding?'

He shuffles in his chair. 'Mr Meavy, I can supply whatever you or anybody else might want. I wonder though how you will be paying the price required for such a shipment?'

I lean over and remove the leather pouch from my belt. I loosen the drawstring, pour the contents into my palm then reach forward to drop them onto the desk. Bronze smiles with one side of his face, picking up the coloured nuggets.

'This I can't take for guns. Too Indian.' He drops the piece of turquoise onto the desktop close to me. He takes the other nugget in his right hand, feels its weight then swaps it over to gauge it with the other hand. 'Silver will work. Particularly Mexican silver.' He holds it up against the daylight from the window, showing his profile. 'Forty-five dollars a gun, and your watch and chain.'

There's only one way to deal with this man. I place the turquoise back in the pouch, lean forward, take the silver, put that with the turquoise and pull the string tight. Tying it back onto my belt, I stand and start walking.

He calls after me. 'Mr Meavy, how do you think Colonel Waldron would react to the news that the former Captain Meavy was trying to arm the Akote?'

I stop and turn. He flinches. 'Bronze, we are several days' ride across the plateau. Every piece of country, every rock, canyon, cave and stream bed is known to the Akote. If Waldron did come looking, I'd make sure he knew where we were buying the guns. Where would you hide?'

His mouth pinches before he responds, his face red. 'We got off on the wrong foot. Please, let's talk about a different price between new friends, but you appreciate that the cost will have to include the silence of the shippers, and those I use along the way?'

'They are worth thirty-five dollars. We will pay thirty-eight apiece to include ammunition.'

We settle on forty dollars – half payable within two weeks in silver and the remaining payment to take place with the handover of the shipment two weeks after that, at a place on the Silver River three days east of Los Huertos.

Coyote

He howled his warning as Crowsfoot led the hunting party out just after dawn. They heard it but did not heed it. Only Bright Flower, in her hogan, felt it in her heart.

Later, from the ledge, he watched Pale Horse in the settlement below, planing arrow weed in his powerful fingers. The warrior held the shaft up to look along its length, gauging if it was true, then lowered it. He remained focused on the far rim of the canyon, on the lone figure high on Bear Rock. Coyote knew who that was. The man who killed his brother Mountain Song. He bared his teeth, moving from his vantage point to witness what was coming.

The stillness of the settlement was broken only by the movement of smoke from the hogan fires bearing the scent of cooking into the breeze. It rustled what few leaves remained on the trees. The women were working on skins and at their looms, and many of the children had gone with the flocks to the high ground. Eagle shrieked. Coyote looked up. Suspended above the settlement in a counter current, she looked down for long moments before her wingtips flickered and she made east, her shadow stroking the rock, the earth, and the brush.

He turned to watch Bright Flower in her hogan setting a pot of water on the fire, herbs and mutton beside her ready to be added. She saw the ripples on the surface. She had been expecting this moment. She could feel that they came in numbers too great even for Pale Horse and his men, that she would have to move the earth and the sky to defeat them. She stood and took the pot outside, emptying it in one quick throw. Darting back inside, she snatched the white stag's hide from Raven's bed and cut two small squares from it.

Raven. She wept his name aloud as she placed an arrowhead he had made in the first of the leather squares. To this, she added a lead ammunition round smelted by Francis Meavy. She knew that her son had the best of her and of his father, but she also knew that he did not yet believe it himself. He was so like Francis Meavy in this. Both outsiders within, neither of them yet capable of sharing their common difference with the other. So like his father – but stronger. To his strength, hers, Hawk's and Willow Tree's and that of all the ancestors had been alloyed. He would stand. He would not buckle. The anticipation of his grief, of her separation from him, doubled her over with sobbing. She forced herself straight and folded the square, binding it tight for her son with her own yucca twine. Her fingers moved fast like the jaws of a spider spinning its web.

The second bundle she made for her husband. As she bound the arrowhead and the ammunition into the skin, she ached for him, prayed for him. She had loved him the first moment she had seen him in her mother's hogan. She knew that she had given this wounded man peace, that she had been his resting place, his only wholeness. He would suffer greatly at her loss. Her father had come to love him, a respect hard earned but inhabited only rarely by Francis Meavy. Her mother had seen from the start, as she herself had, that this was the choice of which Mountain Song had spoken so clearly.

Bright Flower's tears made dark spots in the earth on which she knelt. She knew that her parents would suffer their own grief in silence, to give strength to Francis Meavy and to Raven. Her spirit called out her gratitude to them, called out to them the love she had always felt for them and would always feel. She placed the cooking pot hard against the wall of the hogan and placed the bundles inside it. Coyote whimpered. She prayed to the Holy Ones that once she was gone the binding between son and father would hold tight like the yucca twine – robust and healing. She filled the pot with stones from the hearth and went deep into the hogan, pulling one of Meavy's rifles from its buckskin slip. With her other hand she located the powder horn and ammunition pouch and, pushing all other thoughts from her spirit, started to load.

She rammed a round into the barrel, then smudged the tears into her cheeks to stop them falling into the open gunpowder magazine she was dragging to the centre of the floor. As she poured a trail of powder to the back of the hogan where she had left the rifle, she knew that she would not see the canyon again, and gave thanks for the peach orchards, the children playing in them, the bluebirds against the sun. She pictured in her mind how it would go. She could not reveal herself until the moment was ripe, until the evil winds blew into her hogan. Then, her blood would return to the rock.

*

Coyote felt the pounding hooves of the approaching horses up through his paws. Pale Horse strode to his hogan to fetch out his bow and lance. Against his frame they looked like the weapons of a child. He took ten arrows and stabbed their heads into the earth in front of him, his lance next to them. He shouted for the other men to come to him. They were only a handful. Two he told to conceal themselves in the cottonwood stand, one behind the hogan east of him, one beyond that and one to stand with him. All of them to await his signal.

Willow Tree shouted for the women and elderly to follow her and hide. They dropped their weaving, grasped the hands of the young, clutched the babies to their chests and started up the sides of the canyon to the ledges and caves.

Coyote looked towards the mountains. The raiders were visible now, the thunder of their horses swelling. There were fifty, Anaii, some with lances and many with rifles. They came on at the canter. When they saw Pale Horse, they drove into a gallop, whooping and shouting. He stood his ground, looking east towards them and up again at the lone figure on the rim. The man at the head of the raiders raised his hand, fingers spread, motioning them to halt. They pulled up twenty paces from Pale Horse. The leader edged his horse forward. Above his buckskins, a deep blue army jacket and in the corner of his mouth the butt of a cigar. His right eye was covered by a pale headband slanted across his head. Coyote knew this man too. He had watched the evil winds blow his spirit into darkness.

'You are the great Pale Horse.' His words bounced around the canyon and ended with slow laughter. He took the thick cigar from the corner of his mouth, spat on the canyon floor, turned the stub over, blew on it and sighed. 'The last time I was here, something was taken from me.'

His hand reached down to his belt, unsheathing a knife. The blade hissed, grey and long. He tapped the flat side of the tip against his temple next to the ruined eye, then pointed it at Pale Horse. 'Today, Pale Horse, your friend with the rifles is not here. Your men are in Corazon or away hunting.' He grinned. 'It is true that you are the biggest Akote warrior I have seen, but there are fifty of us. Before we leave here, I will have your horses, I will take your woman for my slave, and I will burn your village.'

Coyote stretched his neck towards the sun and called. Up on the plateau, Arrowhead and Raven were in the hunting party. His howl made them turn in their saddles. They spun their horses around, galloping back up the pass to the canyon's rim. Far below, like ants, they saw the Anaii raiders facing Pale Horse with one Akote warrior at his shoulder. The fastest way down was west, then to come into the canyon heading east. They turned and kicked on.

*

Pale Horse lifted his bow arm just enough to scratch his armpit with his free hand. The Anaii flinched as he made the movement. He laughed, then raised his voice so that all the horsemen could hear. It rolled deep across the space between them, echoing back from the rock face.

'You want my horses and my woman. So do I. So, we must fight. Fifty of you shooting us with your guns would be no contest. So why don't you and I fight, without weapons?' He reached down and placed his bow on the ground. 'If it is a question of my size, we can make it more even – two of you. Unarmed. One of me.'

The other raiders looked towards One Eye, muttering among themselves.

'Or if you choose, two of your men to start with while you summon your courage?'

Pale Horse opened his arms wide and took three steps forward, distancing himself from his lance and bow, whispering to the warrior at his shoulder as he moved away. 'I'm an old man! Which of you younger, fitter men wish to be known for bringing down Pale Horse?' He grinned and waited. 'I'm getting older!'

One man kicked his horse forward out of the group. He handed his reins to One Eye and jumped down, landing lightly. He was of average height, but his head was massive, and his upper body had the bulking of a buffalo.

'Blackrock,' One Eye shouted, 'remember. His horses and his woman come to me.'

Blackrock's eyes locked onto his huge adversary.

He nodded in silence, acknowledging the order. With no warning, he was hurtling towards Pale Horse who shifted his weight onto his right heel and stood. At the point of impact, the taller man's frame swivelled around his heel and Blackrock went through him headfirst. Pale Horse crooked his left foot, tripping his opponent face down into the dirt. He rose, shaking his head, blood smeared across his lips. Pale Horse raised his eyebrows in invitation.

Blackrock sidestepped and burst forward, lower this time, feigning left to meet Pale Horse's waist shoulder on. As he executed the feint, Pale Horse sprung from his knees and hips, so that Blackrock's shoulder met his disappearing shins, adding momentum to the somersault. He landed on his hands rolling forward twice. Blackrock had already turned, and anticipating the move, dived into the space where Pale Horse would have risen had he rolled once. As he hit the ground again, he glimpsed Pale Horse rise to standing, his back towards him. When he lifted his head from the fall, the other's moccasin was close to his face, flicking up the sand. Blackrock yelled, staggering to his feet and lashing out.

The raiders' horses shuffled and snorted, legs rising and falling, hooves beating on the canyon floor. The men were silent. Blackrock stumbled, blinking, rubbing his eyes until at last he faced Pale Horse who stood five paces distant, arms crossed and waiting.

A movement from One Eye. His knife landed point down in the earth. Blackrock snatched it up, rubbing his tears with the free hand. Pale Horse crouched and circled so the raiders had to twist their shoulders to see.

Blackrock came on with more confidence now he was armed. He moved towards Pale Horse, within a lunge's length, slashing right to left then back again. He nicked the older man's buckskins on the return swipe and hesitated, surprised at his opponent's lack of speed. He recovered, glanced at his left hand, passed the blade into it at the last moment and shot forward for the killing stroke.

Pale Horse seemed wrong-footed, spinning away from the knife sideways to Blackrock who switched it back to his right hand and lunged again. Pale Horse pushed himself back a step, barged his hip into Blackrock's flank, grasped his wrist with his right hand and clamped his arm. He hammered his right knee forward and up to Blackrock's locked elbow. The crack of the bone breaking, and Blackrock's grunt, filled the stillness. Pale Horse turned towards his concealed men.

'Now!'

The first flight of arrows hit the raiders in their back and sides. The hidden Akote loosed three volleys before their enemies could respond. Pale Horse raced for his bow. The Anaii charged their horses into the cottonwood stand and round the hogans, rooting out the bowmen. Ten of the fifty had fallen. Pale Horse notched an arrow and drew the string, scanning the blurring mass of riders. He found One Eye too late, his target was already aiming his rifle back at Pale Horse. The smoke of the discharge hid him for a moment. Pale Horse fell to his knees, his left hand still gripping his bow, his right clutching his chest. Amid the confusion,

One Eye walked his horse forward, a younger man on foot beside him. He pointed at Pale Horse. The young man approached the fallen war chief with caution. As Pale Horse swayed, the Anaii stepped behind him, and raised his knife.

In her hogan, Bright Flower rested the rifle on a stool and fired. The raider jerked like a puppet then fell forward. One Eye looked beyond the fallen man; gun smoke roiled from the doorway of the hogan. He shouted for his men to kill whoever hid there. They stalked forward, staying clear of the entrance until they reached the walls. The first to rush in, blocking the daylight as he filled the doorframe, fell to a round in the chest.

One Eye shouted, 'Now, while he reloads.'

They burst in. The smoke was thinning. Bright Flower faced them, kneeling at the back of the hogan, a small fire in front of her, a rifle on the floor. Seeing the woman and the discarded gun, the Anaii laughed and leered. She leant forward, chanting and swaying. A hissing flame raced from her lap across the floor to a banded metal box. The raiders turned too late.

*

The hunting party raced home, skirting quicksand, and jumping fallen trees to keep a straight, fast line. The explosion banged back and forth across the canyon when they were three hundred paces off. Their horses stumbled, losing the rhythm of the charge in the shock of the blast. As they closed the gap to the village, burning timber and blankets bounced down the rock face to lie smoking in the silt.

A charred crater had replaced Bright Flower's hogan. The place stank of rotten eggs and the blood soaking into the rock. Raiders lay dead or dying. Twenty or thirty were already distant, galloping towards the mountains, driving a herd of snatched ponies. Raven crouched by Pale Horse, his calves folded under his thighs, the breath foaming at the corners of his mouth.

'I'll fetch water.'

'Stay,' Pale Horse rasped, his teeth pink with blood. His hand found Raven's and clasped it, his eyes like the night sky. 'Raven, your mother was in the hogan. She killed many of them.' He swallowed, wincing. Then a deep rhythmic sound from his throat – laughter. 'I always told your father. Never anger an Akote woman unless you can live with the consequences.' His laugh became a hard cough. His hand released Raven's. His spirit left his body. It was as bright as sunlight, as bright as any Coyote had seen.

Francis Meavy

We have ridden in silence since the meeting in Corazon. Now, reaching the canyon, the women and children stand motionless outside their hogans, watching us pass. Something has happened. My mind labours to make sense of it. Something terrible. We rein in.

Aspen Tree, headman of the village, walks towards Hawk, shaking his head. 'You don't know?'

The sound of a galloping horse. Arrowhead pulls up so hard his pony trips. He yanks its head back and around to stop it falling. Breathless, looking at the ground, he addresses Hawk. 'The settlement was attacked. We were hunting. They came when only Pale Horse and a handful were left with the children and women.' He looks up then down again. 'Francis Meavy... Hawk... Bright Flower is —'

'Yaaaah.' I kick my mount from standstill to gallop.

*

Blowing fit to burst, my horse stumbles into the settlement. I kick off the stirrups and throw my leg over its lowered head. My knees give out as I land. My buckskins are dark with blood. The rifle slipped forward between my thigh and the saddle and wore the flesh raw. I scrabble to my feet. God be merciful. Be merciful, Almighty.

'Bright Flower, Bright Flower?' I run from hogan to hogan, I cannot find her. 'Raven? No. No, Lord Christ, no.' I am spinning round, searching, crying out in English and Akote, 'My boy, my son?'

Raven ducks out through a doorway, his eyes red, the rims swollen. He cannot look at me. I grab him, pull him into me, into my body, my bones, where he will be safe.

'Thank God, thank God, thank God.' I push him away, holding him at arms' length. 'Bright Flower? Where is your mother?' Hawk and the others canter into the settlement. They watch from their saddles. The wind, twisting anticlockwise, hooks up sand and leaves, dancing them round us. Raven shakes his head. A sob forces its way up through his throat. I fight for breath. 'Where?' I shake him.

'Dead. She is dead, Father. Raiders came, Mother, Pale Horse, the others –'

'Raiders? Where were you?' I am shaking him hard. 'Where?'

'Hunting, Father, the rest of us were up on the –'

The realisation crushes over me like a rockslide. 'Alone? She was alone?' Dear God, she was alone. I'm looking up into the sky for answers, for something. It bursts in me then. With a full twist of the shoulders, I strike my son. Raven spins at the blow, touching his fingertips to his bleeding lip as he turns back to me. My hand. My hand hit my son. I hit my son with this hand. I stare at my hand. All I can see is the hand, it burns. I can't think, I can't breathe. The canyon is a sand painting. I'm on my knees.

I register Hawk dismounting, nodding two of his men towards me. They carry me towards a hogan, I hear Hawk speak, 'Grandson, come. Tell me.'

*

Somewhere in me I know that Hawk and Willow Tree bring me food: baskets of bread, piñon nuts and dried meat. They stack the wood high on the fire in the cave. I don't move. I cannot move. I don't want to move. I look down at my body. I am naked, staring into the flames, the darkness inside me ebbs and flows. I have been here at least two days and two nights.

It is dawn again. Now I know what needs to be done. It came to me. I wrap myself in my buffalo hide and stand mid canyon, facing east, waiting. Footsteps crunch through the gloom towards me; it will be Hawk. I turn. It is. I tell him what the fire revealed to me. 'Fifty will not be enough. We need more guns.'

He says, 'Show me your maps.'

We walk back across the canyon through clouds of our own breath. As we come closer to the alcove, thick black smoke and the bitter tang of burning cloth hangs in the greyness. Hawk looks at the charred remnants of my old army uniform smouldering on the fire. I fetch my leather map tube from the back of the alcove.

'The land to the north of here,' he says.

We kneel and I flatten out the battered map on the floor of the cave. Hawk's eyes flick back and forth across its creases. He points at a range of crudely marked mesas, several days' ride to the north.

*

Daybreak reveals the canyon frozen white and silver. Riding without rest, Hawk leads Raven and me to where the plateau smooths into broad plains and distant mesas stand tall and narrow like branchless copses.

On our fifth day of travel, in a narrow ravine, he urges his horse through damp sand, the walls either side just beyond the reach of outstretched arms. There is insufficient space to turn a pony. The ravine seems endless. At last, we emerge into a vast pasture. The waters funnelling down from the mesa tops make for abundant grazing. The rock, hundreds of paces high, provides protection from observation and intrusion. To one side where erosion has undercut a deep overhang, a group of Akote ponies nose the ground. Hawk touches his heels to the flanks of his tired horse, wringing a last canter out of him across the turf. The dull thump of hooves betrays the heavy richness of the soil. As the three of us approach the cliffs, there is a cave cutting deep into the rock, scorch marks on its outer lip.

Hawk speaks, 'Mountain Song brought me to this place. It is where the Holy People came through into this world. It is sacred and protected. Few know it is here, and none outside the Akote. The day is coming when we will have to lead our people to a new home. This is where we will come, it is our past and our future.'

I dismount, give the reins of my horse to Raven, and scan the place. Bright Flower will love it here. I turn to my son. 'Your mother will love this –' I cannot speak. My hands cover my face. 'We should have been there, Raven. I should have been there when she –' The weeping takes my words.

*

We cook an antelope over the fire in the cave and talk as darkness falls. The evening is stolen from time, the sacred mountain sheltering us from the world outside. As we fall into a peaceful silence, Hawk holds a hand out towards the flames, palm up. On it are two pale shapes.

'Francis Meavy, Raven, these medicine bundles were in the ruins of Bright Flower's hogan. She had taken care to see they would survive her sacrifice. She made them for you.' He nods slowly at Raven who rises and approaches his grandfather. He takes one bundle. Hawk gestures for him to take the second as well and points towards me with his nose. Slowly he walks over to me, holds out the second bundle for me to take it. I resist for a moment, then reach for it. Both of us hesitate to untie the skin.

At last, something in me breaks and I undo the parcel. Inside, one of Raven's arrowheads is bound, by Bright Flower's yucca twine, to a round of my ammunition. I feel like I am high on the edge of the canyon, one step from the drop. I hear Raven's sob, but I cannot look at him for fear of falling.

*

Before first light we set out for Los Huertos, making far to the east to lay a false trail. In the early afternoon we rest the horses in a cottonwood stand by a stream in a rocky valley. I choose a boulder to sit on and look south. A vortex of wind spins leaves across my field of vision, then moves up and down the valley east to west, west to east.

Hawk is sniffing the air. Over the ridge, a flock of rock doves flutter into the turquoise sky. He runs to his pony, shouting to me and Raven as he mounts. 'Raven, with me. Francis Meavy, into the trees, arm yourself.' Raven springs up onto Spider's back, driving his moccasins into the horse's ribs. He draws level with his grandfather. They gallop only four strides before Hawk points off to the left. 'There, behind those rocks.' He turns his own horse right towards the opposite side of the valley.

I have loaded my first rifle and am ramming the second when they come into view. Five New Mexicans in broad hats and short coats, herding horses, shouting, and laughing to each other across the animals' heads. They slow to a walk, moving the herd towards the water, into the sun. I watch them from the trees. Then I notice Pale Horse's war pony. One by one I recognise the Akote stock. When I see Bright Flower's brood mare, the calmness settles on me. I step out from the cover. The stolen horses shy away in surprise. The New Mexicans turn towards me, drawing their pistols. I keep my rifle at waist height, one hand round the barrel, the other round the stock.

'Where did you get the horses?'

They look at each other. The eldest, a man in his forties, rides forward, the muzzle of his gun skywards. 'We did not see you there. Are you alone? My men –'

'Where did you get them?'

The man tilts his head to one side and raises his hand, palm towards the sunlight to shade his eyes. The others scan the valley. 'Well, that is my business, but since you ask me, I bought them from Anaii army scouts. I believe they relieved the Akote scum of them, one way or another.'

I hoist the rifle to my shoulder and pull the trigger. Misfiring, the cap releases a timid hiss and a thread of smoke. The New Mexican levels his pistol, squinting against the glare. The round kicks the dirt up at my feet. I come to my senses, turn, and run back into the trees, discarding my first rifle to take up the second.

The herders' leader is shouting at them. They split, two galloping left; two swing right, circling the stand like spinning wheels. I fire again. A man at the rear clutches his shoulder and slumps into his saddle, his head bouncing with the rhythm of his horse. He pitches forward over its flank, smashing into the hard earth. It gallops off, wooden stirrups dancing like puppets at its sides.

The leader dismounts. Two of his men, circling counter-wise, speed towards each other behind him. His pony jumps away, corkscrewing to the side. He has one foot in the stirrup and both hands grasping the saddle, hopping on his free leg. As the others are about to cross, an arrow thumps into the ground. The horse on the outside track naps into the path of the other.

They meet head on, squealing, crushing bone and tearing muscle in their somersault. Their riders collide skull on skull, their hats dulling the noise of the impact before they crumple lifeless in the dirt, as if discarded.

The leader has freed himself from the stirrup. Seeing the arrow and the carnage, he ducks and comes running, pistol in hand. I'm ramming the second rifle. Rustling in the poison onion to my right. The fifth New Mexican barrels through the tall stalks towards me. I raise the gun with the ramrod in it.

'Drop it!' the leader shouts.

My head snaps from the man at my flank to the leader and back again. I drop the rifle.

'You saw the arrow?' the fifth man asks.

'Yes. Hold him. They'll be coming.'

The New Mexicans hold me between them, the leader pushing the muzzle of his pistol up under my jaw. A loose Akote pony gallops in from the right, across the field of vision. From its far flank Hawk drops to the valley floor. The animal races on. In one movement, he stands, draws back his bowstring and starts to walk towards them. The New Mexicans look at each other for a moment before the fifth man turns his pistol from me towards Hawk who looses the arrow and has another drawn before the first strikes its mark in the man's chest. His knees fold, he drops the gun and pitches onto his face, pulping the purple berries in a patch of Oregon grape. Hawk's bow creaks as he stands with it aimed at the leader.

'Don't move or I'll shoot him,' the man shouts, hoarse. Hearing rustling from the back of the cottonwoods he looks over his shoulder as a pony barges through. Raven has dropped the reins onto Spider's neck and is steering with his legs. His rifle is pointed at my captor, and he adjusts the aim moment by moment as he moves towards us. The man shouts again, 'No closer!' He prods his pistol up under my chin. 'Drop the rifle.'

'Shoot him, Raven. Shoot him now.' As I call to him, Raven halts, still for a moment, he takes in the lie of the situation. He puts his thumb over the hammer and releases it, then holding the rifle by its muzzle, eases it down it so the stock touches the ground. He pushes it away, so it topples into the undergrowth. I am screaming at him, 'No! No!'

The New Mexican sees his advantage. Grinning, he removes his pistol from my face to aim at Hawk. As he extends his arm, the gun flies from his hand, pierced by an arrow from behind. Raven's bow is still raised from the shot. I grasp my bayonet and ram it up under the man's ribs, pushing the hilt deep with the palm of my free hand, shoving him until he topples backwards on the ground. I piston the knife back and forth. My arms are red, my vision is red, the earth is red and there is a noise, an animal noise. It is coming from my mouth. I am howling.

Coyote

Hawk sent out riders from Los Huertos. Coyote observed their ponies pumping clouds of breath as they sped across the plateau.

Two days passed. In the early afternoon, under the glare of a pale sky, Juanito and ten warriors cantered in from the west, steam rising from their horses. Within hours, Cloud Shadow and his men were sighted to the south.

The council took place in the alcove, away from the settlement.

Juanito spoke first. 'Los Huertos has suffered fewer attacks than other parts of our lands. Raiders have been aware of the strength of its warriors and have stayed away. This recent raid has significance. They were armed with guns. Had Pale Horse not surprised them, and Bright Flower not made her sacrifice, then the women and children of this settlement could have been taken for slaves and the returning hunting party slaughtered.' He paused, the flames flickering on the surface of his eyes, the furs over his shoulders rising and falling as he breathed the cave air. To Coyote, he looked like a wolf gauging when to strike with his teeth. 'The Anaii fought alongside the Mexicans against us. Now they work with the soldiers from Corazon. We cannot defend ourselves against an enemy whose every man has a rifle, nor can we counter raid to take back our women and children.'

Francis Meavy was staring at the wall.

'We will see whether the soldiers will protect us under their treaty, but if they do not and they set their Anaii dogs loose across Akote territory it will be too late for us to resist if we remain unarmed. We should expect this attack to be the first. They will be more prepared next time.' Juanito looked at each of the men present. His eyes came to rest on Cloud Shadow. 'Whether we trust the soldiers or not, the Anaii are our enemy and have been for lifetimes. Now they become bold.' He sat.

Hawk now. Moving closer to the fire, he rubbed his hands together and held the palms towards the heat. The updraughts caught the feathers in his hair, making them jostle. He stamped his moccasins so that the bison hide soles slapped the sandy rock beneath his feet. When he spoke, it was as if he thought aloud. 'The raiders came when we were in Corazon. How did they know? They were Anaii, not Ute or Mescalero Apache. Their leader was here years ago. If he returned for revenge, why did they not come before? Why Los Huertos? This was an attack on our spirit. It is a message. The Anaii were its carriers.'

Now he addressed Cloud Shadow. 'When we met Waldron, and saw for ourselves the soldiers and the cannons, Francis Meavy remained in Corazon to buy guns. He made a bargain for fifty rifles and ammunition.' He turned towards his son-in-law, inviting him to speak.

Francis Meavy was unshaven, his face lined with the tracks of tears through filth. One leg of his buckskin trousers was tucked into its boot, the other hung loose. Under the buffalo skin around his shoulders, his shirt was open. 'We need more rifles than I have bargained for. In a few days I return to Corazon to make the first payment to the supplier. I propose to double it in return for twice the firearms.'

Before he could sit, Cloud Shadow rose. His wrinkles were filled with shadow so that his face was like a canyon system at night, framed in the mist of his hair. 'So many guns. Have you changed our agreement? Do you plan to defend yourselves against the Anaii, or to make war against the soldiers?'

It was Hawk who answered. 'Crowsfoot was wise, he did not counter raid after the attack on our home. It is clear that the weapons are needed to protect our people. Pale Horse and my daughter have shown us this.'

The cave fell silent but for the snapping and spitting of the burning wood. Juanito broke the stillness. 'Francis Meavy, tell me, how much more silver will be needed? My men will bring it to you.'

Francis Meavy

Mid-Autumn 1863 — Canyon de Los Huertos Ocultos

It has been weeks since I shaved. The edge of the blade is thick with bristle and grime. Under it my face has changed. My brow is furrowed, my mouth pulled back at the ends, stretched tight by tension in the jaw.

I set out with Juanito's lieutenant, Deer Antler, carrying the silver for Corazon, escorted by fifteen warriors from Los Huertos, the western plateau, and the Great Harvest Canyon. Overnight the vanguard of winter has swept across the land, encasing the earth with the first deep frost. The men discard their linen britches and shirts for buckskins, blankets, and furs. They ride with lances and bows, knives swinging at their waists.

Corazon already. I do not remember the journey. I am awakened by the noise of human voices, the whinnying of horses, and the tolling of the blacksmith's hammer like a chapel bell. My trance made us vulnerable. There is stillness in the movement of the men flanking me. Quiet vigilance. They scan the street back and forth as their ponies trot on. An Anaii man standing on the boardwalk of the Corazon Hotel watches us, his hand on the horse rail. Above his moccasins, dark blue army breaches and a buckskin shirt wrapped with a poncho blanket. Another leans against the timber upright next to the plate glass while a third sits, his back propped up against the wall.

We pull up at Bronze's store. 'Deer Antler, you and I will go inside. The rest of you remain here and be watchful.' We dismount, untie the saddlebags from the horses and yank them over the beasts' spines to get the weight clear.

The store hushes as the staff and customers register our presence. A balding clerk in his late twenties, but with the serious face of a man twice his age, scuttles into the back to reappear with Bronze. He hesitates at the counter before rushing forward, his blushing mouth pouting close to my ear.

'We did not agree that you would bring your Indians in here.'

I breathe deep and slow. 'If you can take his silver, you can take him being in your store. Do you want to complete our trade, or do you want us to stand here scaring your customers?'

'Please, please, come into my office.' His voice is loud. He dances around us, an arm ushering us towards the doorway. I go ahead, into the back room, slide the saddlebag off my shoulder and dump it onto the red leather desktop. It shudders down through the floorboards. Bronze's eyes glitter, he twitches a look at me then at the desk. He sees the saddlebags weighing on Deer Antler's shoulder, and frowns.

'It's your lucky day, Bronze. We are adding to the bargain. Same price again, twice the order. Guns and ammunition.'

He rubs his hands together, his eyes wet. 'That is a sizeable order, Mr Meavy.' He draws in air through his teeth. 'I shall have to see if we can meet the agreed timescales. As to the cost of transport, the shipment was large before you doubled it, twice the expenses are inevit –'

'Bronze, you've already got men and wagons lined up, the cost won't be double. It will be less than that. We have the silver here, now. The deal is we pay you today – same timescale, same terms – or I find someone else. We both know that there are enough men out there looking for a profit to sell guns, even to us.' I unbutton my watch and place it on the desktop with the payment. 'Yes, or no?'

Bronze's eyes caress the watch and move on to the saddlebags. He scratches his groin, exhales, and relaxes his shoulders. 'Yes, of course. Of course.' He smiles his oily smile.

Coyote

Coyote watched Francis Meavy lead his men around the bend of the Silver River where the plateau started its climb into the mountains, Raven and Arrowhead among them. Here, leafless trees stood like skeletons against the winter sky. Like Coyote, they witnessed the passing of the men and their horses in the land of the living.

This was the agreed meeting point for the delivery of the guns. It was a place marked by the mummified remains of a herd of ponies struck long ago by lightning. Coyote nosed at their desiccated hides stretched over ribcages and skulls, breathing deep the scent of lingering shock. The riders drew clear of the willow bordering the riverbank.

Francis Meavy

Late Autumn 1863 — The Silver River

Three wagons. The number of rifles only warrants two. Re-run the arithmetic. Same answer: the shipment requires two wagons. The horses crunch through the pebbles at a walk. At a hundred feet the teamster by the first wagon hears the clattering of hooves and looks over. He waves, rises from beside the fire and spits a jet of black liquid into the flames. It lands an arm's length from a rabbit roasting in the smoke, fat dripping to hiss on the wood burning beneath it. Two men are smoking pipes in the lee of a fallen aspen off to the left while another emerges from the tree line pulling his braces back over the shoulders of his undershirt. I untie the thong on my rifle slip.

The first two wagons are flat backed, their loads protected by grease cloth tied over and secured along the sides with rope. The third is covered. I wave my men into single file, presenting the narrowest possible profile to the camp. We rein in at twenty paces.

The teamster calls across, 'You Meavy?'

'Why the third wagon?'

My question is answered by the sound of splashing water and hooves on rock. Cross leads a group of eight men across the ford at the bend of the river behind us. Only three of them are soldiers. The remainder are Anaii wearing blue army jackets over buckskin trousers and moccasins. Cross has a pistol in his right hand pointing skywards, his reins in his left. Each of his men have pistols at their belts and rifles in slips on their horses.

I placate my men, 'Calm, brothers, remain calm.'

Cross halts his group twenty feet behind us, fanning his men out so they have open lines of fire, undoing our advantage. He shouts towards the camp, 'Sergeant.' Soldiers jump from the rear of the covered wagon. They form up: two firing rows aiming their rifles at us.

Cross walks his horse forward. 'Good morning, Mr Meavy. No greeting? Please do not assume we are here in an official capacity alone – to punish you and your fellows. I am also here in the spirit of free enterprise. First things first though. You will surrender your firearms.' He eyes the saddlebags on my horse.

'What else?'

'Very astute Mister or I should say, Captain Meavy.'

'I'm done with the army.'

'You have already made that clear, which is how I know what grave mistakes you have made. Refusing to serve your country and arming these Indians to bring hostilities against the United States. Well, what can I do but arrest you? In my capacity as a private businessman, I will return these rifles to their supplier, less my fee, naturally. The silver, please. You are smiling, Captain Meavy. I cannot imagine any good reason for you to be enjoying this moment, so enlighten me, what is the cause of your amusement?'

'It's you, Cross. I judged you right at the start. You're a thief in an officer's uniform.' I hand over the saddlebags.

He holsters his gun to take the weight of them, the anger blushing up his neck into his face. 'I understand you were overwrought at the loss of your Indian woman.' He lets the words hang in the air, like a whip crack, 'Of course, this interception will have repercussions on your precious Akote, Meavy. We have been preparing for an event such as this. I will take you now to Corazon. There you will be held for trial pending the return of Governor Waldron. As you can imagine, I shall be recommending that you face the ultimate penalty. As for your friends here,' he waves his hand, 'they are free to go, to carry news of your capture and the loss of their guns and silver to their settlements, and to spread word that our cavalry will shortly arrive to give notice that all Akote must report with their livestock to Corazon by the end of the month. Any Indians found at large after that date will be deemed hostile. If they do not cooperate, they will die in their droves. I will bring artillery and cavalry and we will scorch them from their hovels. Now tell them.'

'Son, you've heard what he said, they are taking me.' Raven shakes his head to speak. 'No, listen now, you must act. Go to your grandfather. Tell him now is the time to take the people to safety.' I unsheathe my bayonet and pass it to him. 'Then take my maps and clothes and head for Argento. Travel as a white trader but stay hidden. Find Abe there. Tell him what's happened here and to come and help me in Corazon. He is my only hope with Waldron.'

'Father –'

'No argument. Go, quick as you can. They want my

head. Don't let me die alone, son.'

Raven shakes his head. 'The air is good, Father.'

'The air is good, Raven.' Cross signals for the men to move out. I raise my hands, 'You're not going to bind me?'

'That will not be necessary.' He unholsters his pistol and scans the men behind me. As he fires, Arrowhead urges his pony in front of Raven, taking the round in the shoulder. The Akote whoop war cries and kick their ponies towards the enemy. The soldiers in the firing line cock their rifles.

My hand high, I bellow at them, 'Hold!'

Cross smiles. 'You see for each attempt at escape, Akote will die. A bargain which inspires in me the confidence of your cooperation.' He turns his horse, heeling it into a trot back across the ford, the others falling in as he passes. Cross' men barge me forward.

I turn to my son. 'Scorch the wound. Get him to Los Huertos.'

*

We reach Corazon at dusk, the darkness finding its foothold earlier as winter gains ground. They shove me into the cell. I trip, use my hands to protect myself from the full force of the fall, but my head strikes the edge of the bunk. I roll into a sitting position, legs outstretched, vision grainy as the door clangs shut and the lock clicks. The guard hangs the ring of keys on his belt and stands aside for Cross who looks down at me through the bars. I stop shaking my head clear for a moment, and nod forward as bile pumps up into my mouth, drooling down my chin to pool on the floor between my thighs. It's like I'm watching myself from the outside. Cross turns and strides out, smiling. The guard snaps to attention.

*

I come to. I feel like the heat will cook me alive and the pounding in my ears will split my skull. Lamps light the cell and the guardroom beyond; there are flames raging in the belly of the corner stove. My nose and lungs fill with the stink of tobacco breath, and I dry retch, becoming aware that I am parched and famished. A slow laugh draws my attention to the door. An Anaii man wearing a cavalry jacket over buckskin trousers grins at me, his head at an angle so his one good eye is closer to its focus. His long hair is streaked silver.

'They honoured you for what you did, for the stand you made,' he growls. He laughs again. 'I have only one eye, thanks to you, but I see only one man standing here.' I try to focus, to fit the man's face to my memory. The one eyed Anaii continues, 'You do not even remember taking it from me. I will ensure that what I take from you is burned forever in your heart. I have started with your wife and Pale Horse.'

I know him now and it surges through me, clearing my mind, focusing my vision. My hands are behind me, the heels pushing down on the edge of the bunk as I rise.

'My men,' One Eye starts.

'I heard ten of your men were no match for my woman.' He lifts his chin to listen. 'And Pale Horse broke your best man as easily as correcting a child.' I stand rod straight spitting the words, my fists ready, tight by my sides.

One Eye exhales, relaxing. 'That is what I will do. Discipline your child.' My breath catches in my throat. 'My brother is among your people. He tells me who is where and when. I will track your son and discipline him, as Pale Horse disciplined Blackrock – before I shot him.'

I throw myself across the space between us, smashing into the door. My right arm jabs out between the bars, skinning the knuckles. As One Eye springs back, my fingers brush the front of his coat before closing on air. The door to the guardhouse opens. A soldier steps inside, closing it behind him. He looks from One Eye to me. One Eye turns to leave. I call after him.

'My son. Please.'

'When I was a boy, your Akote took my brother from me. You have no son.'

*

It is morning, finally. All night I have been awake, imagining One Eye and his men hunting Raven through the landscape, picturing what they will do with their knives. I have not been fed nor given water. My blood beats a throbbing rhythm in my temples.

'Soldier.' The guard sits at the table chewing a wad and whittling with a pocketknife, brushing the sawdust from the top of his gut from time to time. He ignores me. 'I need water.'

He scratches his yellow whiskers, puts the whittling on the table, picks up a tin pitcher and cup and crosses to the bars, rolling from hip to hip. He stops and dips his head. 'You thirsty?'

'Yes.'

He holds the cup out in front of him close to the bars. I come forward. He spits a jet of tobacco juice into my face. 'I heard you like it brown. That's with my compliments.' He chuckles, waddling back to the table. I wipe my face with my hand.

The door opens, admitting more of the morning's greyness. Patrick steps into the room, the floorboards creaking beneath him. The guard looks up and, recognising the visitor, stands to attention.

'No need for that, soldier. You sit back down while I speak with Mr Meavy here.' He crosses to the bars. 'It pains me to see you like this, Francis. They are saying you bought guns for the Akote to attack Corazon.'

'I was buying guns, Patrick, but there was no attack planned on Corazon. We were double-crossed.'

His eyes scrutinise my face. 'Who?'

'Bronze.'

He snorts. 'I just gave him the last rites.'

'What?'

'His neck was broken. They're saying it was an accident, that he tried to carry his mother downstairs and fell. I don't believe it. She hadn't moved from that bed for months. Francis, the last time I was there she sent me away, told me that Bronze was a problem that she would put right. I think that's what she did. She's still alive, but barely.'

I smile. It is the first time since the ambush on the Silver River, and it feels good. 'Patrick, I need to talk.' I nod towards the guard.

Monaghan turns. 'My son, I wish to speak with this man. Will you let him out of the cell and leave us in private?'

The guard's eyes widen. He shrugs. 'I can't do it, Father, the prisoner, he can't. I can't let him.'

Monaghan puts his hand on the man's shoulder. 'I'm sure your orders don't include preventing a man of God doing the Lord's holy work with a sinner, do they?'

'Well, no, but I can't let him out, Father. I just, he must stay behind bars, the Major –'

'Did Major Cross order you not to permit this man to confess?'

'No, Father, but I can't let him out of the cell.'

'Ach, Lord, if only there was a way of him staying behind bars *and* being able to take confession.' He glances at me, then waits.

Light dawns on the man's peachy face. 'Father, if you could be alone with the prisoner, but he stayed in the cell, would that do it?'

'That would be perfectly satisfactory my son, but how could it be possible?' He steals another look at me and rolls his eyes.

'I could step outside, Father. You would be here in the guardroom and the prisoner in the cell.'

'Heavens be blessed, the Lord himself has inspired

you!' He slaps the man on the back as he leaves.

'Patrick, the Anaii raider who killed Bright Flower and Pale Horse was here. He works for Cross. He has a man in Los Huertos, and he knows Raven is headed for Argento. They are going after him, Patrick. They're going to kill my son and then they're going to hang me.'

He stares at the wall. When he looks back into my face, he notices something in the crease of my nose. I wipe it with my fingertip. 'Tobacco. From the guard.'

He takes a deep breath. 'When does the watch change?'

'Midnight.'

'Be ready at nightfall.'

*

I wait, stretched out on the low bunk. I'm vaguely aware that my back and arms ache, but I am elsewhere. In my mind I trace the plateau and mountains from Los Huertos to Argento, trying to think the route as my son would think it.

Daylight yields to dusk through the window. The guard drifts in and out of snoring, shaking the floor with the noise before waking himself, removing his boots and setting to picking his feet, adding to the stink of the thick warmth in the guardhouse. The noise of horses outside brings my attention back into the cell. The guard hears it too. He succeeds in pulling on only one of his boots before jumping to attention as Patrick fills the doorway, beaming at him. He wears a long coat and riding boots.

'Now then, stand easy, stand easy.' He reaches inside the folds of his coat and holds up a honey-coloured bottle, 'This is what they call "the good stuff" and since you were instrumental in the Lord's work earlier, I thought I should reward you on His behalf.' He casts his eyes to the ceiling and crosses himself with his free hand. The guard copies the gesture. The priest steps towards him around the side of the desk. 'Let us thank the Almighty before we partake. Kneel my son, to receive what you deserve.'

The guard is eager. He steadies his weight on the desktop and lowers himself to his knees, panting. His neck rolls up as he dips his chin. Before he can clasp his fingers together, a platelike hand shunts his forehead into the wood with a noise like the striking of a drum. He falls sideways with fluid grace, his skull bouncing a second beat on the timber floor. Patrick drags him over to the cell, snatches the ring of keys from his belt and unlocks the door.

'Get guns and ammunition,' he whispers then bends down, puts the keys in the unconscious man's hand, douses him in whiskey and leaves the bottle coughing up next to the body. I hand him a pistol, pushing another into my own belt, then two handed, toss a rifle towards him. He catches it, hefts it to his shoulder, looks along the barrel, grunts, and lowers it. 'Two horses outside, let me go first.' He opens the door, steps into the night, returns and nods.

We mount up and leave Corazon at a slow trot. The moon is tinged red.

Part Three

Raven

At daybreak, from the cover of the cottonwoods, I watch Father say farewell to Mother. She lingers as he rides away, then ducks back into the hogan. I cross to the canyon wall and climb the same path as the day before, but faster. I roll up over the edge at the top and stop. Arrowhead lies stretched out, his hands cradling the back of his head.

'What are you doing here?'

'I was here first. As usual. What are you doing here?'

I lie down next to him. The ground is cold. 'You were.'

'What?'

'Here first. I'm not as good a climber as you.'

'You're better. I don't make sure of the holds, you do, and that slows you down. One day it could make the difference between winning and falling.'

'You don't care, do you?'

Arrowhead smiles and wrinkles his nose. 'Life's too short to hesitate.'

'It will be if you carry on like that,' I tell him, but I wish I felt the same. I hate my carefulness. He reaches out a lazy arm and delivers a half-hearted slap to my chest. We lie watching the clouds wheeling overhead. I break the silence. 'I'm not like you.'

'No, you'll live longer.'

'I don't mean that. I'm just, you know.'

Arrowhead rolled onto his side. 'No, I don't. You're not making sense.'

'I've got two names.'

'You've got more than that. We all do.'

'No, I mean I've got an Akote name and my name from my father's people.'

'I never really thought about it.'

I wish I'd never started this conversation. Now that I am saying aloud what I feel, it is shaming.

'I just mean I've always thought you had your name, and it was part Akote, part something else. Like from another tribe. Not two names.'

'That's how it feels.'

'When is Francis Meavy coming back?'

'You see, you use his white name like it's Akote.'

'So what?' Arrowhead stands on the edge dropping stones down the rock face.

'It's obvious, isn't it?"

'Not to me.'

'I don't belong here. I'm not wanted.'

'Listen, you are not making sense. Are you saying that people don't want you here for having your father's name?'

'I'm going.'

'That's no answer but go if you want.'

I climb back down. I step off the rock face onto the silt and feel a sharp pain in the centre of my scalp. A stone falls at my feet. I look up. Arrowhead is holding a rock the size of a small pumpkin above his head as if to drop it. I pounce backwards, falling onto my backside, I hear my own laughter echoing.

Arrowhead's voice cascades down the canyon wall. 'I should drop it. I would not miss, and it might help you think.'

There is a pebble beneath my hand. I stand, lean back, and skim it up at him. 'Here's one for you. Use it as a brain, it's bigger than yours.'

*

It's the middle of the day. I am alone reading Father's battered Bible. The Gospel of Mark. I study the words in silence until I have a sense of them, then I say them aloud, listening for the meaning in my voice. I do this every day, always in the alcove. As I read, the echo in the language of my father's people makes it feel like I'm among those I've never met, my ancestors.

Grandfather and Grandmother are at the far side of the canyon, looking over. She beckons me. Grandfather appraises me as I approach. Have I done something wrong? They stand at the rail of the corral. Grandfather has kept his best mare close for weeks here in the canyon while the herds graze on the plateau. She has borne a foal, mottled white and rust, which stood within moments of birth.

'Raven, look at this foal, he's kicking already.' Grandmother points with her nose. We watch the mare and her offspring in silence. The foal bucks so high that it falls forward onto its head and has to untangle itself like a piece of wool, hooves and legs blurring in frustration. We laugh aloud.

'Uncommon,' Grandfather says.

'Husband, as usual, the little you say hints at a much bigger truth. When have you ever seen a newborn use its legs so quickly? He is strong and spirited, full of life and hope.'

'Yes. He will be strong and clever.'

I feel a pang of envy.

'Like our grandson,' Grandmother adds, 'A foal like that takes skill and patience to make it, but the horse it will become, could be the horse of a lifetime.'

There is unspoken meaning in this conversation, but I cannot make it out. Grandfather looks at me. 'The foal is yours, Grandson. Make him good.' He walks away, watched by Grandmother who is waiting for more. It does not come. I do not know what to say.

Then, breaking with taboo, Grandmother puts the palm of her hand on my face and smiles at me. 'You will make him into the best of horses.' She follows Grandfather. I do not understand the meaning of what just happened.

The foal, encouraged by his dam's head to suckle, breaks loose in a whirlwind of head tossing and whinnies. He runs at the rail of the corral, turning at the last moment, tripping into a confused heap. Hoof by hoof he untangles himself and stands, legs spread wide, trembling. He raises his head and squeals his irritation.

'You look like you have eight legs instead of four and tangle yourself up in your own web of limbs. I'm naming you Spider.'

*

The fruit trees are in full blossom, perfuming the soft air. Grandfather stands watching, arms crossed. Grandmother stands alongside him. The boy next to me whoops, bringing me back to myself. I try to focus on the rock face. The others are off, racing up the canyon wall like lizards. I leap, reaching above my head for handholds and scissoring my thighs against my ribs, pulling myself towards the rim. I'm gaining on the leader. He glances down mid haul, frees his left foot, and presses it onto my shoulder, laughing as he uses me as a step. I sink under the weight, then brace, and heave upwards again.

A toehold. I launch myself towards the disappearing ankle and grip it like a rope, using it to climb level, the move is ruthless, and I laugh aloud. The boy above takes the weight through his shoulders and arms, they tense like cords. He removes his free foot from its ledge and uses it to scrape my grip from his other leg. I'm falling and cry out as I swing sideways supported only by my fingertips. The other swarms up the final section without break, disappearing at the top. I regain my balance and haul myself over the lip ahead of the three boys beneath. If I'd held him tighter, I would have won.

It is evening. I step into my grandmother's hogan and stop to enjoy the smell of the stew. She looks up. Grandfather comes in behind me, placing a hand on the bare skin of my shoulder. It is heavy like rock.

'You are tall like your father and grandfather,' Grandmother says. I smile at her and sit down.

'You have the same smile as your mother and grandmother,' Grandfather tells me.

'Did you speak with him yet, Husband?'

'Not yet, Wife. I –'

She interrupts him, 'You are a fine young man, Raven. We watched you racing the canyon wall with the others earlier. Have you thought about finding a girl, starting your own family?'

I want to run, to hide myself from them, from everyone.

My parents appear in the doorway. Father answers, 'Willow Tree, this is a matter to be discussed at another time, we –'

She shrugs and hands him a steaming bowl, 'Have you noticed anyone, perhaps in one of the other settlements of the canyon?'

'Mother!' My mother cuts in, 'He is to be allowed his own choices. As I was. Mountain Song made this very clear.'

'He is in his fourteenth year – Husband, you know what I am going to say – it is long past time for a wife, and we don't want Raven going far, do we? We should start talking to the families of the other settlements in the canyon.'

*

Afterwards I stand by the wash, staring up at the sky. There are several hours of light left. I look around me. Akote men and women. I know that I will not marry. Who would want me when they could have one of their own?

I set out to find Arrowhead, heading east along the canyon to beyond Bear Rock where he lives with his new wife, Peach Blossom. As I walk into the next settlement, I am awakened from my thoughts by a movement in the stillness of the scene.

Sat in front of his hogan, his skin camouflaging him against the brown of its walls, Shadow Bloom's eyes are locked on me, his head swivelling to follow. I avert my look from the older man and call out, 'The air is good.' He watches me in silence.

*

Arrowhead is walking away from his new home. He has a yucca halter looped over his shoulder. I slip behind the loom so that neither of us can see the other and I laugh. Arrowhead's moccasins are visible beneath, turning, puzzled.

'Don't worry Arrowhead, you're not hearing voices in your head.'

He steps clear, grinning. 'I'm going to check the sheep on the plateau, are you coming?'

We examine the canyon wall as we approach it for foot- and handholds. Arrowhead jumps and latches his fingers onto a ledge. I do the same, remembering the last time we raced each other. I push hard, hands, legs, hands, legs and although this section of the rock face is unfamiliar to me, I stay level with him until we reach the lip. Arrowhead is not taking the brilliant risks which earn him victory in race after race. We pull ourselves over the rim and stand, catching our breath.

'Mountain lions have taken two sheep in the last month. I'm checking them regularly.'

'I assumed there must be some good reason for you to be away from your wife.' We walk shoulder to shoulder. He backhands me in the chest. I laugh, winded.

'You sound like a dog.'

We both see the tracks in the same instant. The width of a man's palm, four toes and an irregular pad, the fore prints larger than the hind prints and lacking claw marks. Arrowhead draws his knife. I do the same. We creep forward. The breeze from the north is in our faces. We can see the stragglers now, littered around the body of the flock, grazing. Between us and the sheep is a narrow slab of rock rising to the height of a man's shoulder.

Flattening itself, shimmying up towards its edge, a mountain lion raises its head to gauge distance and check the awareness of its prey. Its focus is absolute. We are downwind, it has not picked up our scent. We stand motionless.

The memory of the race up the rock face and the talk of me finding a wife spins in my mind so my head hurts. I sprint forward and when I am but a few paces from the lion, I bellow at the top of my voice. It leaps and looks back in one movement. The sheep bolt west, so the cat lands in clear ground. It turns and stands, watching me through unblinking eyes as I come on shouting spittle in my war rage. I hear Arrowhead's desperate voice.

'Stop! It will kill you!'

The predator punches a hole in the brush and is

gone, the scent of sage from the broken twigs mingling with its muskiness as it disappears.

Arrowhead spins me around by the shoulder. 'What is wrong with you? Do you want to die?'

I laugh at him, 'Come on, let's count the sheep. I shall tell your wife how you fought with the lion and drove it off without even a scratch.'

As we return, shards of the talus scatter beneath our heels. Arrowhead sees Peach Blossom dipping back into their hogan below. 'Listen, come and have some of my wife's cornbread. Don't tell her I said so, but it is even better than my mother's.'

I stare at his stomach. 'Oh, that's what it is. I thought you were carrying your first child.'

*

Walking back, I look out for Shadow Bloom. By the door to his hogan is a cage of branches bound together with yucca twine. Inside, a coyote, its head low. As I pass, it turns, watching me go. I stop, scan the place for the medicine man, then stalk up to the cage. I untie the twine and let the creature out. It lopes up into the rocks.

*

I shiver with the early chill as we turn south for the Great Harvest Canyon. Arrowhead and I are part of the escort to Grandfather and Pale Horse, a great honour. Father rides ahead of us with Crowsfoot. They laugh and he reaches out with his free hand. They wrestle one armed until Grandfather looks over his shoulder and they stop.

Arrowhead grins at me and whispers, 'I thought we were supposed to be the youngest.'

It's like father is Akote in everything but appearance, his hat and boots betraying him.

As we come in from the east, the Great Harvest Canyon is beyond anything I have imagined. The canyon floor is three or four times the width of ours and the walls stretch hundreds of paces into the sky. Arrowhead nudges me as I'm looking up. He points ahead of us with his nose. I peer between Father and Crowsfoot. They are thousands strong. I have never seen so many Akote men in one place. We are among them now. All of them show Grandfather and Pale Horse great respect, averting their eyes as they greet them. I feel proud that I am his grandson. Many of the men greet Father too, but differently, with less formality and more fondness, calling him by name and waving. I didn't realise he was so well known, so popular.

*

We sit with our backs to a fallen cottonwood in the dusk, watching the chiefs in the alcove opposite, their shadows long in the firelight. Arrowhead leans across and snatches a piece of smoked venison from my hand. My arm flicks out and I grasp his wrist, twisting it around as I drive up with my legs, rolling him onto his face to kneel on his back. He's laughing so hard he starts to choke. I take the venison back and release him. He coughs a piece into the silt.

'That's how I treat scavengers,' I tell him.

He hisses and grunts like a vulture and flaps his arms. 'I am defeated. Anyway, when did you become so strong?'

I don't answer because I am watching the profile of the man speaking at the Council of War Chiefs. It is Father. Arrowhead follows my stare and grins.

*

I saw them afterwards, walking in the moonlight. Something is wrong. Now Father and Grandfather leave for Corazon with other war chiefs. Arrowhead and I are to return to Los Huertos with Pale Horse.

Once they are gone, we set out, riding behind Pale Horse and Crowsfoot, travelling north in silence. Just after noon, Pale Horse calls me forward. Usually, he would get us to describe the lie of the land in pairs.

He nods towards the horizon. 'Tell me, Raven.' I open my mouth to speak, but he cuts me off. 'No. Do not. I will tell you. With my great medicine I will tell you your own heart.' He laughs, 'You ask yourself why your father did not take you with him, why he and your grandfather have gone with other men of the Akote.' He hesitates for a long moment, then, 'It is not for me to tell you that.' He laughs again, 'What you must know is that you will need to hunt when we return. The food of Great Harvest Canyon is nothing compared to the venison and antelope of our part of the plateau, and I grow hungry for it. I have promised Hawk that I will protect the settlement, so you and the others will have to hunt well – and soon – if the emptiness in my stomach is not to scare the game away.'

*

We leave Pale Horse and a handful of others in the village. He has assembled stalks and arrowheads to work on outside his hogan. As Crowsfoot leads us out, Pale Horse calls, 'Be quick, before my roaring stomach drives them off!' Crowsfoot laughs and kicks his horse on. A coyote howls somewhere close by.

By the time we reach the plateau, the sky is already bright and hot. Hotter than it should be at this time of year. We follow antelope tracks into an arroyo, forming two ranks to fit through. Arrowhead is by my side. Somehow, we always end up with each other. He feels me looking at him and glances up. He nods but says nothing. Strange.

Crowsfoot pulls up sharp. Ahead, a coyote trots into our path with a limp snake in its mouth. It drops it into the dirt and sits. An eagle calls, its shadow passes over us caressing the earth and the rock back towards the canyon. As one we turn our horses and gallop to the rim. We rein in hard. Shards of rock from beneath the hooves of our ponies fly over the edge into the void. I stop breathing, my mind blocked. Below, Pale Horse faces forty or fifty raiders. I left Mother in her hogan. And Grandmother, where was she? Crowsfoot shrieks his war cry and gallops east along the rim, so close to the edge it crumbles as his horse passes.

We are in the canyon now, racing back east, going so fast one of us must surely fall. Spider jumps a fallen tree then jinks left to skirt quicksand. We are in front, the wind whipping dust up into our eyes. Faster, faster he goes. Stay in the hogan, Mother, hide in the hogan. The ground shakes and a wave of sound sucks the air from my body before filling my head. Other horses falter and stumble, but Spider is undeterred. Burning timbers and smouldering blankets fall around us. The air stinks, bitter and bloody, the smoke stabs at my eyes and throat. I see Pale Horse. He is fallen. I jump from my horse and try to lift him. I look for Arrowhead but see instead the burning hole in the earth where Mother's hogan should be.

*

I weep through the night until my eyes ache and no more tears come. I feel nothing. There is no me, no now. I have left myself. I sit in this hogan and breathe the emptiness. A horse outside. I hear Father's voice, wild, terrified. I stand, my bones heavy. He holds me to him, crushing me so hard I can't breathe. He asks me something. I hear my own voice. The canyon spins and I'm here. I'm here again. I taste the blood in my mouth, feel the sting of the blow, my anger raging up within me. He struck me. I close my fists and turn to him, but something holds me back.

Grandfather's hand around my forearm. 'Tell me, Grandson.'

*

Late Autumn 1863 — The Silver River

This place reeks of death. The dried corpses of horses, the skeletons of trees. The noise of hooves on pebbles is like the hissing of ghosts. Father feels it too. He orders us into a single file. I watch his fingers untie the slip of his rifle as he looks ahead at the wagons. His face is grey like an old man's. He is not the same. He lost his mind in the canyon and at the Sacred Mountain – the way he spoke of Mother – and then the New Mexicans. It was like a death wish, a wish to die and to kill.

We are in the open here. Grandfather would never have chosen a place like this. They call our name, 'Meavy.' Father does not return the greeting. He knows something is wrong. They come from behind us, the Anaii and Cross, they are all armed. We are caught between them and the soldiers pouring out of the wagon into firing lines. Arrowhead draws his knife and kicks his horse towards them. Father orders us to stand, to calm ourselves.

Cross approaches him, demanding his guns and the

saddlebags of silver. He is a thief and Father tells him so. As Father prepares to hand them over, Cross looks us up and down. His eyes linger on me for a moment longer than the others. He recognises me from last time. He knows about Mother, about what happened. How could he know that? Father will surely kill him now, but he does not. Instead, he listens while Cross tells him that he's taking him, that the rest of us should return to our people to tell them to surrender.

Father hands me his knife. I try to tell him to attack, that this is where we must stand, but he stops me. He gives me a message for Grandfather, that this is the time to lead our people to shelter, that I should deliver this and then go find Abe Knox to intervene with Waldron. Cross draws his pistol. He pretends to aim at random, but he and I both know his sights will settle on me. So does Arrowhead. He kicks his horse in front of me as Cross fires.

*

The others hold Arrowhead down. I pour powder into the wound and clench my teeth as I light it. My friend screams and passes out as the smell of burning flesh and the stink of powder fills the cold air. It should be me lying there. We tie him to his horse and gallop northwest across the hardened plateau.

After two days we reach the eastern end of the canyon. The aroma of herbs stewing with mutton and the sweet earthiness of Akote bread welcomes us home. Children wrapped in blankets leave the warmth of their hogans to watch us race past, ponies blowing hard. Grandfather emerges from his hogan wrapping his buffalo hide round his shoulders. We dismount and lower Arrowhead to the ground. He is pale and feverish.

Grandmother takes over. 'Bring him inside. Fetch Shadow Bloom.' Arrowhead's moccasins disappear as he is carried into the hogan.

'Come, Grandson.' Grandfather's hair is grey at the temples and thick with feathers. Greyer than when we left for the Silver River. The wrinkles at his eyes are like the dark streaks on the canyon walls. Still, I see Mother in his forehead and cheekbones. Does he see her in me? Or only Father? Enough. There is no time to grieve her now. Grandfather walks towards the cottonwood stand. My back aches from the ride. It cracks as I stretch it. We are at the far side of the trees, concealed.

'They were there, waiting for us, Cross and his men.' I tell him Cross' ultimatum. 'Father gave me a message for you, he said it is time to take our people to safety.' He looks north. 'And Grandfather, I'm riding for Argento to find Abe Knox.'

*

I wash in the river downstream of the settlement. The water is slap cold. Scrubbed and dried I take up the skin pouch. My hands shiver as I unstring the neck. I pinch the cornmeal inside and shower in it. The second pinch is for the earth, 'Mother,' I throw it down; the third, for the air, 'Father,' I toss it into the breeze. Kneeling,

I face East and bow my head. 'Lord, grant me swiftness of foot and of mind.'

Time to dress: the cotton shirt, Father's coat and trousers, Father's boots. I sling his map tube over my shoulder. Grandfather and Grandmother stand next to Spider as I strap the rifle into its slip.

Grandmother scowls. 'You have enough cornbread and dried meat?' Before I can reply, she speaks again. 'Must he travel alone, Husband?'

Grandfather nods. 'This man is the son of Bright Flower and the grandson of Willow Tree. He knows what needs to be done. He will do it. Raven, you have an enemy in this journey who cannot be avoided and who will kill you more surely than any other. Respect the cold.'

I draw my blanket around my shoulders and pat the second one strapped to Spider's saddle. Grandfather shakes his head and goes to his hogan, returning moments later with a buffalo skin.

'Grandfather this has great value, I –'

Grandmother interrupts again. 'Then take good care of it and bring it back safe.' She takes the hide and rolls its shaggy bulk as best she can, tying it to the cantle. I take up the reins, throw my leg over Spider's back and lower myself into the saddle. Already Grandmother is chanting under her breath, 'Fast and far he travels, fast as sunlight, far as the moon.'

I head the horse east, touch my heels to his flanks, and turn to wave. Passing through the next settlement, Shadow Bloom is in the doorway of his hogan, staring. I press Spider into a trot. Within hours I see the end of the canyon, and beyond it the mountains, Ute country.

*

It would have been best to leave the canyon from the western end where the wash is broad and cuts north then east before heading up through the Ute mountains. That way I'd distance myself from Corazon, moving deep into Akote country, avoiding the areas most raided by the other tribes. Prudent, but it would have taken days longer to reach Argento, days crucial to saving Father from Cross and his trial.

Instead, I strike out northeast towards the forests and the mountains. I know the path well. This stretch of plateau is crisscrossed by the Akote and other tribes for hunting and raiding. I stay below the horizon in arroyos and the lee of escarpments, riding on hard ground to leave the faintest trail. The terrain is uneven and fragmented, but we push on to a point two thirds of the way to the mountains by nightfall.

Twice during the day, we approach herds of deer grazing the last of the green before the snow hides it from them. Each time we slip past in silence, the commotion of fleeing wildlife could alert human eyes to our presence. I make camp beneath the overhang of an arroyo. The water has scooped the flesh from the red rock, creating a shallow cave before eroding the riverbed to a level several paces below the ledge it has carved. Despite the late autumn cold I do not light a tell-tale fire. I relieve Spider of the saddle and packs. At the back of the cave, I lay a bed of brush, cover it with a blanket and lie on it, pulling the buffalo skin around me. It smells of the smoke in the hogan of my grandparents. I breathe it deep.

I brush sleep from my face with both hands. Remnants of the dream still linger – I am being woven into a cocoon of spider silk, my legs bound. I see the spider, large as a buffalo, looming over me, spinning as I struggle to free my arms before the thread imprisons me.

Awake now, I watch as a spider suspends itself from the underside of the rock by a gleaming thread. It hauls itself back upwards. It's an hour before dawn. I chew dried venison while I feed and water Spider, and we wait until there is enough light to see our feet and the ground in front of us. The predawn is crisp and damp with dew, the last of the autumn's warmth exhales its sage sigh from the earth. Our breathing and movements are loud in the stillness. My shoulders rock with the rhythm of the horse. I stretch my neck back to see the stars. This is a shadow landscape, the clumps of brush visible only in outline, the sky a pall of smoke hanging above the charcoal earth.

Perhaps this was what the world looked like to the Holy People as they ascended through the four worlds to live on the land. Or, when God created the Earth, it might have been like this before He lit the Sun. The Sun. Mother sang in the sunshine, gathering peaches with Aspen Leaf, while Arrowhead and I held the baskets for them in the warmth of the canyon.

The glow of a spark shooting into the cold sky saves us. My breath stops in my chest. I pull Spider up and dismount, creeping forward to the ridge. In among the rocks, a group of Ute are sleeping. Their fire has burnt down but casts a low glow on the rifles at their sides. Without the warning of the spark, I would have ridden into them. I take Spider by the bridle and lead him around. After a hundred paces I remount and trot away along the dry riverbed.

The country is changing. Great escarpments of rock in rainbows of red and brown rise and fall on the plateau then give way to undulations painted with wild grass and wooded-in patches. In full daylight, the pale green of the trees opens out to a rolling plain between us and the mountains. I keep to the lower ground as far as possible, or just inside the tree line where the dappling of the light and the countless lines of trunks and branches break up the shape of a man on a horse. I have been here before. The place is in my memory. The track stretches up the side of the mountains now, ascending so steeply that, in places, the tops of the trees downslope are level with us. It leads to a path just below the spine of the range. We thread our way along. Spider stumbles constantly on loose shards.

The ground flattens out. Pines form a long clearing which funnels to a cut through the rock. The air up here is cold and sharp with resin. The aperture is the crossing point from one side of the ridge to the other, and passing through it, we start a gentle descent onto a rolling plain covered with pale bristle. The trunks of a juniper forest have burned, leaving only the uprights to weather, white. They stand like a ghost army awaiting orders. We pick our way through, over the crisscross of fallen branches until we reach the far edge of the plateau where it drops into a wooded canyon with fractured sides.

When Father and Grandfather brought me here, they took a path to the west. It was invisible from above, descending the rock face for several hundred paces before reaching the deserted pueblo in the canyon wall concealed in a natural undercroft. I take this path now, Spider's ears flicking as his feet slide on loose stones. The only other means of access is by hand- and footholds up the sheer cliff to the lip. Inaccessibility has ensured the survival of the pueblo. This place will be our last chance of manmade shelter and the warmth of a fire for days. The path is already forty paces beneath the canyon's rim and its narrowness presses us against the wall. My knee grazes the cliff. To my right, the drop is sheer into the river below.

At last, we round the final outcrop onto an area of level rock between the pueblo and the canyon beneath. Spider stops short. I kick him on, scanning each alcove and shadow.

There. Crouched low on a roof, hard under the stone ceiling. A mountain lion, ears back, muscles tense, eyes slits. It has dragged a freshly killed antelope over the edge of the parapet, leaving a crimson trail in the sand. I have seen it too late; we are barring its escape back up the path. Trapped, the cat will make the only choice it can.

I draw Father's bayonet and flick Spider back around, kicking him on hard towards the drop. His front hooves find the edge, his eyes roll white, and he rears, vapour billowing from his nostrils as he rises. Glancing over my shoulder I see the lion pounce. I lean back in the saddle with my full weight, tearing at the reins. Spider topples backwards and sideways. As we go over, I kick my feet out of the stirrups and push clear to avoid being crushed. The stink of musk fills my nose and I feel the draught of the cougar's leap over us. It lands upslope and races away. I topple from Spider into a clump of dead brush, the thickest of its limbs snapping as I fall, spearing my thigh through the buckskins, gouging a channel just beneath the skin and holding me up like an effigy at an angle to the path. My howl bounces back and forth across the gorge. A flock of mourning doves take flight from their hiding place in the trees.

I press my hands against the rock face, twist slowly and reach down to grip the wood just below the wound. I try to raise the leg, pushing with the other as I do so. I turn my head and throw up. Spider is back on his feet, intact but for a flap of skin above his eye, hanging loose and bleeding so the whiskers of his muzzle drip scarlet. I call him over, grasp the front of the saddle with my left hand and slap his hindquarters with my right. His rear dips as he surges. I scream, the wood snaps and I pitch forwards, free at last.

The branch is the thickness of a finger, poking out of my thigh by a hand's width. I shuffle so my back is against the rock, bend forward, grasp the shaft and yank, twisting from my shoulders. My vision becomes grainy, but from the doorway of the largest house in the pueblo, I see a shadow emerge. Two yellow embers glowing in its head. It slides out onto the ledge, taking

form in the daylight. Low and grey, its mouth hangs
open, tongue lolling as it trots towards us. Spider shies
away as I reach up for the reins. I watch the horse go.
The coyote pads up to me. I try to raise myself against
the rock, but my legs jack-knife. Darkness.

Coyote

He watched Raven's respect for the cougar, his understanding of its nature. The boy's heart was true Akote. He was a gift, as his mother had been. The mother whom Coyote had brought from the North, who should have lived long.

Raven fell from his horse. Coyote felt the pain of his body, smelled the blood on the rock. Uncleaned, the wound would fester. He left his hide. At the edge of consciousness, the boy saw him. While he was in darkness, Coyote bit the wood from the wound. It was dirty. He cleaned blood and sand from the flesh with his tongue.

Raven

The rock beneath me is cold and wet from the rain. I try to stand. The pain in my thigh stabs up along my back. I retch. It's better still than moving, but even then it burns and throbs. The wound is clean and scabbing. Somehow, a bloody fragment lies on the ground next to me. Spider shelters under the overhang. I try to put my weight on the leg again. It's unbearable to start with but I can move. One hand on the rock face, I hop to the pueblo, taking care not to slip on the rain slick slab. I climb the stairs to the place where Grandfather showed me a natural chimney, a fissure in the rock which draws the smoke into a network of cracks to dissipate on the plateau above where the pueblo is invisible. I feed and water Spider, then, hobbling, drag the antelope carcass by its leg from the parapet.

I make a fire, butcher the animal, and impale it on sticks to roast above the flames. I eat as much of the hot meat as I can, stocking my body against the journey ahead and feeding the injury. With water heated on the fire I clean the wound on Spider's head. I try to reckon how long it will take to reach Abe Knox in Argento. Is it even possible for Abe Knox to intervene in time? I question whether Father has asked the impossible of me, making me responsible for what happens next. He blames me for not being in the canyon with Mother, but neither was he. I need the guidance of the ancestors.

Father's Bible. I take it from the saddlebag and read aloud.

'Be strong and of a good courage: for unto this people shalt thou divide for an inheritance the land, which I sware unto their fathers to give them.' The walls of the pueblo bounce the words around me, like the voices of others.

The itching of the wound wakes me. It is first light. The space retained the heat of the fire still burning. I am revived by the rest, hot food, and deep black sleep. The leg hurts with every movement, but I can stand. One hand on a low wall, I try a shallow squat. The muscle feels like it is stretching to snapping point, but I can hold the position. I can ride. I eat more of the meat, saddle up, pack the Bible and the remaining antelope into my saddlebags, and bring Spider alongside the pueblo steps, using them as a mounting block.

As the first sun of the day cracks fissures in the sky of the plateau, we crest the rim of the canyon. North now, climbing through green valleys, the temperature dropping despite the bright autumn sunshine which casts great patches of light and shade on the earth. Rich pasture carpets the troughs of the valleys. How fat Mother's sheep could grow here. She will never see that, and I will never see her again. The darkness rises up inside me, flooding me. I push it back. This is not the time.

I pass like a ghost through the landscape, as Grandfather told me. The soldiers will expect me to take the path around the feet of the mountains, longer but easier. An Anaii hunter will expect me to do the opposite, to double-bluff. Father would say, 'Throw a coin.' The mountain terrain will be harder on my leg, but we will be concealed, truly alone. The pace will be slower but the route direct. I nudge Spider up into the hills.

As we climb, the hills gain a pelt of countless pine trees clinging to the steep slopes and bowing north together as if in worship. Into the forests we clamber, tacking in places to make the ascent possible. Spider picks his legs up high to clear fallen trunks, the progress exhausting him. I cannot dismount to share the burden on foot because of the wound. Bleeding or fever now could finish me. And Father.

A day's slow climb. At last, we crest the high ridge. Starting down the far side Spider stumbles three or four times, pitching me forward and forcing me to brace against clenched hips. The wound is agonising but, despite my fears, it does not reopen. I dismount at dusk, taking the weight through my good leg like an old man. A wall of trunks fallen across each other serves as shelter. I stuff the gaps with undergrowth and branches, the larger ones across the top to make a roof. It will not stop rain, but it is tall enough for Spider and will keep off a frost. The horse's wound looks clean enough, but I think I feel the beginnings of heat in the edges of it. I bathe it with the cleanest piece of cloth I have – one of Father's shirts.

Dusk comes fast and is short. The shelter, barely visible in daylight, will be invisible by night. Only the vapour of our breath might betray us up close. In any case, I will hear any enemy before they can see us. Pile the earth with small pieces of bark and pine needles as insulation against the cold of the forest floor with a blanket over the mound. Hooting in the distance. I bed down, but soon afterwards I awaken to the beating of wings. The owl perches outside the shelter and blinks, twisting its horned head away from me. When it screeches, my body jolts as if I have missed a step.

Asleep again. The owl's face fills my vision, its yellow eyes flickering flame. In the fire I see my mother, my father, myself. It flares up, startling me. My eyes open, adjusting to the darkness. The snap of a stick ruptures the silence. My nose fills with rich musk. By the light of the crescent moon, I peer through the gaps in the shelter. Upwind, among the pines, a herd of deer tiptoe through the sharp air. They stop and flick their ears. Spider wickers and they bolt in a rustling blur, floating across the forest floor and clearing the trunks of fallen trees like a storm racing across the plateau. I stay still for long moments to ensure that the horse, not a predator, spooked them. I look for the owl, but it is gone. Seeking a spot where my body weight has not yet flattened the pine needles into the cold ground, I pull the buffalo hide over myself, check Spider, and close my eyes.

Dawn. The unbroken chill of the night on my face has made my jaw and nose ache, and my eyes burn. My neck cracks. Best to move, to get warm that way. Pain shoots through my foot and my hip as I flex my leg. Stiff, I saddle up. We need water and to eat before the day's push across the mountains. Through the trees, the peaks beyond are twice the height of anything so far and covered in snow. The clean pine air pinches my lungs as I sigh.

Descending the slope through the forest, I hear the crashing of a cascade. To the north a stream falls from high on the mountainside, cutting a path through the greenery, baring the black stone beneath. I rein Spider towards it. As we tack our way down and across the slope, the noise of our breathing and the clacking of hoof on rock is drowned out by the sound of water punishing stone. It pools at the foot of the drop then heads northwest. A sparkling river of quartz; glinting, it hurdles jutting boulders midstream and winds down into the valley where trees grow on small islands strung between rock beaches. A woodpecker rattles. The air bites less here but the fine mist from the waterfall is drenching.

Along the tree line to an inlet, a green cove where the trees are separated from the river by a narrow curve of rock. The water is still. I crouch, peering for fish. Nothing. A dark patch at the edge of the trees. The smell of putrefaction fills my nose and throat as I approach it. The bones in the otter spraint show that trout are plentiful here. I turn back to Spider to fetch the bow and wait, arrow notched. The wound burns and my leg trembles at the effort of holding still. A fish the length of a man's forearm slides into the stillness. It swims within two paces of the shore, hovering in the unseen current. I loose the arrow, its splash followed by the thrashing of the impaled trout, its freckled body folding from one side to the other, light gleaming off it like metal.

Spider has his head down picking at the grass at the foot of the trees. The fish meat is clean but still I heave at its rawness. A fire could ruin everything if it led to discovery now. I breathe through my mouth, chewing little and swallow it down with icy water. I wash my hands and bayonet in the current. The blood stretches into crimson strands, paling to pink in the flow.

In the tree line I sit on a fallen trunk to examine my wound. The scab is thick and itches like lice but there's no heat in it. Good signs. I prod the channel the branch dug into my thigh. The pain makes me grunt aloud, but no discharge oozes from the edges. I look up at the peaks encircling us. They are capped in snow and cloud. To the north, a pass cuts like an axe mark into the high ridge. I call Spider, use the trunk to mount, and head towards it.

The air grows colder again as we climb, the vapour from our breathing thicker. I pull the buffalo skin round me and twist to delve in the saddlebag for Father's rawhide gloves. As I pull them over my fingers, I think about the Meavys. What would they make of my Akote family? What would they make of me, the white Indian? If they held to the Book, they would accept me as another child of God, as Father Monaghan did. But I've seen the others, heard how they speak to the Akote, how they speak about us. I pass for a white man with Father's green eyes and pale skin, but why should I? I am Mother's son also.

I pull Spider to a halt. We are halfway to the pass. It's mid-afternoon. We cannot make camp this high; the trees are sparse so there is no cover, and the cold will sap our strength. In the open, on the bare slope, we will be visible from afar until the darkness hides us. If I camp while the light is still good, I'll be wasting precious time we need to use covering distance. The longer we delay now the greater the risk to Father. I kick on. Spider keeps his head low to the slope, brushing the ground with the breath from his muzzle as he hauls us both up the mountainside. The sweat foams at the edges of his saddle. I stop for a few moments' standing rest and his chest heaves, repaying the effort.

We move on again. If I allow the horse to get cold from a sweat, he will take a chill in his lungs or a fever in his blood. We crest the ridge just before dusk. Crossing the high point in the pass, the wind stings my ears. Spider starts to pick his way down, tiptoeing on his forelegs, half crouching on his hindquarters to keep his footing. He grunts, the effort rolling through his shoulders with each short stride. We have covered thirty paces. A hoof strikes a rock, and he stumbles. I feel the weight shifting over our centre of gravity and lean back further, pulling hard against the reins to lift him by his mouth. Spider throws his head from side to side in protest but raises his chest, regaining balance. I halt him, his hind hooves sending a shower of rocks down the slope ahead. I allow him a moment to recover then push forward again, my legs rod straight, my thigh singing with pain. There's little light left and over two hundred paces of near-bare rock to descend at a crawl before we reach the trees.

I let the horse establish a slow rhythm then keep him to it. We grow in confidence as the yards pass one by one. Then, in the half-light, neither of us notices the seam of scree like a tear up the mountain. A pica, close but invisible, cries out. Startled, Spider shies and slips on the loose surface, his right forefoot snags on a lip of rock and his shoulder goes over it, the weight of us both moving forward beyond his legs. We start to fall. Once more I slip my feet from the stirrups as the slope leaps up to meet us.

Coyote

He came up through the four worlds with the others, rising towards the sun. But there were those who would not follow, who remained to face the Evils. They were swallowed in darkness.

Hawk called together the headmen of Los Huertos. Mid-morning, they met in the alcove. The War Chief bided his time while their conversations settled to a murmur. When he stood, they gave him silence.

'We have been betrayed by the gun trader. Francis Meavy is a prisoner of the soldiers in Corazon. When they took him, they gave our men a message to bring back to us. Soon they will come here to order us to surrender ourselves, our land, and herds. If we do not, they will round the Akote up and take our homelands for themselves. Francis Meavy was born among them. He foresaw that they would do as they have done.

The Anaii are allied with the soldiers. They know the movements of our men. Many of us will now leave for safety in the north away from the soldiers, beyond the land they patrol. We will take our animals. There we will live as we always have, in a hidden sanctuary, sacred to the Akote. It is clear that the Anaii have an ally among us. For this reason, our journey must remain secret.

Those who wish to come with us are welcome as our brothers and sisters. If you wish to join us, you must prepare to leave with whatever you can carry. Our progress will be slow with our animals and possessions.

Now we have spoken of this we must leave without delay. They will come for us.'

The headmen looked at each other in silence. Aspen Shake replied, 'Hawk, you ask us to give up everything. The plenty of this place where our fruit orchards have grown for generations, our corn and flocks multiplied and thrived.'

Other voices broke out in agreement.

'My flock is thirty strong now.'

'We cannot take peach orchards with us.'

Once they dwindled, Hawk spoke again, 'I do not ask you to come. That is for you to decide. We are leaving to make again the homeland intended for us. Not by shedding blood but by doing as the First People did and building a new life out of the darkness. We have lived in this place for generations. Our roots are deep in the canyon floor. Those who wish to stay are free to do so. We will remember you in our prayers. For those who wish to come, we set out at dawn three days from now. Be prepared by sunset the night before, herds and flocks in and ready to be driven, horses loaded and every man, woman, and child to meet here by the cottonwoods.'

*

At dusk, two days after the council, Hawk was on his knees in his hogan rolling arrows and knives into buckskins, tying them off with yucca twine.

Willow Tree threw back the blanket at the doorway. 'Come with me.'

He finished the knot, stood, and followed. Once outside, he stopped short. The villagers were so closely packed that the canyon floor was hidden. Willow Tree smiled at him and nodded. He edged his way through the mass towards the trees. The full moon was rising. He stepped up onto the fallen trunk. Silence spread across the Akote like a breeze on a lake.

'You are gathered and ready. We will not leave at dawn. We will leave this evening. The moon will light our way. For the next three nights, we will travel by night and shelter unseen during the day. To any seeking us we will have disappeared.'

One voice rose from the crowd. Shadow Bloom. 'It is inauspicious to travel at night. We should delay until dawn.' As he finished, Coyote howled.

A gust from the East lifted Hawk's hair as he spoke, 'The First People travelled up through darkness to this world. The night will cover us. We will chant and pray as we travel and in such numbers the prayers will be answered.'

He awaited Shadow Bloom's reply. None came.

*

Raven

My side throbs. Blood and grit in my mouth. Sweet horse breath warming my face. I can't move my arm. I'm wedged against a rock. A warm drop lands on my lips. Spider above me, dusty, trembling, his muzzle dripping blood from the reopened wound. I roll onto all fours, sharp rock pressing up through my buckskins to my knees and through my gloves to my palms. Check my thigh, it's bound to be wet with fresh blood. No, it's still dry. How far did we fall? I turn my head upslope and follow the line of the scree. Hundreds of paces. I stand up. I'm shaking. The world is grainy. I lean on Spider and suck in the thin air until the blurriness sharpens and the sound of my breathing and the whistle of the mountain joins the tap of the horse's hooves on the slope as he fidgets.

What now? Below, the ramp of the mountain steepens again, but we will soon be in the tree line, sheltered from the blustering cold and less visible to hostile eyes. I run my hand along Spider's back feeling for injury. Behind his withers, beneath the saddle, a patch twitches to the touch and makes him toss his head and snort. I form a tube with my fingers and palm and run it down each leg. They're sound with no warmth to indicate damage. His back needs to be rested or he'll become unrideable. I lead him in hand down the slope. The tenderness might respond to active rest.

Darkness halts us in the forest. I step up alongside Spider for my canteen, to rinse the wound on his head and my own mouth. It's gone. The thong that had held it is torn. The powder horn is also missing. Father's rifle and the bow grandfather gave me are wrapped in a buckskin sheet tied to the saddle. Both rode up during the fall and have been saved from Spider's full weight as he rolled. The bow will allow me to hunt silently for game. The rifle is deadweight without powder. Check my belt. The pouch heavy with silver is still there, so I could buy powder, but that will make me visible and leave us vulnerable to pursuit. Check Spider's back again. The flesh is less tender. The rest from weight bearing and the movement descending the slope into the trees have loosened him up, but he's trembling. Shock, stress, cold – I don't know which – he needs to get warm, that's for certain.

Now we're in the trees, smoke will reveal our presence to an observer, but not our identity. I'm weak from the fall and the thin air, but I drag as many fallen boughs as I can up against the raised trunk of a wind-felled pine. The branches are still heavy with needles, I can use them for a windbreak. I stack timber according to dampness, ensuring warmth as long as possible while we sleep. The fire belches thick sharp smoke as the moisture of the pinecones fights the heat. The flickering flames lull Spider. And me.

*

Ember tips glow in the fire. It's mushroomed during the night. The sun is rising but has already lost the battle with the cold of the clear sky. Mother would have chanted in the last darkness to welcome the dawn, the smell of cornbread cooking in the earth floor filling the hogan. The grief rises in my chest like a whirlwind, bursting its way out of me in sobbing groans. I block the weeping, forcing calm on myself.

Spider stands, more alert than at dusk, trembling less. The bruising on his back barely twitches to my touch. I'll lead him for a few minutes before riding once more. Best stack the wood up on the fire to draw interest while we put distance between ourselves and the camp.

I take the reins in hand and set off between the trees down the slope. As we drop, the full valley stretches before us. I stop. Below, the buildings of a town hunker like moss. From them a silver ribbon unravels towards the foot of the slope beneath. There it switches back to form a pool with rocky beaches sheltered by encircling trees. The promise of water draws us onwards.

I'll find them. I'll save Father and then I'll find the raiders. I will hunt them. The hard stillness fills me.

Coyote

He watched Francis Meavy and the priest as they made for the high mesas to the north, then cut east. They found no sign of Raven. They rode as hard as they could without ruining their horses, pushing through the pale green woodlands onto the plains which rolled away before them to the foot of the mountains. They headed for the cliff pueblo – if Raven had been there, there would be a trail. Francis Meavy located the concealed path down from the canyon rim. As Patrick Monaghan rounded the last kink in the track, Francis Meavy halted ahead of him. He dismounted on the ledge and crept forward, scouring the ground.

Coyote curled himself up in a shadowed corner of the pueblo. He watched them find the tracks: Spider's, the mountain lion's, and his own. The boot prints and blood in the brush told the story. They searched the pueblo. The smell of fire on the rock lingered and blood clotting the sand revealed that Raven was here only two days before. Dusk leached the colour from the canyon.

'He was here. He cooked and was injured in a struggle with a cougar. His horse fell but he rode out.' Francis Meavy looked across the gulf to the darkening sky. 'We'll leave at dawn. There is blood but I don't know how badly he was hurt.'

They camped as Raven had camped, making fire on the rooftop. When they had eaten, and fed and watered the horses, they sat. Francis Meavy stared into the flames, becoming aware that his friend watched him.

'I'm sorry about Bright Flower, Frankie, I –'

He looked away, back at the embers. When he spoke, his voice failed to a whisper. 'She was alone, Patrick. I let her die alone. And now Raven.'

Coyote felt the gnawing of the man's guilt. It was older than Bright Flower's death, older than his father's death, older than Francis Meavy himself. He felt the bottomless blackness of his loss. He puzzled at the man's blindness, his inability to see the past in his own life, trapped in the belief that he alone was the craftsman of his present suffering.

'We will find your son. That's why I'm here.'

'They'll be hunting us, Patrick. I hope you don't live to regret what you've done.'

The priest picked up a stick and prodded the embers. They spat sparks at the undercliff. 'You know, I've been a priest a long time now. Far longer than I was a soldier. When it comes down to it, it's about doing what's right.'

'I hope you still feel you've done that. We owe you –'

'Ach, will you stop with the thanking? Giving that whoreson guard communion with his desk was reward enough.'

Coyote observed them until the darkness shrouded everything and they finally laid themselves down, two black shapes asleep on the rock.

Raven

Early Winter 1863 – Argento

We trot north along the tree line by the water's edge.
It's just cold enough for our breath to steam. The path
of the river takes us closer to the town. The question
is whether or not to buy powder. If I do, I'll regain the
use of the rifle, but I will be seen. I feel my rough chin
and jaw with the back of my hand and scratch my beard.
I catch my reflection in the water. Unshaven, I look like
a man ten years older. I could get a hot meal for myself
and good feed for Spider while I eat it. I peel away from
the river, past pools of rust red water.

Argento's Main Street is ten paces broad. The
buildings are painted pastel colours, shingle above
brick walls with timber verandas. The ground hasn't
yet frozen for the winter and the carriageway is a
brown blur. The enticing smell of meat cooking is
overwhelmed by the stink of shit and mud. Over to the
right, dark smoke glows with sparks as it rises. The clang
clang of the forge echoes in from a side street, then
the whoosh of the bellows chases it up the mountain.
There's a sign for the livery out front. All part of the
same establishment. To the left, the largest building in
the town is the noisiest.

A tall man in a clean, dark coat, his face shadowed
by his hat, pushes the door open, loosing into the street
the sound of a piano and a tangle of men's voices. I ride
up to the stables, remove my headband from under

Father's slouch hat and tuck it into the saddle. A young man in a leather apron comes out carrying a wooden box as long his forearms. He stops, evaluating me from boots to head.

'Anything I can help you with?' The rhythm of his speech is strange, symmetrical.

I should speak like Father speaks to men in Corazon. 'Yes. Please feed and water my horse while I attend to my business.'

He smiles. 'That's what we're here for. How long will you be?'

'The time to eat and buy powder.'

'You been to Argento before?'

I shake my head.

'Well then. That over there is the store. You get your powder there. Then there are three choices for eating but a couple of them are no choices at all, so if you have the money, I'd take myself to the Argento Hotel.'

I thank him and nod at the horse. 'I don't shoe him.'

The young man has his back turned, positioning the box at the front of the building. He calls over his shoulder, 'I saw that.'

I'm glad of Father's boots as I cross this street. I stamp the muck off on the pine steps of the store and walk in. The storekeeper is greying with a rough beard and a kink to his back.

'Good morning. What are we getting for you?' His voice is jaunty, but his eyes are hollow.

I take the opportunity to lay a false trail. 'Powder and dry provisions. I've got a long ride south.'

'You a trader, or a trapper maybe?'

'Trader.'

He nods. 'Well, I'm going to ask you how you will be paying for your goods today.' I untie the pouch and roll a lump of silver into my hand, taking it between finger and thumb and holding it up for him to see. He nods and chuckles, 'Wouldn't be much of a silver town store if I didn't take silver now, would it? You got a horn for the powder?'

'No. I lost it. I need one, and a canteen.'

'We can do that for you. You staying in town?'

'No. Just stopping then heading out.'

'Well, if you're going to eat, eat at Mr Knox's place. The others will only do you if you're drunk beyond seeing.'

Abe Knox's place. I breathe deep before responding. 'Where is it?'

'The Argento Hotel, right next door. Should call it Maggie's place since she runs it now, but it belongs to Knox like the mine and plenty else besides round here.'

I pay for the goods and arrange to collect them after eating. Stabbing pain in my leg wound. I limp along the boardwalk to the hotel, push open the door and am hit by heat, noise and the odour of liquor, food, and unwashed men. Some are dressed like me, buckskins or rough fur. There's a space there at the polished counter. I walk over to it. The woman behind the bar wears a dark red dress. She turns towards the room. I remember her smile and the sadness I felt in her as a boy in Corazon. Maggie.

'Welcome to the Argento Hotel, what can we get for you?' She only glances at me and now examines the countertop as she polishes it with a check cloth that clashes with her dress. I study her face, the lines from her nose to her lips and the downturn at the corners of her mouth. She's too thin. I remember the softness in Father's voice when he spoke to her. My silence betrays me. She looks up and I see the seed of recognition struggling for light.

'Hot food, please.' I look down again, hoping the brim of my hat will stem her recall.

'Meavy, Francis Meavy, are you? You can't be. You must be the son. You are the picture of your father, boy. Remember me? From when your father brought you into Corazon?' I nod, look up. She seems younger, invigorated by memory. 'So, what brings you up here to Argento? Are you alone?'

I decide I will trust her. 'I need to find Abe Knox.'

Her smile evaporates. 'Why would you be looking for him?'

'I need his help. Father told me he would be up here. He said Abe Knox would –'

'He's not here. You best eat and head back south. You wasted your journey. I'll stand you a plate of mutton and bread. I'm sorry for your trouble.'

'The shopkeeper told me Knox was here until a week ago, can you tell me where he is now?'

'No. I can't. He owns this place and the mine just out of town, and he comes and goes. I'll fetch you that food.' She disappears into the kitchen.

I turn to face the room. Against the far window, overlooking the street, a group of five men have finished eating and are drinking and smoking. Among them the tall man I saw earlier. The others with him are also clean, expensively dressed. Between them and the next group are three or four unoccupied tables, then a cluster around which ten or so men drink and banter, their clothes rough and worn, their faces dirty. As they joke with each other they cuss loudly. Maggie's voice behind me breaks the spell.

'Mining foremen. This is a silver town. They are noisy and none too clean, but they don't make trouble if I tell them not to and they spend hard. Better than the higher-class patrons.' She nods towards the table by the window. 'Here's your mutton. Take a seat.'

I take the plate and start into the room to sit between the two groups – a man at ease with nothing to hide. I want to eat alone, get whatever information I can about Knox from Maggie, pay her and leave. The piano starts up. A girl is playing over by the door, her back straight, tense in concentration. She's Ute, you can tell at a glance. I pass closer to the miners, and my throat rises at the stink of their bodies and poor tobacco smoke like smouldering dung. I keep going to the other side of the table and sit by the window facing the bar, showing my back to no one, but solitary. The miners make me feel less conspicuous in my worn buckskins.

From the group to my left drifts the rich waft of whiskey and expensive cigars. I eat with my hat on, my head tipped forward. I feel eyes on me and look up. A man with a red stain across his face and a balloon nose looks away. As I swallow chunks of mutton and bread hot with gravy, the warmth of it creeps into my muscles. I have been so cold, so hungry. I remember

Spider, finish up, and take my plate to the bar where Maggie smiles at my manners and thanks me. I take out my silver pouch. She shakes her head.

'It's my pleasure to feed Francis Meavy's boy.'

'Thank you. My father said there's a hotel in Nebraska territory which Abe Knox –'

'You're wrong. Forget about Knox.'

I smile at her, remembering the crush I had on her as a boy, broad and clean like the plateau. 'Thanks again.' I touch my hat as Father did when we went to Corazon and turn to leave.

She calls after me. 'Meavy.' I turn at Father's name, my name. 'He is. In Nebraska. The Stag Hotel in Saratoga Hot Springs. Be careful.' The tall man in dark clothes comes to the bar. She turns to him.

I leave, the Ute girl staring.

I pick up my supplies and cross the street to the stables, walking round the side to the covered barn. I glimpse Spider through the gaps in the planking and my chest aches with recollection. The gift of the foal to me by Grandfather and Grandmother. The days and years of training. The power of the horse that day on the plateau when we heard the eagle above and saw the Anaii far below. When Mother died. Her voice, the smell of her hair. The inside of the hogan when I was small. The taste of dried peaches. The warmth of the blankets and furs.

'He's fed and watered.' The stable hand is walking towards me, heavy buckets stretching his arms, 'But he's not right. He was shaking before. I checked his legs, they're sound, but that cut on his head is warm.

You want to watch that. We have the room to rest him overnight, if you –'

'No. We keep going.' I pay and saddle Spider up. He wickers, smelling the hard feed from the store.

We ride out of Argento. White wisps drift across the mountaintops, unkempt against the pale blue sky. At the end of Main Street, the track leads to the foot of the mountain then curls north around it, taking us out of view of the town. Above us the sheer face reminds me of the canyon wall. I kick Spider into a trot.

The path climbs, taking us upwards once more to narrow waterfalls crashing down slick black teeth of rock. The mountainsides blaze apricot with the turned aspen, and folds of green velvet stretch away ahead of us. On the lower slopes, great slabs of rock jut like piles of discarded Bibles, sheltering the racing river below. We crest the ridge, the path tacks down the far side, so steep that we ride once more among the treetops. The river cuts a broad trench along the valley and the milling of it echoes off the mountains. Ahead the land stretches into broad flat pasture beyond which the ridges running parallel relent, losing height towards the horizon. By the time we reach the valley floor and have followed the stony beaches of the tree line for a while, the day is fading. Coming down the mountainside I see a rock slab overhanging a hollow in the slope opposite. I push Spider back uphill towards it.

As night falls so does the temperature. We are lower here than before and sheltered, but the autumn is yielding fast. The chill is coming in. We'll need a fire. I drag dry wood inside from the near slope, piling it to waist height. At the far end of the cave the ceiling is blackened at the gap between the overhang and the lip of rock beneath. It forms an underbite, venting four or five paces above. I light the fire there and haul the soft branches across. The shadows jump and fall against the back wall and the ceiling. It's like the fire which Father, Grandfather and I made at the Sacred Mountain. I asked Grandfather who else knew about the place.

'Only us, Raven.'

A noise. Spider whickers at it. The echo reverberates back at me from the walls.

'Us, Raven. Us, Raven.'

Coyote

He watched Willow Tree lost in her thoughts. She guessed there must be a thousand of them with their sheep, goats, and horses. None of them her daughter. Would Bright Flower's spirit stay in Los Huertos or come north with them? Her grief could wait. She knew that they must bring their people to safety, that they must remain strong and appear certain of what they were doing. Her resolve was unbending, but still she felt tears on her face. She wiped them, looking instead at the tide of villagers flowing towards the western mouth of Los Huertos along the path of the wash.

They formed into working parties. Mounted men kept the herds of ponies to one side of the mass of people, women and children chivvied the goats and sheep. Horses dragged travois carrying baskets, blankets, and the old. Humans and animals moved as one, with none wishing to fall behind or become separated in the night. They travelled without speaking, voices rising only to shepherd the stock. For this, Willow Tree was grateful. She rode with Hawk at the head of the column. He had made it clear that the first night of travel, fresh and with the best of the moonlight, was their opportunity to cover the ground fast. The people of the canyon pushed on.

At the end of Los Huertos, where the rock walls petered down to meet the plateau and the wash pooled before flowing south, they turned north. Heading out into the desert night, many looked back over their shoulders. It was colder here but the work of travelling warmed them, and the moon was so full and bright they could see better than at dusk.

Coyote breathed deep their prayers, their fear and hope. They had never had to leave their canyon home, but some among them recalled that they had not always farmed Los Huertos and the Akote lands, that their ancestors, wanderers, had settled the place and long before that, the world had begun with the Holy Ones emerging from their travels in the darkness. He blew on these memories, making them glow, making them warm the men and women who held them. They would need that warmth for what was to come.

They headed for The Horseshoe, a tall outcrop of rock half a day's ride to the north. A place sometimes used for corralling horses when large herds were moved. They reached it before dawn, then made camp and started short-lived fires from brushwood to keep them warm until daylight. Smoke in the daytime sky would have betrayed them. Hawk sent men out to conceal themselves among the higher rocks as sentries to warn of any threat from the desert. The people ate, speaking low, smiling slight smiles at reaching their first goal. They took turns to rest and tend the animals, warming themselves on the embers of the fires peppering the camp, keeping close to each other as day broke.

'Come walk with me, Hawk,' Willow Tree said, and they went among their people, stopping to speak with the elderly. At last, when they returned to their possessions, they sat down to eat. 'What do you think, Husband? Is it good so far?' He scanned the camp. She knew what he was thinking, 'You're wondering who it is.'

'We will not know until they show themselves. We have mounted warriors concealed in every direction as we travel. We will know if anyone leaves the drive.'

'Why would they leave? They do not yet know where we are going.'

He continued to survey the sea of people. 'They are most likely to leave once we have arrived, so they know where to lead our enemies.'

'If they succeed?'

'We cannot let them.'

She thought for a moment. 'A few stayed in Los Huertos, perhaps he is in the canyon?'

'Do you believe that?'

Now she looked out over the camp. 'No.'

Coyote knew what would become of the traitor, and the parts he and Hawk would play.

In silence they ate piñon nuts, dried meat, and peaches. Hawk spoke with the sentries, returning late in the morning. He sat on the ground next to Willow Tree and wrapped himself in his buffalo skin, bolstered by the packs taken from their resting horses.

Willow Tree noticed the silver hair across his face rising and falling with his breath. There was a time when he would not have even considered sleeping in such a situation, she thought, brushing the strand away with her fingertips. When they were younger, when Bright Flower was a child. She watched the hair settle behind his ear and felt her tears come once more. She jumped when she saw his eyes were open, watching her. He cupped her cheek in the palm of his hand. She saw the tears in his wrinkles.

Raven

Early Winter 1863 — Northwest of Argento

I awaken in the firelight, shouting and sweating, Father's bayonet in my hand. My mind and body full of the memory of the dream – the great vulture coming out of the sun, snapping its wings to glide, swooping into the canyon to snatch Pale Horse in the talons of one foot and Mother in the other.

My chest rises and falls with deep breaths as I kneel. The morning is pushing through the gap in the rock and sparks off the frost on its rim. I am looking through a perfect web linking the slab overhead to the basin of rock beneath us. Mountain sunlight makes it glow silver white. Grandfather taught me: 'Whichever thread you touch, it is felt in every strand.' I remember why I am here, the desperate need to get going.

Spider lies on his flank. The fire has burned low but the embers glow and the heat of its prime still lingers in the rock. I whisper his name. He rocks himself over, stands and shakes. I feel his back and legs for soreness. They are sound but the head wound is warm to the touch. I feed and water him, secure the packs onto the horse's back before leading him out onto the slope.

To the north, the mountains soften either side of the valley like a dropped blanket. Below them a broken line of willow shows the path of the river where the grass is lush. As the slope levels out, I remount. It is greener here than anywhere I have seen. The going is flat. I canter Spider in long stretches, rest him in walk then canter again. The mountains flanking the valley subside into rocky hills and, before dusk, I see that ahead they disappear altogether, revealing a plain undulating to the horizon.

To the west, the last thicket of trees visible for miles. It is warmer here than on the slopes, but there will be a frost overnight. We have travelled far today, but even so, Spider is too weary. We camp here among the trees where the riverbank has been swept away, leaving a scooped shelter covered by fallen willow. I untack the horse and leave him loose to drink from the river and snip the fat grass. I set a fire but won't light it until it's safer, after dark. The only souls I've seen all day were a party of ten or twelve Ute cresting the hills to the east. We stayed hidden until they disappeared over the ridge. The goat meat tastes smoky, like home. It makes me sleepy.

I come to in shock, arms pumping, legs tightening together. Father was standing in the open, loading his rifle. The great vulture swept down upon him. Grandfather and I galloped after, urging our horses up the talus just as the vulture disappeared over the rim.

The shelter is cold, but I'm wet with sweat. I toss more wood onto the fire. It takes and the flames warm me. I wrap the buffalo skin around myself and lie back down.

Out onto the plain at first light. We are in the open and visible. I check the horizon framed with low hills, a good day's ride off. Spider is warm now. I take him into a steady canter. The ground is covered in short, rough grass and rolls into the distance like a cloth drying in the wind. I alternate the paces of the horse, resting him in fast walk, then trotting and cantering once more. Mid-morning, we stop at a stream cut into the earth. I remove my boots and stand on Spider's back, curving my soles to his contours. I scan from horizon to horizon, looking for signs of people or herds.

Away to the northeast a heavy wagon takes a course which will cross ours. A wagon. I remember the soldiers emerging from the third wagon at the Silver River, the sounds of hooves on rock and splashing water as Cross and his men cut us off through the ford. If Arrowhead had not shielded me, who would now be seeking Abe Knox? No one. It would be too late, as I was too late to save Mother. I start to shake, my whole body shuddering against my will. I clench my fists and jaw as I lose balance. Favouring my injured leg, I jump to the ground. Although it's not winter-hard, the impact jars up my spine. I pull my boots back on, hands still trembling, and remount.

The day started ice blue and clear of clouds, but closer to the hills the sky darkens. To the east, the mountains rise again, lower than before but with steeper slopes. Mid-afternoon and the greyness has summoned the cold. The icy rain is spitting on my face. We near the point where our trail crosses the wagon's, the plain rises to a low ridge. Smoke hangs in the air at the far side. I think of the smoke and wreckage in the canyon when I found Pale Horse dying, when he told me Mother was gone. Dismount now. My chest rises and falls, my breathing noisy. I bunch my fists again and bite my jaw tight to stifle the howl that will betray us.

The smell of cooking. I'm hungry. I creep up the ridge on my belly as the first blast of thunder shakes the earth and the sky. The rain falls in silver shafts. I take off my hat to look over the edge. The ground drops away, flattening out before the river cuts through it. Where it is level a timber stockade stands peopled with Ute, white men and women in heavy skirts and rough bonnets. The wagon from the plain is being laden with bales of fur and there are several similar around the trading post. As the rain sweeps across the place, the man loading the wagon ducks under its high belly. Others pull clothing over their heads and run for cover.

Only a few are left at their work, showing their contempt for discomfort.

I return to Spider, my boots sliding on the slope slick with rainfall too heavy to be absorbed by the earth. We head due east, under the cover of the ridge. Constant drips fall from the brim of my hat onto Spider's withers. Everything is a blur of wind and rain but there are trees in the distance, far enough away from the trading post. It'll be worth taking a chance and making a fire to get us warm.

Coyote

He watched the hundred cavalry and ten Anaii guides strike out from Corazon in the chill dawn. They rode in formation to the Akote settlement at Hole Rock. Their horses stamping and fidgeting.

Cross shouted the decree from his saddle, 'As a consequence of the continued raiding of livestock among neighbouring tribes and New Mexicans, in contravention of the treaty of Corazon, by order of the Governor of the territory and its military commander, all Akote – together with their belongings – are to report to the camp northwest of Corazon. There they will be processed and relocated to a place of settlement at a location to the southeast where they will reside permanently under the supervision of the authorities to ensure no further violent incursions against neighbouring inhabitants. All land currently occupied will revert to the use and ownership of the government and any, and all, livestock and possessions discovered on it after the date of convocation will be confiscated. Any Akote found still in occupation will be deemed hostile and be subject to summary capital punishment by the authorities in whatever circumstances they are found.'

The cavalry and their scouts crossed the plateau from settlement to settlement with the proclamation. After a week they reached the Great Harvest Canyon. They came from the east and delivered the decree to the first two villages. News from the Silver River and Los Huertos had travelled, and the Akote of the Great Canyon watched impassive as the Anaii One Eye translated the soldier's words.

Three days more and they reached the eastern end of Los Huertos. A few goats and sheep wandered unattended. Hogans stood smokeless. The aspen shook in the icy wind, whispering secrets left behind. They rode deep into the canyon. Each settlement was deserted, but for a few stragglers; old men and women, huddled on ledges in the canyon wall or peering from behind trees.

Opposite Bear Rock, One Eye dismounted. He crossed the silt to Shadow Bloom's hogan and threw back the blanket over the doorway. He emerged after a moment with a leather pouch from which he pulled a piece of paper. He examined it, crushed it in his hand and tossed it aside. He remounted. All hundred and ten horsemen turned east, pushing cavalry mounts and Akote ponies into a fast trot.

As dusk came, they neared the end of the canyon. A rider galloped towards them from the southern plateau. His Anaii pony kicked up the earth as he urged it on. Cross held up his hand, halting the column. The messenger pulled his horse up before One Eye.

'Meavy has escaped from Corazon with the priest Monaghan. They have gone north.'

Raven

We reach the line of aspen and willow, but the weather has set in. We're soaked and cold to the bone. I turn Spider towards the cover but pull up short. A hundred paces ahead, thick smoke from a new, damp fire climbs above the tops of the trees. I rein Spider back east. Ahead the turf gives way to rock and sand dunes with scattered brush and clumps. The desert stretches away into the rain. It's endless. As we stand here the cold leaches the life from us.

I press on, I see Father in my mind, the boots and rifle butts of the cavalrymen who hold him. Why didn't he make a stand there on the Silver River? Why didn't we fight? I know the answers even as I ask the questions. Time. He was buying time for the Akote, for us.

I heel Spider into a trot. We ride through the downpour for hours, taking a line between the dunes to avoid the effort of climbing. We cross from one small valley to the next. Now the dunes are yielding to broad pastures fertile enough to grow anything and fatten stock. Dusk is chasing away the daylight. The rain finally stops. Fighting a passage through a thicket, I bring Spider into a clearing then close up the path behind us, knitting the branches back together. The best shelter I can find is a damp spot under a bush which might spare me from the frost. From the hearts of fallen trees I lever rotten wood with the bayonet, using the powder from Argento to start the fire. It takes enough to get some heat back into my muscles. My spine aches from the hours of hunching against the wet and the cold. I sit on a fallen tree, my back to the struggling fire to ease it enough to sleep.

*

I am hunched over, chilled through and soaking. Spider stands two paces away, shaking. It's not yet dawn. In the struggle between the darkness and daylight, the air is like soot. My heart is still drumming. I check Spider's legs and back. They're wet and cold to the touch, but his wound is warm. For the moment, he's keeping the fever at bay. This journey to save Father could take his life. It could take mine, then Father will die too. What if I don't find Abe Knox? What if he can't help, or it's too late? Alone. Father would die alone. And Grandmother, it would be too much, even for her. I'll find Abe Knox. I will free Father and I will find the raiders, the men who killed Mother. And then. My mind finds peace. It is cold and hard and still. I will do what needs to be done, and to do that I will ensure my own survival.

It is barely light when we turn northeast out of the thicket. Ahead, mountains drop into a lake framed with willow and gold aspen. The sky is clear, and the edge of the lake is in a patch of sunshine. Spider needs water. My clothes are still damp. Yellow-bellied marmots sprawl on an outcrop, sunbathing. They scatter at our approach. The rock is warm. I cast a blanket onto it and stretch out.

Coyote

He willed them to dismount as they crested the high ridge. They did so. The slope below was steep and stretched hundreds of paces to the tree line. Francis Meavy and Patrick Monaghan led their horses across the uppermost edge and saw the drag marks long and straight. Far below, a small brown object trailed a strap. They tacked down the mountainside on foot. Francis Meavy left his horse with his friend and scrambled across the seam to Raven's powder horn. With his eyes, he traced the marks down the slope to the bloodied boulder and the tracks just below, where Raven led Spider in hand following their fall. He motioned Patrick Monaghan to lead the horses down.

The priest brought them across the slope. 'What is it?'

He showed the powder horn. 'There is blood, but here –' he pointed at the tracks, 'They are both walking.'

They found the shelter in the trees and pushed on through the forest. At night they kept watch in shifts. The next day was colder. Just after dawn they rode out of a hollow into a clearing. Three Ute warriors were crossing it on horseback. They saw Patrick Monaghan first, whooped and urged their horses towards him. Francis Meavy rode out from the trees, pistol in hand. The Ute turned and kicked on to the southeast. Later, they thundered past a pool of rusty water. Its surface danced with the beat of the hooves. They pulled up in the tree line outside Argento.

'What do you think?' Monaghan nodded towards the town, 'Can we risk it, or shall I leave you here and go in?'

Francis Meavy stared at the buildings, then turned to face his friend. 'No. We'll go in together.'

They trotted their horses side by side across the meadow. Despite the chill of the air, the sun had been warming their backs through their coats. Now, as they reached Main Street, clouds feathered the mountaintop, plunging them into cold shadow. They slowed to a walk through the stiffening mud and halted at the livery. Francis Meavy greeted the stable hand.

'Feed and water please, we won't be long. An hour or so at most.' He surveyed the street as he spoke, 'I'm guessing provisions from the store opposite?'

The young man sighed. 'Wish I had a penny for every time I've sent a customer over there.'

Patrick Monaghan laughed. 'You get a lot of visitors?'

'We do that. Argento's a mining town and they're always coming and going. Then there's those just passing through needing provisions and maybe some company before they head into the mountains or out onto the plains. This is the last chance for those this side of the ridge.'

They dismounted. The young man stepped forward and untied the cinch of Patrick Monaghan's saddle, lifting it onto the wooden rail. The stirrup snagged. The priest leant over and tugged it free.

'Is that right? Well, maybe you saw a young man come through here. My height, green eyes, and dark hair?'

'There was a fellow like that two days ago. Quiet. Looked like he might have ridden all the way from Old Mexico.' He turned to Francis Meavy. 'He looked like you.'

'Was he injured?'

'Don't think so, just used up. Must have had a fall though, his horse had a cut on the head. It was warm too. I told him to take care it didn't get a fever. Now I come to think of it, he limped a little.'

Patrick Monaghan handed a coin to the boy. 'That's for you. I'll settle for the horses later.' They crossed the street, Francis Meavy's boots growing heavy as the mud and filth clumped to them.

'You take the door. I'll question the storekeeper.'

A bearded man in furs and heavy boots left the store. He had two packages of a sack-like bag slung over his shoulder. The storekeeper watched him leave then greeted Francis Meavy as he closed on the counter, heels banging through the wooden floor with each stride. The old man scratched his patchy chin.

'What can we help you with?'

'Dry provisions. Do you have powder?'

'Of course, you got a horn you want me to fill?'

'Do you sell them?'

'I do but I'm out. Just sold the last a day or two ago.'

'I guess this being a silver town, the miners clean you out?'

'They do, they do, but this wasn't a miner, he was just passing through, some kind of trader.'

'Did he look Akote?'

The storekeeper hesitated. 'I'm not looking for trouble and I don't go telling strangers about my customers and their purchases.'

The storekeeper flinched as Francis Meavy reached for his belt. He pulled out a coin and slapped it on the counter. 'Was he Akote?'

'No, he was a white man with boots and a hat.'

'Boots and a hat don't make a white man.'

'No but he spoke English like you and me and he had green eyes.' The man's voice trailed off as he registered Francis Meavy's eyes.

'What did you sell him?'

'Powder, a horn, supplies for his journey. He said he had a long way to go, heading south.' Francis Meavy laughed. The storekeeper kept talking. 'I sent him next door for food. He looked like he needed it. His pants were ripped and bloodied.'

'Injured?"

'I think so. Is he wanted? I didn't know he's wanted. I don't help outlaws, it was a genuine mistake, I –' He paused, 'I would have helped him if I'd known.' His voice kicked up at the end, questioning.

'No, he's not wanted. I'm just trying to find him that's all.' The old man wrung his hands, eyes fidgeting. Francis Meavy knew he had something to hide but unless it concerned Raven, he wasn't interested. 'You sent him next door you say?'

'Yes, to Maggie's at the hotel.'

'Maggie?'

'Yes,' he blathered. 'She runs the place for Abraham Knox.'

*

Francis Meavy was behind Patrick Monaghan as he pushed through the door into the fug of the hotel barroom. Six or seven men, boots scuffed and old, shirts beyond scrubbing, sat round a table in the middle of the room smoking and drinking from small glasses. Three clean, well-dressed men in long jackets stood at the bar facing the door. A woman with red hair, her elbow on the mahogany, made conversation. They smiled and laughed, then their expressions changed.

She turned to look. Recognising her, Francis Meavy turned away, pulled his hat low and joined an old man in a top hat, asleep at a table between the counter and the piano. Patrick Monaghan touched the brim of his hat as Maggie gazed across. She nodded, said a word to one of the patrons then moved down the counter towards the newcomer.

The priest put one boot on the brass foot rail, his hat on the bar, mopped his pate with a kerchief and smiled at Maggie. 'A tot of whiskey please, ma'am.'

'Father Monaghan, what brings you to Argento?'

'Well, that would be Maggie's famous hospitality.'

She laughed. 'And how far has my fame spread that you've come all this way?'

He looked at his boots, then back at her. 'Well, at least as far as the stables across the street.' She laughed again and pulled a bottle from beneath the counter. He raised his glass to her. 'We miss you in Corazon, Maggie. I'm looking for a friend. I know he passed through a few days ago.'

Her face hardened. 'This is a long way from anywhere to be looking for a friend. Is he in trouble?'

Coyote felt Francis Meavy's' frustration, the impulse to jump up, to implore her, to make her know something, for her to say that Raven was here, safe. He forced himself to sit motionless.

'Not yet. We want to find him before it goes that way. It's Francis Meavy's boy. Perhaps you remember him, tall, dark hair, green eyes.'

'Did you ask at the livery?'

'I did. He said he sent him here for food.'

Maggie put her hands on her hips, her eyelids halfway closed. 'Well, if you asked in there, why do you need to ask here?'

He shrugged and looked around the room. 'Did he say where he was headed?' She turned to go. His hand shot out, gripping her forearm. 'Maggie, why won't you help? It'd be better for him if you tell me. Did he say where he's going?'

She glowered at him. 'Yeah, he did. He said he was heading west to California to find a piece of land and start a family.'

He sighed and nodded, looking around the room once more, then released her arm and took a coin from his pocket. 'For the whiskey.'

'I don't want your money.' She bustled away from him.

He put the coin down, paused, lifted the empty glass, and stuck his tongue into the bottom of it before walking past Francis Meavy. The Ute girl had started playing. He took out another coin and placed it on top of the piano.

The girl spoke to him, her fingers still dancing. 'He was here.'

'Who, child?'

'The man you seek. The white man who is Akote, who looks like your friend,' she nodded towards Francis Meavy.

He looked up from the table. 'You know where he went?'

'He turned north, round the mountain.' Patrick Monaghan took another coin from his pocket. She held out her hand. He put it in her palm. She continued at the keys as before. Francis Meavy rose and turned to go after Maggie. Patrick Monaghan put a hand on his chest.

'There's no time, Frankie.'

Raven

The sound of my own voice echoes back to me across the lake from the far mountain. 'Mother.'

I don't know how long I've slept but my clothes are almost dry, and the day is warmer. I call Spider to me. My voice rasps in my throat. He seems stronger for the rest. We make northeast. Rivers split slabs of rock the colour of seasoned oak, jutting blocks suspended above the current. More mountainsides plunge sheer into the water. We climb into the pine forests, rising and falling with the slopes in the clean sharp air. The scent and the sunlight buoy me. There is a peacefulness in travelling beneath the protection of the canopy, tiny and invisible. We are not alone here. I saw freshly skinned beaver carcasses along the river. Scat and tracks show that we share these mountains with wolf, bear, and caribou. Last night the bugling of elk blared through the forest.

It is our second day in the pines. I take down a young deer with my bow. I cook it over a fire, taking the entrails far from the camp to draw away bears. I sleep. The meat, the air, and the stillness of the forest calming me and Spider. At dawn we push on as fast as the terrain and Spider's stamina allow. Do not risk lameness, Grandfather always says. My spirit aches for Mother, gone; for Father, imprisoned. My mind is calmed by the rhythm of Spider's footfall, the creaking of the leather, the sound of my breath in my ears.

The mountains level out, the forest thins. Rushes betray the paths of hidden watercourses. We climb an outcrop whose summit is two parallel obelisks shaped like the head of a rabbit. I remember the cottontails on the plateau, the fractured landscape where I brought down the stag with the rifle, my shot not clean. I have one shot now.

Coyote

He crossed their path to warn them. Francis Meavy reined in. Patrick Monaghan did the same. 'What's wrong, Frankie?'

'Coyote'

'What about it?'

'It cut across ahead of us. The Akote believe that to cross the path of a Coyote brings ill fortune.'

He glanced up at the charcoal clouds squatting beneath a low sky. It had rained overnight and frozen. The ground lay slippery under the surface. Their horses stumbled up to the ridge. Shivering, they looked down on the trading post, built around a lumber stockade, wagons piled high with pelt bales. The smell of cooking meat gusted in then dropped. As they walked their horses down towards the buildings, women in heavy skirts and tight bonnets looked up and scuttled away. The closer they came, the faster the townsfolk disappeared. The threat pressed in on them, colder and more uncomfortable than the freezing dampness of their clothes.

They halted outside the livery. Francis Meavy dismounted. An old man inside scooped feed from a sack into a bucket. He stopped, looked briefly at the stranger, then scowled across the expanse beyond him. The animals jumped as the shot echoed back-and-forth, then Meavy's mount barged sideways into him as Patrick Monaghan's horse fell on its side. The priest bellowed as the weight of it slammed him into the ground, pinning his leg.

Francis Meavy slapped the rump of his horse. It cantered off. He crouched down by Monaghan, pistol drawn, looking for the smoke. It billowed from a window opposite. He levelled his gun. Four more rounds buried themselves in the dead animal. The Priest's face was purple with the struggle to free his limb.

'Get under cover,' he gasped, then bucked and yelled as a shot glanced off his collarbone. Meavy dropped the gun and stood with his arms outstretched to the sides. The ground shook as thunder announced the rain.

'On your knees,' a voice from the livery ordered him. He lowered himself. 'You have lived a lifetime among the Akote, but your powers of observation remain those of the white man.' One Eye stepped into the rain. The end of his cigar hissed. 'You are mine to do with as I wish.'

Nine more appeared from behind cover. They drifted in, grinning. Patrick Monaghan bled into the dirt. The raiders lifted the horse to free him. He cursed as he put weight on his leg to stand.

'This man has risked everything to help you.' One Eye nodded appreciation. 'He is your brother.'

Meavy cut him off. 'It's me you want. Leave him, he's already injured.'

'He is. We must put an end to his suffering.'

Coyote watched from the ridge. The Anaii held Francis Meavy and started to bind Patrick Monaghan's arms behind his back. The rain ran over his face, so he had to blink it out of his eyes. His hat lay in the mud. One Eye bent to pick it up. His men brought forward two horses from the livery and tied the other end of the rope to one of them.

The horse shied as Meavy started to shout, 'No, NO!'

One Eye whipped its haunch with the hat, and it bolted. One of the others jumped on to the second pony and galloped after Patrick Monaghan as he was dragged, spinning one way then the other. Meavy slipped the grip of the man on his right, head-butted him, twisted left, then stopped, feeling the hard muzzle of a pistol in the back of his neck as the hammer clicked its death warning. The rider drove the loose horse out towards the river before herding it in a wide arc back to the livery.

Francis Meavy stared down into his friend's ruined face. Blood ran from the corner of his mouth. His eyes flickered open, he focused on One Eye and spat, choking on it. One Eye straddled him, lifting his head from beneath so the throat was bare. He unsheathed his knife and struck. Meavy closed his eyes. This was his fault. Patrick Monaghan died on his account, as had Bright Flower and Pale Horse. As would Raven.

One Eye turned to him. 'Now we go north to find your son.'

Raven

Winter 1863 — The Plains

The cold pinches me awake. The sky breaks blue far across the plains but still there is too much light. I peer out from the cave; the landscape is covered in snow. A few embers glow in the fire, and I add an armful of twigs for quick heat before checking Spider's legs. There's scabbing from brush scratches but they are sound. I turn to face the blaze before loading the packs and saddle onto the horse.

On foot, I lead him out of the cave and down the steeper rocks before remounting. The plain billows white towards the mountains on the horizon. We walk. Spider stumbles often, recovering less quickly each time. God be with us. May the blessings of the Holy Ones be with us. A great black cloud of buffalo thunders away to the northwest, shaking the ground. I trot Spider for hours, trying to reach shelter. The hard ride drives off the morning's cold but as the day wears on, Spider misjudges brush and rock, striking his hooves and tripping, his head sinking lower. My thoughts are elsewhere. I run through what I will say to Abe Knox when I find him. A wave of sickness rises in me.

Movement ahead catches my eye, bringing me back into the landscape. I slip Father's rifle from Spider's side. My fingers are stiff. The horse carries me forward. As we draw closer, I see the stripped corpse of a buffalo calf, its underbelly gaping raw red against the melting snow. Wolves, more skin and bone than muscle, tear at the few remaining scraps. I cock the lock and slip the cap onto the hammer, steering Spider wide of the pack with my legs. As we draw level, thirty paces east, the alpha stops ripping and raises its bloodied muzzle, yellow eyes following the horse. They sniff the air. Some break north, some south, always focused on Spider. I know what they plan. I take aim at the leader of the first pack and fire. The report of the rifle is followed by the dull whipping sound of the round piercing muscle. The wolf somersaults, yelping and thrashing. Smoke engulfs me for a second before being swept away by the wind. The sound of the shot reaches the second pack, and they jump backwards. Spider walks on. I turn to see whether they will follow at a distance, but they do not. It is as if Spider has been unaware of them throughout.

Coyote

He watched Hawk as his thoughts unfolded. The Chief stood atop the outcrop looking north. Grasslands for half a day then bare earth and scant sagebrush. He turned to scour the camp beneath. To the south, outriders watched for pursuers and signs of anyone slipping away, emerging from some hiding place in the rock after the Akote had moved on, to head back and guide the enemy to them. He examined the sky. They needed it to be dry for two or three days yet, then he hoped they would be granted a storm. If no storm came, he knew they would have to wait. The snow or the rain and the wind would be needed to hide their tracks in the sand on the final leg.

Willow Tree climbed towards her husband. 'Is it as busy on the inside as it is quiet on the outside?' She pointed at her head then his.

Hawk remembered the first time she asked him this, it was a lifetime ago and the question was so worn and comfortable it had lost its query. 'It will soon be time to pray for bad weather.'

She looked towards the mesas in the distance and smiled at him, her eyes glittering in a lattice of wrinkles. 'We have made such progress.' She brought an arm out from under her blanket to take in the camp with a gesture. 'Who would have thought it with so many of us travelling?'

'We are not there yet, Wife. Without the weather we need we will have to delay.' She reached up and stroked his cheek with her hand, then faced northeast. He allayed her thoughts. 'Raven can move among them invisible. He will find Knox.'

'I dreamt of him last night. He is in danger.'

'We all are.'

'I never met a man who says so much with so few words.'

'Perhaps you were talking.'

'Perhaps. Perhaps I will go and look for him now instead of preparing our food.'

They turned for the camp below.

Raven

Winter 1863 – The banks of the River Platte

The snow comes again. We slog on, the plains either side of us rise up into mountains. I can no longer feel my feet. To the right, a river flows north-south, sunk deep in the bed it has worn through the ages. Willows, aspen and pine make up mixed woodland on short steep slopes which fall to broad banks. The trees could provide shelter and cover on the approach to Saratoga Hot Springs. The wind tugs at the map. I fold it and start to lead Spider down the bank but there are men up ahead. Ragged, dirty, hauling equipment on their shoulders, steam rising from them and their mules. They dump the tools at low cabins that are white with snow. They have good shelter and no doubt food for themselves and their animals.

I take off a glove. My hand is the colour of bone. Spider is trembling, his eyes glazed. What reception will these miners give a lone stranger in their camp? They could take my gun and boots and slaughter Spider for meat. Maybe they work for Abe Knox? The thoughts come slowly. Spider's breath is rapid and shallow. I take up the slack in the reins and turn for the cabins.

Men wearing bone breastplates and elk skins creep from a ditch ahead and surround the camp. The Ute close in on the largest cabin like a drawstring. Dead still. Stay dead still. One of the miners emerges from inside, closing the door behind him. A warrior pounces from the corner of the building and holds a knife to his throat. He raises his hands above his head. Five more men join them, spinning the man and pushing him back towards the door. They carry rifles. They open the door, shove the man through it and barge in behind him.

Through the wind I hear shouting and gunfire. Leave now. Turn back towards the water, lead Spider down the slope to the flat eastern bank. The snow lies knee deep on the level and I fight the resistance of it. The river's frozen over with the flow visible only in gaps in the ice. Steam wheezes from Spider's mouth as he lifts his feet, shoulders and hindquarters straining. Behind us, smoke rises high above the trees.

Ahead, on the riverbank, a Ute camp stands ruined, the tipis torn, half-collapsed, and four or five fires still smoking. The smell of charring hide embitters the air. Blood stains the snow and strakes the skins of the tents where shots have pierced them. No corpses nor wounded to be seen. One tipi stands intact at the centre of the camp, a trickle of smoke curling between its pole tips.

Inside. It's abandoned like the others, but baskets and skins litter the floor and it's warm, thank God and the Spirits. I push back the flap and pull Spider into the space through the gap, closing and tying it behind me. Move the wood from the edge of the fire onto the embers. There are food baskets. Dried fish and buffalo meat, berry and grasshopper cakes, and choke-cherries.

I lift the packs from Spider's back and feed him the last handfuls of corn from Argento, the kernels slipping between my frozen fingers. Spider sighs with the effort of chewing. To survive, he needs rest. I scavenge wood for the fire from around the camp to keep it burning until dawn. Pull off Father's boots and put them near the flames to dry, maybe I'll regain feeling in my feet overnight. Bed down in these soft elk skins.

The spasm in my guts starts to bring me out of my dream. Spider had been outside in the night, ringed by wolves. He bucked and reared, flailing at them with his hooves as they darted in for the attack. He melted into darkness. The wolves shapeshifted into warriors closing in on the tipi while I slept. They took a burning torch and set it alight.

The flames are crackling.

Wings beat close by. I open my eyes as a crow flies back up the chimney. Spider is on his side, his ribs rising and falling, the rhythm fast. My stomach rises. Shrug off the skins and barge through the flap. The glare off the snow in the dawn blinds me in the freezing air. I throw up. Heave after heave, hurling the noise of it across the river and into the trees like a bull moose calling. I spit and look around. Still no one. More snow overnight. Fires which were burning when we got here are now white mounds. To the west, the sky is pink and grey, overhead it breaks blue. Spider's head emerges from the tipi. The edge of his wound is livid.

Trudging the flat bank northwards, I break the ice at the edge for water, wading through fresh drifts.

Around noon, a fox watches from the willows, its fur puffed with the cold. We stare at each other as I move past. Catch sight of Spider over my shoulder, bones lumbering under hide as if to tear it with the effort. We galloped breakneck along the canyon floor,

Spider stretching and pumping his legs as if he would never tire, jumping rocks in our path, weaving left and right around the quicksand, the wind whipping dust between his ears into my face. Other horses stumbled at the blast, but Spider thundered on.

Now he struggles to keep pace with me, breath short, hooves dragging. He stops, rocking, on the point of collapse. We have been walking for hours, entranced, freezing. Lift the packs from his back, grunting with the effort. Drop them into the snow. Untie the cinch and yank the saddle sideways so it slides to the ground under its own weight. It hunkers at my feet like a lost creature, far from home. Unwrap the buffalo hide from my shoulders and tie it round his back, secure only the rifle and bow to it.

Coyote

They were readying themselves. As he had always known they would. He had known from the time he saw the first of them come from the East. From when the first wanderers marvelled at the mountains and the rivers and the buffalo.

Cross stood by the office. The door to the building banged open and Waldron swaggered in. The men at their desks rose to attention. Waldron ignored them, gesturing for Cross to follow him and close the doors.

'Well?' His orderly removed the pale duster from his shoulders. He unholstered his pistol and laid it on the blotter, slumping into the chair.

'Sir, the Akote have been notified that those of them failing to surrender themselves and their livestock by next Monday will be considered hostile and their possessions forfeit.'

Waldron leant back. The chair creaked. 'Note this modification to my orders. Instruct the men that, from Monday, they are to kill all adults of the tribe on sight without question and take prisoner the children along with livestock and possessions of value. These they will bring back to Corazon. The children will then be sold quickly, and the funds remitted to me for onward transfer. Did you meet with the informant on your patrol?'

'No, sir. We penetrated the Canyon – formerly home to Francis Meavy – but it was practically deserted.'

'Deserted?'

'Organised with great care.'

'Where are they? They can't have just disappeared.'

'The tracks show they headed west along the canyon. We believe our informant is with them. He left information for our scouts in his hut to say he will send word.'

'Information? How could he leave information?'

'A note in Spanish, Governor.'

'A note? They can't read or write.'

'Some of the Anaii can, sir, the older ones. Our informant was captured as a boy. He was originally Anaii, sir.'

'I want them all, Cross. Every last one. Their horses, their silver, their land. This is a war. If the Lord had intended them to exist here, he would not have made them savages. Do you understand, Major?'

'Sir.'

'Well then, see that the holding pens are prepared for when they come in. And ensure arrangements are in hand for their animals to be taken from them on arrival. You have the salt and the axes?'

'Yes, sir.'

'Good. We will ensure that these animals put the idea of inhabiting this land out of their minds once and for all.' Cross saluted and turned away. Waldron called him back. 'Meavy and Monaghan?'

'No word. They have left the area or are in hiding.'

*

In the gloom before daybreak, he shadowed Cross and his cavalrymen as they cantered north through the brush. When they came across stray livestock, the soldiers butchered it, cooking it over their campfires to warm their insides against the bite of nighttime on the plateau.

After four days, approaching the Great Harvest Canyon, Cross split the troop into groups, ordering one east and another west, to sweep towards each other from opposite ends. He detached four smaller groups to ride along the rims on either side to cut off those who might try to escape to the plateau or to attack from above. The settlements were empty. The larger groups moved towards each other using axes to fell the fruit orchards which had flourished for generations at the edges of the canyon. They doused the earth in salt to make it barren.

Coyote pissed in the dirt, so the dark stain would engulf them.

When the sun began its descent, the cavalrymen met at the canyon's midpoint. They turned to leave but the noise of an infant wailing bounced back and forth on the rock face. Cross halted his men with a raised hand and squinted against the sky. From a pueblo tucked high in the rock like a wasp's nest, the crying echoed again briefly and was cut short. Cross gave the order to fire a volley into the pueblo. Guns flashed and cracked, dust and fragments erupting from the walls. The air filled with the stink of powder and the sound of coughing as the breeze dropped, leaving smoke hanging on the soldiers. When the shots had stopped resounding,

Cross sent twenty up the talus. They fanned out, stumbling up the slope, taking positions behind rocks.

'Reveal yourselves now, or we will fire again.' He signalled. A second volley pocked the pueblo walls, hurling more dust and shards out over the canyon.

An old man came first, followed by fifty old men and women and small children. The cavalrymen surrounded them, herding them like sick sheep down the talus to the canyon floor, to Cross, where they knelt as they reached him. An old woman shuffled towards him clutching a baby. She stroked its back, held it at arm's length to look at its face then tipped her head back and howled. A soldier shoved her forward. She was immune to his violence as she hugged the lifeless infant to her chest.

Cross called a young officer to him, 'Lieutenant Armstrong?'

'Yes, Major.'

'Gather whatever ponies you can find, take ten men, and escort these people to the garrison. We will continue upcountry to finish the sweep then rejoin you on your way south with the prisoners.'

'But, sir, our orders were to kill the adults on sight and take the children for sale, Governor Waldron expressly –'

'I am giving you your orders. You will take these prisoners towards Corazon and ensure that when we find you, they are alive. Remain here tonight so the elderly and infants can at least shelter before setting out. Start at first light.'

Armstrong's pale blue eyes were sneering. 'Yes, sir.'

Cross led the main party east out of the canyon and north on the plateau. By nightfall they were a day and a half from Los Huertos. They made camp in the cleft of a ravine with lookouts on the rim. His men got fires going and tended to the horses. He took his pipe and a saddlebag out onto the plateau. The tobacco smoke rose to merge with the inky sky. Coyote howled. Cross twitched at the sound, then returned to his pipe. When it was finished, he placed it on a boulder, pulled a locket from inside his coat, prised it open and smiled. Clicking it shut, he took a rope from the bag, noosed it, and fed it round the trunk of a fig tree oversailing the ravine. Placing the loop round his neck he stepped into the void, fingers clenching the locket as the rope cut in.

Raven

The snow comes thicker, whipping past. Ears stinging, flakes in my eyes before I can blink. Lights ahead, shelter. This is the place. Knox will be here. Darkness casts itself on the land. We come up the eastern side of the river. Clouds of steam rise from the water ahead. The ice has retreated. It forms a great bite from the far side to midstream.

Sleep. Maybe fall into the warmth, sleep forever. Drifting now, slowly as Spider, the bridle loose in my hand. In among the willow facing the far bank and the lights.

The frozen river lies between. Reach into the snow to feel for a rock, teeter with the effort of balancing. Lob it. It bounces across the surface into the night. Untie the buffalo hide from Spider's back. Wrap it round Father's rifle and Grandfather's bow, tuck them under this boulder beneath the trees. Lead Spider onto the ice. It squeaks as we tread it.

Halfway across now, it flexes under our feet, thin from the melting warmth of the springs. Keep us moving. A loud crack, Spider grunts. Turn to see him down at the rear, a hind leg piercing the surface. Yank the bridle, yelling for him to follow. He lurches, unbalancing himself, pitching forward before regaining his footing. Flat-footed now, across the last few yards and up the bank. Climb to where it levels. The reins jolt up through my numb hand into my shoulder, spinning me round.

He's fallen. He's on his side and is gaining a blanket of snow already. Crouch down, my head level with the lowest pine branches. Lay my hand on his head, stroke his cheek. The last cloud of steam leaves his nostrils. He's gone. Spider's gone. I'm alone.

A hundred paces ahead, the Stag Hotel glowing gaudy yellow against the white and black of the night. One street only. Frozen ruts, hard as steel. Haul myself up the plank wood stairs. Shoulder the door open. Snow and pine needles fall from my blanket. It slams behind me. The wail of the snowstorm hushes. A man. Seated by the fire, chair tipped back against the wall, stroking the barrel of a revolver with a fragment of cloth. He doesn't look up. He says one thing. 'Meavy.' The room is hot. Pressing heavy on my throat and lungs. My vision is like sand.

*

The light through the window is wan, the sky still clinging to streaks of dawn. I'm in a bed, the sheets white and clean. The room is warm and smells of stew. I recognise each of the herbs, they smell like home. Male voices below us, a door bangs, juddering up through the floor. Horses whinny. Count the hoofbeats. Ten, maybe twelve riders. They'll have a barn, shelter for Spider. Spider. I remember.

The door opens. A slender young woman with black hair tied back comes in carrying a bundle of logs. She looks up at me and scowls, clear dark eyes, fine, high cheekbones. My lips crack into a smile.

She makes eye contact for a moment. 'There is food. Dress, come downstairs.'

'You are Akote. What is your name?'

'New Star. I am Anaii Akote.'

'Anaii?'

She nods and puts the logs next to the stove, points with her nose at my clothes on the chair. 'Dress. He is waiting for you.' She turns her back, leaves in silence.

I dress as quickly as I can, the weakness in my body slowing my limbs. I open the door to a corridor with a staircase at the end. The smell is stronger here, meat and vegetables. I grip the polished banister and descend. I am so hungry I shake. Feeling has flowed back into my legs overnight. Take the stairs two at a time. There are voices from the room at the bottom, I barge through the doors. Abe Knox. He sits at a mahogany table eating from a china plate with silver cutlery. He wipes the corner of his mouth with a napkin and gestures towards a seat. I pull back the chair, it scrapes across the floorboards. He calls over his shoulder.

'New Star? Food for –' he hesitates, 'our visitor.' As he turns to shout, his coat swings open revealing the ivory butt of a pistol. When he turns back again it is covered. He smiles at me. 'Young Francis Meavy. I had a feeling you might come looking for me. I didn't expect you to fall through the door of my hotel half dead from the cold with no horse.'

He stops talking and raises his eyebrows. New Star comes in. Her blanket skirts brush the floor. I look into her face. She puts a plate of stew in front of me and a basket of bread on the table between us. Abe Knox leans forward and rips off a chunk, waving it towards me before dividing it again.

'Have some breakfast.'

The words fall out of me. 'My father is held prisoner in Corazon. He was betrayed and now the army say they will hang him. Cross knew where to find him buying guns and they came for us. They are using him to say we were making war on them. They are going to attack the northern Akote lands. They said if we don't surrender, they will kill us on sight. Anaii raiders are working for the army in Corazon as killers and scouts –'

He is nodding. 'Continue.'

'He told me when they took him that I should find you. They will kill him unless you help him. His trial is when Waldron returns.' I draw breath.

He takes a small leather case from inside his coat, removes a cigar, lights it, and when he sees the tip glow he speaks again, batting the smoke aside. 'What will your people do?'

'There is a place known only to a few where they will live in peace, away from enemies.'

He draws on his cigar, then looks through the window, assessing the daylight. He turns back to me. I look down at the stew. He nods at the bowl. 'Go on. You'll be needing your strength.' I become aware of the pain in my body. I am ravenous. I gulp down the meat and the liquid. Abe Knox laughs, he shouts towards the hallway, 'New Star! More of your very special stew for young Francis here.'

She carries in another bowl of stew, full to the brim and steaming, wrapped in cloth for the heat of it.

She puts it in front of me, removing my first one, then turns to him, looking down and speaking quietly.

'Food for the men?'

'No. I sent them to Riverside. They'll be back tomorrow once they've taught the Ute a lesson.' She leaves. Knox smiles again. 'Her stew certainly is special today, isn't it?'

I nod. It scalds my mouth.

'Listen, boy, your father.'

I put my spoon down. The food is too hot. He leans in, removes his revolver from his belt and places it on the table. I see the silver watch chain hanging across the front of his waistcoat. Father's watch.

'I'm not going to help him.'

I hear the words. My mind tries to make sense of them. My gut twists hard like I will foul myself.

'He brought this on himself. Playing families with savages. It was never going to work out.'

Under the table, I work my hand to my belt, searching for the bayonet but find only Mother's medicine bundle.

'We traded all through that territory, but when I learnt only this year that there was gold in the plateau, well, if God had intended those Indians to be rich, that's what they would be. But they're not. They are savages occupying land intended for us, but being a white man was not good enough for your father. At least in his way he has helped rid us of the vermin.' He reaches down as if to scratch an itch. He straightens, waving my knife. Father's knife.

'I see you carry his bayonet. You Indians love army

equipment. We gave One Eye a cavalry coat and he never takes it off. You know who I mean?' He does not wait for me to answer. 'You should. He works for me. Has done for years. He knows your father.' He is smirking. 'He knew your mother, and that animal Pale Horse. Knew them well. Kept them company in their last moments. Son of a bitch gave me New Star, his own daughter, as a trading gift. Can you believe that?'

The cold hard stillness settles on me. I hold his stare. My breath slows. I take in the details of the room, the distance across the table, the revolver, the bayonet next to it, the space immediately behind Knox, the stew, steaming. I see how it will go.

'Cross thinks One Eye works for him, that we have a partnership. The fact is my interests are beyond his horizons. I own the hotel in Corazon, the mine in Argento, the hotel there, this hotel, and tens of thousands of acres to the south of here where I'm mining copper. My mines will produce more money than I can ever spend. You know how I got started? Trading up and down the country with your father, then further south as Indian Agent. I took and sold supplies destined for the Indians for money you would not believe, and I didn't pay for any of it. Your people and their land paid for everything. Of course, I ensured your father was caught buying the guns. When the army have done what they need to do, the land – along with the gold and minerals in it – will find its way to me. Even your medicine man is on my payroll and I've no doubt he's travelling with your folks to this secret place of theirs and will tell Cross exactly where to go to finish off the last of you.'

The stew is still steaming. I touch the medicine bundle once more.

'And young Meavy, since we are being honest with each other, that stew you're enjoying so much – we found a horse over towards the river in the snow. White and brown, I'd say dragoon horse cross Akote pony. Waste not want not.' He nods towards my bowl.

I fling the scalding liquid into Knox's face. He bellows, pushing back off his heels, rubbing his eyes with one hand, reaching for his gun with the other. The chair tips, teeters, then corrects. He's blinded, holding on with his legs. I grip the table's edge with both hands, bend my knees and surge upwards. It flips over, taking him with it. He screams as his wrist catches underneath and snaps. His heels scrabble on the floor, rucking the rug as he pulls himself clear. The hand of his broken arm closes on the butt of the revolver. I jump over the table and snatch the bayonet from the floor. Knox is edging towards the door, moving the gun from his limp right hand into his left. He backs into a pool of broth, slips, and falls backwards, dropping the revolver. I close on him and raise the knife. He tries to push up off his broken limb, reaching for the weapon again. I stab down with the bayonet from the shoulder – from the hip and from the soles of my feet, nailing Knox to the floor by his good hand. I can crush him now, crush him like shit under my boot.

New Star stands in the doorway. She is looking at the gun on the floor at her feet. He screams at her, 'Shoot him, Goddammit, shoot him!'

She reaches down for it, straightens, cocks the hammer, and levels it at Knox.

*

Mid-morning snow swirls in the street. A horse and a mule stand tied to the rail of the hotel. I hold my gloves in my teeth, my shaking hands working the rope. I've got Knox up across the back of the mule. I bind his ankles and walk round the animal's head to the other side.

'They'll never take your word against mine, boy. Face it, there's nothing you can do to stop him hanging and you're next unless you loose me. You take me all the way down there, there's only one outcome. You'll hang too. Who's going to believe an Akote savage over a respected businessman?'

I roll a piece of cloth while Knox speaks, stretch it between my hands and hold it to his face. He clenches his teeth shut. I pinch his nose, so he has to open his mouth to breathe, then force the gag in, knotting it behind at the join of spine and skull. I stand to the side so he can see me, I pull my gloves back on.

'I am Raven Francis Meavy Tseyi'nii, son of Bright Flower Tseyi'nii and of Francis Farrer Meavy. I am Akote and the laws I obey are Akote. I will bring justice to you and my father, but it will be Akote justice in the land of our people.'

I bind the last of the packs to the fine gelding I have taken from the barn, grab the mule's lead rope and turn for the river.

Coyote

He felt the pain in Francis Meavy's shoulders from holding the reins with bound wrists. One Eye and his raiders were racing along the riverbank, their horses kicking up white plumes. They rode into the ruined Ute camp early morning and scavenged through the tipis. Some took furs, shedding their blankets in the blood and snow. Meavy scoured the camp for signs of his son. They set off again. Soon afterwards they saw the top of Raven's saddle in a drift. His mind was numb, unable to reason.

One Eye turned to him and laughed. 'He is on foot.'

The day was bright by the time they reached the hot springs. Beneath the willows they found the buffalo skin. Meavy recognised the bow and rifle. His breathing quickened. He ached to sight Raven before they did, to shout a warning to him, to give him a chance at least. One Eye stared across the river at the buildings beyond. The path of the hot current streaked the ice translucent in places. He kicked on further to where the surface appeared solid, dismounted, and walked his horse out, the hooves striking hollow on the frozen skin. His men followed. Only Francis Meavy remained in the saddle scanning the far bank, casting his eyes downwards now and then to keep his balance. The hooves beat like drums as more of them advanced onto the ice. A gunshot rang out. They halted mid river.

A rider came down the far bank towards them, a revolver in one hand and the lead rope for a mule in the other. It bore a writhing bundle slung over its back. A hat fell from one end. It was another man, hogtied. Smoke drifted towards the Anaii from the buildings, sharp with the scent of pine resin. Meavy squinted at the rider who sat tall but was skin and bone. He recognised one of his own hats and called out, 'Raven!'

Raven

One Eye beckons for Father to be brought alongside. The man next to him hands his reins to his neighbour and takes hold of the bridle of Father's animal. He slips, wheeling his arms to stay upright, then leads the horse forward.

I point the revolver at Knox. 'I will shoot him unless you release your prisoner.'

One Eye looks at me, the angle of his head favours his good eye, so the movement is like a bird's. A vulture's. 'My *prisoner*? Your father, you mean?'

I cock the revolver with my thumb. 'Release him.'

'He is a trader. You travel as a trader. We will trade. I will release my prisoner and you will release yours. Then we will each turn back the way we came.'

'No!' Father yells. 'They butchered Monaghan. They'll kill us both.'

'We will make the exchange,' I shout to One Eye, 'But I have my gun on Knox until we are clear. Father, remember Jonah.' Knox is thrashing around on the back of the mule, trying to shout through the gag.

One Eye frowns. 'You must lead his mule closer. He cannot ride bound.'

'Son, no!' Father bellows now.

I ignore him. I kick my horse further onto the ice, pulling Knox's animal along behind. One Eye gestures and the reins of Father's horse are released. I do the same, patting the mule's rump to urge it on. They cross mid river, but Father's gelding slips, lurching forward. Knox tries to bury his head in the mule's flank, but as the animals barge past each other, Father's boot strikes Knox on the crown of his head and his body falls limp. Each is a few strides from home. I am shielded from One Eye by Father's horse. I aim the revolver at the ice between us, shout 'Breathe,' and fire off two rounds. A third and fourth I shoot mid river.

There is a moment's stillness, then a sound like green oak splintering echoes all around us. The horses rear and stamp, legs disappearing into the water. The Anaii turn, abandoning their animals to make for the bank behind them. The fissures in the ice outrace them, swallowing them into the flow. Knox and his mule sink. I jump from my saddle towards Father. My arm closes around him. We both gulp the air as we go down through the ice. The water sears my skin. It clamps my head and shrieks in my ears. Father's horse kicks out, its hoof opening his temple. I have him by the collar, but I can't feel my fingers. With my other hand I scratch at the underside of the ice, pulling us along. I beat my legs against the current. Father's blood mingles scarlet with the water, mine pumps loud in my head. I am dizzy with the effort of hauling us. Father grows heavier. I kick harder and claw at the sharp surface. The frozen lid glows white and seamless above me. I crane my head back. Behind us, bubbles percolate up through a pool of clear water. I feel the warmth now. We burst up through the puddle, I grip the weight of his body under both shoulders, roar the air in, and shut my mouth again to sink. Boots slipping off the weed on the bottom, I push towards the bank. I drag him out of the steaming water.

New Star is here. She has Knox's revolver in her hand and glares at the river behind me. I struggle to turn my head. One Eye wades towards us, a long knife gripped in his hand. He grins at her. She fires a shot across the ice, it echoes loud and sharp. He stops.

'Leave them,' she shouts.

One Eye's grin cracks, showing his teeth. He starts forward again. She fires another round. He shakes his head. 'We are one Anaii blood, New Star. You will not fire on me.'

I lock my left arm under Father's ribcage and scrabble at my side for his bayonet. One Eye closes in on us, raising his weapon above his head. I twist the deadweight in my left arm and push up out of the water with my right. I look into his eyes as I make the stroke and the sound of the shot deafens me. I force the bayonet up and in. The body falls back. A bullet wound in the side of his head. The water takes him. New Star stands on the bank unblinking, the gun at arm's length, the smoke from its muzzle floating in the still air.

Coyote

An eagle cried overhead. Coyote watched it wheel twice before flying away over the mesa top. He turned his attention to Willow Tree. She knelt on the floor of the cave offering up prayers of thanks for the dream. Outside, the snow-covered grassland was encircled by cliffs shielding the fugitives from human predators. The sun broke over the high rim in streaks of red and pink. She looked into the darkness at the back of the cave where Hawk should have been, wondering what had taken him from their bed before daybreak with his bow. She pulled a shawl around herself and stepped out into the cold.

She saw him with Crowsfoot, wrapped in buffalo hides, bent over something in the snow at the mouth of the rock passage. She drew closer, calling out, 'Hawk, I dreamt that Bright Flower's blood is returning, that Raven is coming.' She checked herself, seeing their faces. 'What is it?' She looked at the ground between them. In the half-light she made out the body of a man, the seeping blood like a shadow beside him.

'You have tracked these hoof marks?' Hawk asked Crowsfoot.

'They are Shadow Bloom's. He fled in the darkness. The prints outside the mesa lead southeast.'

Willow Tree stared at her husband. 'It was him? It was the medicine man? He must be stopped, before he can lead them back here –'

Crowsfoot cut her off, 'I will raise a war party now, we'll –'

'No,' Hawk interrupted, 'I go alone.'

Coyote rose from his resting place and stretched.

*

As he passed through the narrow passage of rock into the world of others, Hawk started the chant given to him by Mountain Song. A secret kept for lifetimes. It was given only to those with the strongest medicine. The chant for calling Coyote.

He galloped to the south of Shadow Bloom's tracks during the afternoon, walked his horse through the nighttime snow, then cut east at dawn on the third day and dismounted at the mouth of a ravine. It formed a shallow slope to the plateau above. He took his bow, sat cross-legged on a boulder and pulled his buffalo skin around him. Covering his head, he saw the vulture circling above. It had followed him day and night from the mountain. The flakes settled and Hawk's shelter merged with the rock. He sat motionless, whispering the chant without end.

He has not yet seen me, thought Coyote, but he is faithful. Only I know he is here.

Mid-morning, during a lull in the snowfall, Hawk's patience was rewarded. He heard the striking of hooves and saw Shadow Bloom through a chink in the hide, guiding his pony down through the rock. He waited until horse and rider were ten paces away, then stood. Shadow Bloom's pony shied. He fought it back under control.

'The air is good,' he rasped.

Hawk said nothing.

'I have been seeking herbs and roots from the desert.'

Hawk was in an outcrop, barring the path. The vulture crossed the strip of sky above them, part of night's darkness broken loose.

'That is not why you left.'

Shadow Bloom sat staring for long moments, then drew a pistol from within his clothing. 'You will fall by my hand, as your daughter and Pale Horse fell to my brother. As Mountain Song fell to us both.' He shuffled in his saddle awaiting a response. Hawk gave him none. 'Then I will ride for Corazon and lead your enemies back to destroy what remains of the Akote.' He raised the gun.

Beyond him, in the ravine, Hawk saw Coyote on a boulder looking back at him. He acknowledged him, 'The Air is Good.'

Shadow Bloom laughed. 'Do not think you will fool me so easily.' He cocked the lock.

Coyote shrieked. Shadow Bloom twitched round at the noise. Hawk's arrow pierced his throat, his head and neck jerked backwards. As he fell from his horse, his fingers clenched on the trigger. The report filled the air between the rock faces like a thunderclap. The round whined in protest, ricocheting off the cedar sandstone. A second arrow pierced the hand at his neck. A third buried itself in his gut. He lay in the snow fighting for breath. Hawk took his pony and walked back towards the plateau. Vulture set about his work.

*

He watched over Raven and New Star, their horses trudging west through frozen landscapes. They spoke little, raising their voices only to urge on the mule bearing Francis Meavy. When they stopped to rest the animals, or to make camp, they would talk about the homes they had left behind, their shared Akote heritage – not the great losses they had each suffered.

She had never met a man like him. As they rode through unknown country, he never hesitated, never seemed to doubt where they were going or why, never questioned that they should be travelling together. She felt, too, in the respect he showed her, a great kindness in him. Within seven nights she knew she wanted him for her husband.

He felt at ease with her in a way he had not felt even with his mother. New Star was Anaii Akote, an outsider from birth as he had been. Unlike the others in the canyon, he spoke two languages, Akote and English. She spoke Akote and Spanish. Each of them was split in two. As they pushed through snow drifts and waded icy fords, riding for distant mesas, he came to know, without doubt, that she would be his home.

*

Coyote's fur bristled. It was nearly dusk. Hawk slept at the back of the cave. At its mouth, Willow Tree knelt to uncover the cornbread from beneath the earth. She rose to peer at the dim figures approaching through the snow. Two riders and a mule. They drew nearer. She knew that she had not seen the horses before. She looked to the mule. It carried a long burden slung sideways over its back, roped on. She looked again at the second rider, a young woman. The man wore a hat she recognised, one of Francis Meavy's hats. She re-examined the mule. It carried a body, wrapped in a shroud.

Raven

I open my eyes. Through the doorway of the hogan the bright line of dawn burns on the mesa top above. Silhouetted against it, Coyote sits, ears upright. I nod acknowledgement to him. He rises and disappears into the light.

From my bed, in the darkness at the back of the hogan, I turn my attention to my wife. New Star is kneeling in prayer, chanting. She stares into the smoke rising from the floor and raises her head, hearing the breeze part the long grass of the meadow. She is listening for guidance. Her sadness flows like a river through my body. Or is it my own? She turns and, seeing me awake, jumps. I smile and sit with her by the fire. She places the flat of her hand on her swollen belly.

'Husband, soon he will be born. And then, when he has grown and discovers who his grandfather was, what he did to these people, to his own daughter, it will destroy him.'

I shake my head. 'You are so sure it is a boy?' She sniffs and nods. The tears flow down her face. I wipe them with my hand. 'My love, the God of my ancestors washes sins away. You gave your father that on the river. You do that now with your tears. Our son will only know that his grandfather was a warrior, killed before he was born.' I stare into the flames, where the truth burns hot. 'As to the rest, it is better left behind.'

Coyote

He had watched the Akote from the beginning. Before then. From the time when the Sun came into being. When First Woman saw the flame of First Man and First Man was drawn to the fire of First Woman. When he and the others emerged from the dark worlds onto this earth. He knew their scent, the beat of their feet in the dust, the cries they made. He had always been with them. Always watching, always hungry. He had brought them gifts from the Ancestors in the North. The spirits of children long yearned for – to reward their faith, their gratitude in prayer for that yet ungiven.

He had brought Bright Flower; he had brought Raven. He had come in the darkness, but still the Akote knew because they were devout. Now he turned away, into the First Light. As he did so, he looked down from the rim.

He heard New Star's prayers and knew her doubt. Coyote had not brought this child to her womb. He would have Akote skin, Akote hair, the arms, and the legs of an Akote man, but his heart belonged to his father. Abraham Knox.

Author's Note

Coyote covers themes of personal, racial, and geographical identity and the human urge to dominate and other, through invasion and colonisation. It is also, in a sense, a personal fable.

As a mixed-race person, writing this book enabled me to reexamine the internal conflict of being both the coloniser and the colonised (the enemy within), to explore how the landscapes of my childhood have shaped my identity and to view – from a very different perspective – the far-reaching effects of catastrophic loss in my own family over generations.

Although most of the plotlines in this novel are inspired by events which took place in the 19th century, it is sobering to note that the same issues remain unresolved today. I hope that *Coyote* serves as a reminder of the costs when compassion and acceptance are forsaken, in favour of violence. I've used a fictitious tribe in *Coyote* out of respect, and to avoid the risk of misrepresenting any particular peoples. I'd like to thank our indigenous sensitivity reader for their help in that, too. The influences in the Akote culture will be clear to anyone familiar with what is now called Arizona, Utah, New Mexico, and Colorado. By way of thanks to the original peoples of that area, 50% of all author royalties from *Coyote* will be donated to charitable organisations in the Navajo Nation.

Acknowledgements

This book germinated in the desert when I was a small boy.

I'd like to thank my parents, Dolly & Bill for taking us there and starting that process. I'd like to thank my sister, Judy, for her cultural expertise & input and for being my fellow traveller all this time.

I'd like to thank the mentors and teachers – knowing and unknowing – who have helped me along the way: Russ Litten, my official mentor in *Coyote*, for his inspired advice and ideas. Suzy Walker who empowers so many writers. Shann Ray for showing me what's possible. Laura Barton, Sunjeev Sahota, Alison MacLeod, Tony Greaves, and particularly Dennis Allan for his unshakeable faith.

Thank you to my manuscript readers and fellow writers for their input and enthusiasm for *Coyote*: Chrissie Knight, Theo Clarke, Alexis Harvey, Robert Levy, Paul Austin Kelly, Ian Comaish, Dominic Weston, Kaya Gupta.

Thank you to the members of the post-Arvon course writing groups I've belonged to.

Thank you to Georgie for our discussions about narrative and form, and for being my favourite only daughter.

Thank you to Don, who knew I was a writer even when I wasn't sure. You'd have enjoyed *Coyote*, I think.

My profound gratitude to Jannat and Samiha at Lucent Dreaming for your hard work and for the enthusiasm, responsiveness, and ambition you bring to publishing, and to the award-winning Cerys Knighton for such wonderful front and back covers.

Finally, my greatest thanks to Xanthe, my wife, who falls into nearly all the above categories – without your initial and ongoing encouragement, support and expertise, I could not have written this novel.

Robin.